# THE SECOND SHOT

by
## Bethany Maines

Blue Zephyr Press
2661 N. Pearl, #360
Tacoma WA 98407

Cover art by **LILTdesign.com**.

ISBN-13: 978-1-7332813-1-7

## DEDICATION

With many thanks to Laurie Ryan, Shannon McKinnon, and Brittney Noble who helped bring this story to life.

# CONTENTS

**SATURDAY**......................................................................................................................1
   Maxwell Ames..........................................................................................1
   Dominique Deveraux............................................................................10

**SUNDAY**..........................................................................................................................14
   Dominique – Misunderstood .............................................................14
   Jackson – The Children .......................................................................21
   Maxwell - Play Date ...........................................................................35
   Dominique – Max Sass ........................................................................46
   Maxwell - Trailing...............................................................................55
   Dominique – Dinner............................................................................60

**MONDAY**..........................................................................................................................71
   Jackson – Marks on the Wall .............................................................71
   Maxwell – Echoes of the Past.............................................................84
   Dominique – Getting Dressed.............................................................88
   Maxwell - Friends of the Rainforest...................................................93
   Dominque – The After Party .............................................................108

**TUESDAY**.......................................................................................................................115
   Jackson – Morning Visits...................................................................115
   Maxwell – Working Out....................................................................126
   Dominique – Emergency Contact .....................................................132
   Dominique – Past Revisited ..............................................................144

**WEDNESDAY**.................................................................................................................150
   Jackson – Deveraux House................................................................150
   Maxwell - The Closet .......................................................................159
   Dominique – The File.......................................................................167
   Maxwell – Stand-Off ........................................................................172
   Dominique – Revelations .................................................................179
   Maxwell – The Queens .....................................................................186
   Jackson – Visiting Hours ...................................................................190
   Dominique – Almost There ..............................................................199
   Maxwell – Show Down .....................................................................205
   Dominique – Batter Up .....................................................................213
   Maxwell – Afterwards ......................................................................231

**THURSDAY**....................................................................................................................240
   Dominique – After that .....................................................................240
   Maxwell – Fatherhood .....................................................................247

**TWO WEEKS LATER**.....................................................................................................250
   Dominique – Here Now .....................................................................250

**EPILOGUE: THE DEVERAUX BOYS**.............................................................................255
   Evan Deveraux – Last Week .............................................................255
   Aiden Deveraux – Last Night ............................................................258
   Jackson Deveraux – Right Now .........................................................261

# THE SECOND SHOT

# *Maxwell Ames*

*I have better uses for my mouth.*

The words were etched in his brain.

Maxwell Ames looked across the room at Dominique Dever-aux and felt himself physically flinch at a memory-driven whip of embarrassment.

An eighteen-year-old Dominique had arrived at college with an ice queen reputation and a pair of legs that had fueled half the hot dreams on campus. But it hadn't been the legs that had gotten to Max—it had been her lips. Max had taken one look at Dominique and decided he wanted, no, *needed* to know what those lips felt like on his body. And he'd declared, drunkenly, to an entire frat party that he would melt the ice queen. He hadn't doubted for a minute that he could do it. He was a senior. He was a nationally ranked college wrestler—his body showed his effort—and he rarely had to do more than lift a finger to get panties to hit his floor. Perhaps it had been the liquor that had made him stupid, but whatever the reason, he'd simply walked over and told her what he wanted her to do to him. He recognized his mistake the second he heard the words come out of his mouth. Her horrified expression only confirmed how badly he'd misjudged. Then she'd gone from shocked to furious, but instead of slapping him, she'd pulled herself up to her full height, looked him in the eye, and declared loud enough for the rest of the room to hear: *I have better uses for my mouth.* And then he'd stood there and let her pour the entire contents of her red solo cup down his front.

And now, six years later, his father had dragged Max into the Galbraith Tennis and Social Club and directly into revisiting one of his top ten stupidest moments.

"Dad," said Max, turning to look at his father.

"She donates two-k a year," said his father, staring across the party hall at a woman in beige everything. "She's worth like eighty million. Would it kill her to scrounge a little more change out of the couch cushions for needy kids?"

"Dad," said Max again.

"Yeah, what?" asked Grant Ames, finally making eye contact.

"You didn't say this was a Deveraux party."

"Uh, yeah?" said Grant, looking away again—probably scanning the crowd for more targets. "Oh, that's right. You went to school with them, didn't you? Dominique and Aiden? They're probably around somewhere if you want to dig them up. Eleanor usually commands appearances from the family at these little shindigs."

Eleanor Deveraux was running for congress. Again. Or still. Whichever. These *little shindigs* were fundraising events masquerading as cocktail parties. Max didn't know why she bothered. Her nearest competitor was a bitter Republican that sounded crazy even to his constituents. But his father, always on the hustle, spared no thought about why the party existed—he simply enjoyed that it did. And of course, it hadn't occurred to Grant to mention to Max who was hosting.

After the frat party incident, Max hadn't even had the courage to apologize to Dominique. His only consolation was that during all their other encounters she had treated everyone in the room with an equal amount of cool disdain—he hadn't been singled out. Generally, she hadn't even acknowledged him, let alone what had happened.

"You said we wouldn't be here long," said Max, looking back at Dominique. Her golden blonde hair was longer than the last time he'd seen her, laying in soft waves against her pale skin. Those lips that had made him lose his judgement were painted a wine red that emphasized their size. Her conservative pencil skirt and long-sleeve, high-necked blouse should have taken her allure down a notch, but as far as he could see, she was even more gorgeous than she had been in college.

Max had been with plenty of beautiful women—hell, his last girlfriend had been a model-slash-actress. Dominique shouldn't have been able to make the impact she did. But here it was, six years later, and Dominique still hit him like a Mack truck to the libido even when the only skin he could see was her knees.

"We won't be long, I promise," said Grant, scoping the room, oblivious to the direction of Max's gaze. "I need to make the rounds. Say hi to a few people and then we'll be off for burgers."

It was a lie. Max didn't know why he'd thought his first visit to his father's in over a year might warrant special treatment—particularly, since his entire childhood held evidence to the contrary. He wondered if there was a point in adulthood when a parent's failings stopped mattering so much.

Dominique nodded along as the guy next to her talked. He was a lean, good looking twenty-something with black hair and a designer suit. Max watched in surprise as Dominique burst out laughing at whatever he'd said—Dominique had never been very demonstrative in public. Her laugh made the guy grin, but, still talking, he leaned over and snagged something off her plate. Dominique smacked at his hand, but the man leaned further away, dragging the morsel with him, and popped it into his mouth. She flicked at his ear, miming patently faked annoyance. In equally mock penance, her companion lowered his head and held out his plate and Dominique made a show of selecting something in recompense. The only person he could remember bringing out that sparkle of playfulness in her had been her brother, Aiden. It seemed that the ice queen had been melted after all.

Still chewing his stolen goods, Dominique's companion looked up and scanned the room, homing in on the location of the other Deveraux family members. Max followed the man's gaze to the matriarch, Dominque's stately and poised grandmother, Eleanor, holding court by the bar at the far end of the long, narrow room. Then he shifted to Dominique's red-headed investment manager cousin, Evan, amongst a bevy of Wall Street bros in the middle of the room. And last, Dominique's brother, the equally blonde Aiden, hovering by the buffet table in front of a wide expanse of floor-to-ceiling windows.

All of the Deveraux children had lived with their grandmother after a plane crash had left them orphans sometime during their early teens. Max remembered thinking how nice that had sounded when his father had missed every single one of his college meets and was late for graduation. He supposed it hadn't really been pleasant for the Deveraux cousins, but at least they'd had each other and Eleanor.

Max realized, too late, that the scan was continuing on to the new arrivals in the room, which, in this case, were Max and his father. Max found himself awkwardly making eye contact with the guy and knew that he'd been busted staring at Dominique. He broke eye contact and turned to follow his father.

Max pretended to be absorbed in his father's conversation with a white-collared, black-shirted Jesuit priest. After a few minutes of discussing the endowments and scholarship funds, Max's eyes glazed over and he looked around the room, desperate for anything to take his mind off his desire to blurt out a question about pedophiles. How did anyone take priests seriously anymore? He found himself fidgeting with one of the tiny decorative pumpkins placed on the bar-height tables and biting his tongue.

With Halloween and the election around the corner, the party was decorated in a patriotic harvest theme. The red leaves and orange gourds seemed attractive, but Max thought the hay bales by the buffet table seemed a bit too folksy for the Deveraux, not to mention the tennis club locale. He suspected that the entire reason for their existence was to support the stars-and-stripes-bandana-wearing scarecrow. After all, a politician couldn't fundraise without at least a nod to the flag.

He snuck another glance at Dominique and realized that her boyfriend was scanning again. Same pattern—Deverauxes first, then new arrivals, then the rest of the room. There was something professional in the appraising stare, and Max felt the weight of it resting thoughtfully on him. Max checked his watch and angled so he could watch Dominique and her guy. She chatted in an easy, unaffected way, but at a minute fifteen, her boyfriend made another scan. Then again a minute later. It was definitely a more than a casual glance. Max tried to get a better look at the guy. What was he? Boyfriend, bodyguard, security? The suit was expensive, but he was drinking water as he watched the crowd.

Dominique reached out and put her hand on his arm, tugging impatiently, demanding attention. The guy laughed and complied, turning toward her with an affectionate smile. He was definitely not the hired help. For some reason, that burned. In the intervening six years, Max had put Dominique out of his head. Mostly. Sort of. Max would never have admitted it out loud, ever, under any circumstances, including a court of law, but Dominique had always been one of his go-to fantasies. He was perfectly sure that she hadn't thought about him once in that time. So why did he feel jealous of this guy?

Max turned back to his father and tried to focus on the

conversation. Dominique was none of his business. What did he care if she dated someone with an over-active sense of security? None. Of. His. Business.

Grant moved on and Max followed him dutifully, the same way he had when he was twelve. He was a prop to his father's socializing. He met a dozen people and forgot their names instantly. Finally, he turned away from a blocky woman in a Chanel jacket and found his father about to introduce him to Dominique and her date.

"Max, I don't know if you've met Jackson, but you went to school with Dominique. Max is staying with me for a few weeks while—Hey, Frank! Frank! Be right back. I've been trying to get five minutes with that guy all month." Grant buzzed off and left Max staring uncomfortably at Dominique and her date.

"So, Max," said Jackson, his expression derisive, "do you need Dominique to get you another drink? We could send the catering staff out for some beer and solo cups."

Max glanced at Dominique, who was visibly restraining a laugh.

"No," said Max, trying not to feel like an ass—any hope that she'd forgotten him or the incident slipping away. "I think once was enough." Did she really have to tell everyone?

Dominique actually did giggle this time and her boyfriend looked amused by her laughter, but his attention was pulled away.

"Nika, what is Aiden doing?" asked Jackson, looking past Max.

"Um," she squinted toward the door, "exactly what you told him not to do?"

Jackson sighed. "OK, I'll be right back." He ducked around Dominique, his jacket swinging open. For a second, Max clearly saw the strap on a shoulder holster and outline of a gun. Max looked back at Dominque, but she seemed not to notice. She was watching her brother attempting to sneak out of the room and biting into her bottom lip with a frown. She transferred her gaze back to Max and smiled, but it was the same old cold smile.

"I'm glad you can laugh about that uh... incident," he said, deciding to man up and do what he should have done six years ago. He glanced down at the floor and realized that she was only conservative from the ankle up. Her heels were stacked, strapped, and had a black satin bow at each ankle that begged to be untied. "I really apologize for that," he said, tearing his eyes off her feet.

She looked startled and suspicious.

"I was a total asshole," he added.

"Um." She frowned, then smiled—a real smile this time. "Well, apology accepted."

It was his turn to feel surprised. He hadn't expected her to simply believe that he was sorry. "And I wouldn't say total. I'd go ninety-eight percent."

"Ninety-eight percent?"

"Well, I'll give you a one percent discount for being young, dumb and in college."

"Yes," he agreed fervently.

"And another one percent for standing there for the entire cup of beer."

"I knew I'd earned it," he said. She glanced over his shoulder, still following the action across the room.

"Your boyfriend's a little intense," he said.

"My boyfriend? You mean Jacks?"

He wanted to comment on the intimate shortening of their names. Jacks seemed weird, but he liked Nika. On the other hand, it really was none of his damn business.

"Does he always carry a gun?" he asked instead.

"Oh, you know..." she said, trailing off and not answering the question. Max decided that meant the answer was yes. "Grandma has gotten some... Well, they're death threats, really, in the last few weeks. She's chairing that Senate Committee Hearing on Absolex. And nothing brings out the crazies like Big Pharma."

"I don't understand," he said. "I thought that was about government fraud?"

"Absolex falsified research and then sold their drug Zanilex to the VA as a solution to treat complex PTSD. Suicide rates sky-rocketed. Turns out that, in fact, it makes the symptoms of PTSD worse, particularly the paranoia and depression. Or at least that's what Grandma intends to prove. She's going to haul the CEO out on the carpet next week. But ever since the hearings started, she's been getting hate mail."

Max looked around the party. "Where is the Secret Service?"

"None of the threats have been active. It's all kind of vague. And she's not a party leader or anything. So, no Secret Service."

Max frowned. If he had been Eleanor, he would have been putting his foot down and demanding an investigation. He also wouldn't be hosting a party and looking as relaxed as she did.

"Besides," continued Dominique, "we have Jackson. Although, even he couldn't get her to cancel this stupid party. She claimed that we all just didn't want to go."

He raised an eyebrow and she looked guilty.

"That may be partially true. Anyway, Jacks said if she was going to insist on having the party, we should at least be smart about it. He gave us all rules and hired additional security. Of course, Aiden is not following the rules. I would accuse him of being willful, but it's more likely that he's just not taking the threats seriously."

Max nodded. His memory of Dominique's older brother was a sunny personality to whom nothing serious was allowed to adhere and who never seemed to get mad about anything.

"I expect Jacks will tell him about a secret stash of bourbon under the bar and rope him back in."

"Sounds like Jackson knows what he's doing then," said Max, turning to look at the two men who were now making their way back toward them. Aiden stopped to adjust the bandana on the scarecrow with a disapproving shake of his head.

"He does," agreed Dominique, looking up at him with a flash of a smile, "but Jackson isn't—"

Whatever she had been about to say was drowned out by the sound of a car engine and then a thunderous crash as a car exploded through the windows, slammed through the buffet table, plowed across the room, and buried its nose in the far wall.

# Dominique Deveraux

Dominique stared in disbelief at the rubble and then began to run toward the car now lodged in the interior wall of the tennis club. "Aiden!"

She hadn't been looking. She'd turned her head for one second and now she couldn't see them.

"Aiden! Jackson!" She knew she was screaming, but she could barely hear herself over the hot whine of the car engine. She glanced at the car expecting to see a driver, but the car was empty. She didn't have time to focus on that—instead she scrambled over the remains of the buffet table. Max attempted to stop her for some reason, but she pushed his hands off her. She couldn't lose them too. She couldn't. She could still see her grandmother's face, paper pale, and the vase slipping through her fingers when she'd gotten the news of the deaths of her children. Dominque never wanted to feel that again—that horrifying sensation of lives being stripped away by some strange man's heartless words. This was ten times worse. Her lungs felt inoperable, clogged with dust and fear, and her heart pounded loud enough in her ears to overwhelm the sound of the car.

She heard a grunt and saw both Jackson and Aiden sit up, covered in dust and glass. She heaved a sob of relief. Jackson sprang up and ran to the window. Climbing over the rubble, he sprinted out into the parking lot, leaving her to slither across the broken glass on her stilettos to Aiden. The car engine was still revving and creating a din of white background noise, punctuated by the screams of the other party guests.

Aiden was struggling to his feet by the time she reached him.

He looked unsteady on his feet and whirled around as Dominique and Max pulled him fully upright. Dominque grabbed at his arm, trying to make him hold still. Injured people were supposed to hold still.

"Fuck!" he exclaimed, turning around again, trying to take in the devastation. "Fuck! That car! Fuck!" He looked at the car and then back at Max as if confused by his presence. "Where's Jacks?" Max shook his head and Aiden turned to Dominique. She could see her earlier fear reflected in his face. He didn't want to lose their cousin either. "Where is Jackson?"

"He went out to the parking lot!" Dominique knew it didn't make any sense, but it was the only answer she had.

"He's OK?" Aiden's blue eyes were wide, and his suit jacket was torn.

Dominique nodded.

"Stay here," yelled Max, above the engine noise. Dominique did as she was told, clinging to Aiden. Max made his way over to the car and reached inside. Moments later, the horrible revving of the engine quit.

"Cops are on their way," said Jackson, coming back through the window, followed by the security guards he'd hired. He was also covered in dust and had a scratch on his cheek that trickled blood. His eyes, the trademark Deveraux blue, looked hard and angry.

Dominique reached out for Jackson and Aiden wrapped his arms around both of them.

"Yes, OK," said Jackson, resisting the group hug. Dominique hugged harder until he laughed. "I'm OK. Really. I'm OK. Are you OK?" he stepped back to look at both of them. Jackson wasn't any older than Aiden and only two years older than she was, but it was moments like this that made him feel an eon older. Dominique wiped her eyes, which were threatening to leak, and nodded.

"Fuck no, I'm not OK," said Aiden. "I think I just about pissed myself. That car would have hit me if it hadn't been for you."

"There was a brick on the gas pedal," said Max, returning from the car.

Dominique stared up at him, trying to understand his words, instead all she could think was that she had forgotten how tall Max was. In five-inch, stacked stilettos she should have been looking down on him or at least in the eye, but Maxwell Ames was ridiculously tall. Ridiculously tall and, with his square jaw, smattering of freckles and green eyes, ridiculously good looking. It was one of the reasons she had hated him in college—he had no right to be that genetically gifted. In college, every other girl of her acquaintance would have died for his attention, or at least seriously considered doing what he'd told her to do. But this was no longer college. This Max had a grim expression, and he looked like a completely different person from the boy she'd known in college, or the man that had been smiling at her only a few minutes before. She wasn't sure she would have known him if she'd run into him looking like this.

"I saw someone running," said Jackson, nodding. "But they were gone by the time I got out there. Apparently, I should have been less worried about personal attacks and more worried about general mayhem." He turned to the security guards who'd gathered from the various points in the room, converging on Jackson. "Start rounding up the guests. The police are going to want statements. Don't let anyone leave. Be polite but firm. Make sure everyone is OK."

"Post someone to make sure no one else touches the car," said Max and Jackson nodded, pointing at one of the guards and then at the car. The two of them seemed to be speaking on the same wavelength and Dominique watched them in confusion. She was barely used to the switch that Jackson seemed to flip to go from her loveable cousin to the kind of person that could deal with threats. It hadn't occurred to her that there would be other people who could do the same thing, but Max did it too.

"Nika, I'm going to need you to make the rounds and keep the guests calm," Jackson continued. "Eleanor can't do it all and Evan won't bother."

"Right," said Dominique, taking a deep breath. She could do this. It was just a matter of putting off what she was feeling until later. She took another breath and smoothed her skirt down. Deverauxes never looked messy. She straightened her spine, squared her shoulders. "OK," she said and smiled her best approximation of her grandmother's smile. Max was giving her an odd look. She smiled a real smile at him and his face relaxed.

"I'll go with you," said Aiden.

"You don't have to. You almost got hit by a car," she said.

"Yeah, and with three reporters in the room, the last thing I need is to have it all over the internet that I retired to the fainting couch while you handled everything. I'm not incapacitated—I can do the Prince Charming bit."

"Thanks," said Dominique, feeling relieved.

"The cops will probably want exclusion fingerprints from you," said Jackson eyeing Max. There was the barest questioning tone to his comment and a subtle inquiry in his expression. Leave it to her cousin to try and politely inquire about someone's criminal background during a crisis situation.

"Yeah," agreed Max, apparently missing the cue as he scanned the crowd of guests that were congregating toward the back of the room by the bar. "I'll make sure I'm available." He turned back to them. "But right now I have to go make sure my dad doesn't try to sneak out while no one is looking."

## *Dominique – Misunderstood*

Sundays were usually reserved for family dinners at Deveraux House. But Grandma had a meeting later, so the meal had been moved to brunch. Dominique opened her mouth to say the thing that was pressing on her mind—she needed to talk to the police—but the words died in her mouth as she looked around the table at her family.

Evan was silently downing mimosas as he picked at a waffle. As usual, he looked perfect. His red hair in perfect order. His button-up and slacks perfectly pressed. Mouth perfectly shut. These days, Evan never said much at the family meals unless it was about work or if someone asked him a direct question. Not that she minded his silence. Quiet Evan was far better than most other Evans. Quiet Evan might be brooding, he might be ignoring them, or he might be still high from the night before, but at least he wasn't being viciously condescending or outright abusive as he had been for her entire childhood.

Aiden poked at his eggs and stared obsessively at his plate. She didn't think he'd blinked in the last minute. Aiden, despite graduating top of his class and working for a prominent law firm, was known for spacing off in a way that had earned him a dumb blond reputation. Dominque thought it was a self-defense mechanism to keep himself from pointing out the blatant stupidity of whoever was talking to him, but at the moment, she had to admit it looked more like plain zoning out.

Jackson's dark head was down, checking his phone, which,

considering his well-known dislike for the security breach known as social media, probably meant he was emailing someone. Three years ago, when Eleanor's private investigator had found Jackson incarcerated in a Chicago prison, they had all been shocked to learn that Randall Deveraux, Eleanor's oldest son, had produced an heir. It had taken a great deal of fancy footwork from Aiden and their grandmother's team of lawyers to get him released, and Dominique knew that the rest of society couldn't figure out why they'd bothered. But the predictions that he would blow his money on drugs and women and then blow town had been wildly wrong. Instead, Jackson had spent his money on every seminar and instructor who could info-dump how to be a one-man security force into his brain. Their grandmother's security had taken a giant leap forward into the twenty-first century because of him.

Grandma—elegant in a simple gray dress with one of her trademark vintage broaches and a short strand of pearls— read the paper. Dominique remembered happy childhood hours taking all the broaches out of their case and sorting them by size or by color or shape. Eleanor was sitting in her usual straight-backed position, holding the paper at what Dominique thought was a slightly awkward angle to avoid putting her elbow on the table. Because elbows should never ever be on the table.

None of them were looking at Dominique. They weren't even looking at each other. She wondered if this was what other family's dinners were like. Did other people talk to each other? She was willing to bet that Max and his dad talked to each other. Probably over beers while grilling things and laughing. Max seemed like he could manage flames and coals and other hot things. Yes, he could manage steamy things while shirtless. Definitely shirtless.

Dominque shifted in her chair. She should not be thinking about Max. Except possibly in bewilderment. No one apologized for things like that. They slunk away in shame or pretended it never happened. No man, certainly no man who had been the campus god that Max was, actually admitted to being the asshole that ordered a woman to go down on him and then apologized for it. In Dominique's experience, most men thought of themselves as the heroes in a story and admitting, even for a fraction of a second, that they had behaved less than heroically caused a system wide failure of the ego that made them lash out in anger. But Max had managed it. He'd apologized. Sincerely. And then he'd stuck around and helped. Who did that? She wondered how long he was staying with Grant. She hadn't even been able to say goodbye yesterday. She knew where Grant lived—maybe she could… Do nothing. Because she shouldn't be thinking about Max. She should be thinking about the crazy person who tried to kill her brother. And that brought her back to her original thought—she needed to talk to the police.

"I think," said Dominique, and they all lifted their heads to stare her, "I think I should try and talk to that detective again."

"Why?" asked Evan. "It could not have been more clear that he thought you were an idiot. I mean, maybe you misunderstood that. But the rest of us got it."

*Misunderstood.* That was one of Evan's favorites. Maybe she was so stupid that she misunderstood what Evan had meant by stupid. What Evan had meant by whore. What Evan had meant by useless. What Evan had meant by any of the other names he'd called her during her teen years. He had seemed to slow down the name calling sometime around college—now he settled for *misunderstood.*

"Do you really think you recognized that van?" asked Jackson, ignoring Evan. She wished that it was Saturday instead of Sunday. Since joining the family, Dominique and Jackson had taken to having Saturday brunch hash sessions. Sometimes with Aiden, sometimes not, but it had become her habit to discuss and dissect matters with Jackson. Sunday left no room for private conversation and she didn't feel comfortable revealing anything truly real in front of Evan or Eleanor. She couldn't help feeling that if she had twenty minutes alone with Jackson, she could figure out what she was supposed to do.

"I could barely tell it was a van," said Aiden. "That picture was total crap. Why bother paying for a security camera if the image quality is going to be that terrible? For the amount of money we pay that club, I would have expected 4D smell-o-vision."

"Those vans park right outside my window at work," said Dominique, ignoring her brother's commentary and attempting to cling to her point. "I have spent a fair amount of time contemplating those stupid pink license plate frame holders. Someone drove up in that van. Someone got out. That someone broke into that BMW and drove it through the window at Aiden. And then they drove away in that same stupid van with the same stupid pink license plate holder. The police should be investigating the company."

"Was it really pink though?" asked Aiden. "I mean, I kind of thought it had those what-cha-call-em—when pictures get all low res and weird colors start popping up?"

Evan and Jackson both stared questioningly at Aiden.

"JPEG artifacts," said Dominique.

"So nice that you two can share a brain cell," murmured Evan. "Grandma, are you done with the paper? I wouldn't mind reading something instead of listening to this."

"I thought it looked pink," said Eleanor, as she passed a portion of the paper to Jackson to give to Evan.

"Because it was pink," said Dominique. "Images experience color degradation when they're low res and they are successively down-saved or enlarged, but that was a first gen image screen capped out of a video. Pink is not just going to magically appear itself. Not in a consistent field like that."

"If you say so," said Evan, flipping open the paper. His tone was one of absolute disbelief.

She resisted the urge to trebuchet a spoonful of oatmeal over the battlements of his paper. "Yes, that is what I say. I said it yesterday. I'm saying it today. And I think I should say it tomorrow to the police."

Eleanor sighed. "You told it to the police yesterday. I'm reluctant to have you seen going into a police station."

Because appearances are everything—the unspoken Deveraux motto.

"And what if they don't do anything about it?" asked Dominique. "Are we supposed to let this asshole take another shot at you?"

"They didn't get anywhere near me," said Eleanor calmly, clearly choosing to ignore Dominique's bad language. "The reason that they had to use that car was that they realized they *couldn't* get anywhere near me. Our security is working."

"Except that Aiden and Jackson almost died," objected Dominique.

"Meh," said Evan from behind the paper. There was silence from the entire table. That was unacceptable even for Evan. It was also unusual. Of the three of them, Evan had actually been the most certain that Jackson should join the family. Jackson and Evan's mothers had both been Ukrainian, and, periodically, Dominique had heard them speak to each other in their literal mother tongue. Evan might be blasé about Aiden's death, but she thought he would actually care about Jackson, just a little.

"I meant," Evan said, lowering the paper slightly, "that it

wasn't *that* close. It just seemed close because there was a lot of dust and screaming. Mostly from Dominique, but still."

She felt a pang of self-doubt. Was he right? Was she overreacting? Maybe the license plate frame hadn't been pink? Maybe it had been pink but wasn't from the same company. Maybe she was wrong. If she went to the police and it turned out she was wrong then she was going to look like an idiot. And Evan would never let her live that down.

"It looked pretty close from where I was standing with my nose twelve inches away from the bumper," snapped Aiden.

Evan gave a shrug. "I was only agreeing with Grandma."

"And I just think that... maybe someone should investigate," said Dominique, hating herself for the uncertainty in her voice.

"I can look into it today before we leave," volunteered Jackson.

"Waste of time," muttered Evan, putting the paper back up.

"Text me the address," said Jackson. "I'll go knock on the door."

"No," said Eleanor. "We can't interfere in a police investigation. Dominique, if you really feel strongly about it, we'll have Aiden send them a letter. I want to keep everything formal and in writing."

She eyed at Aiden, who looked as skeptical as she felt. A letter was crap. It didn't matter if it came from the Deveraux lawyer on the Deveraux letterhead. Nothing was happening for a letter.

"But," said Eleanor, "thank you for raising the point. I'm glad we could all discuss it." Eleanor smiled at her, and then her hand flicked out, settling her bracelet back into place on her wrist. It was the smallest gesture, but it said louder than anything else that the decision had been made. Eleanor had already turned her eyes back to the paper. Dominique glanced at Jackson, who subtly wagged his phone at her. She smiled. Jackson hadn't grown up with Eleanor— he didn't have the same ingrained instinct to follow her decisions.

Dominique took a bite of her oatmeal and glanced at Evan, who was frowning at something in the paper. It occurred to her that as much as she hated Evan, he had also refused to stick with Grandma's decisions on occasion. Like every year on the anniversary of their parent's death, when he refused to visit the cemetery with the rest of them. Apparently, then, it was just she and Aiden who couldn't stand on their own? She glanced at Aiden. There was always the infamous Cancun trip Aiden had taken against Grandma's wishes and come home with only one eyebrow and a black eye. So… what? That meant it was just her?

It was a florist. The van belonged to a florist. A florist whose delivery drivers she'd talked to on more than one occasion. If Jackson could go knock on the door to a florist, so could she. She was probably overreacting anyway. They would probably just say that they bought the pink license frame holders in bulk or something and that every third white van in the tri-state area had them. It couldn't be that big of a deal. She would go, look, chat, and then come back when it proved to be nothing, and no one would have to know.

# Jackson – The Children

Jackson watched Dominique exit the house into the clear October sunshine. She pulled her hat down and marched out to her cab looking…determined. At the end of the walk, she paused to kick a pumpkin that was part of the festive holiday décor Eleanor mandated for the house. The kick sent the pumpkin skittering out into the road. Dominique didn't go to retrieve it. That wasn't a good sign.

Theo, the Deveraux butler, made a cluck of disapproval as he watched his decorative efforts die a sad death under the wheels of Dominique's cab.

Jackson had been a Deveraux for what felt like all of three minutes, but it had only taken two to realize that when Dominique wanted something, she went after it. Trying to stop her usually just meant that she did it, whatever *it* was, the dangerous way. Dominique committed to her decisions completely—like when she decided a jailbird cousin that she'd never met was going to be part of her family. Jackson loved that about her, but it wasn't always the safest trait.

"She was peevy," said Aiden, taking his jacket from Theo, who brushed a spec of lint off Aiden's shoulder and then disappeared to collect Evan's jacket from the closet. Theo always seemed to know just when to evaporate.

"She thinks she's right," said Jackson.

"Mm," said Aiden, who probably knew his sister well enough to know what that meant. "Maybe I'll…" Aiden trailed off, frowning. Of all of them, Aiden looked the least Deveraux-ish. He had the blue eyes and blonde hair of the Deveraux men but his father's happy-go-lucky personality. The society pages sometimes referred to him as Prince Charming and it was a nickname that seemed to fit. Usually, he was the one to make them all laugh and would never take anything seriously. Usually. Jackson knew that the Deveraux bedrock of stubbornness and steel was buried under that good-natured façade.

"I don't know," said Aiden, looking distressed. "What should I do? Call her? I can write Grandma's stupid letter. But I don't think it will do any good."

"Don't worry about it," said Jackson. "I'll check in with her later."

Aiden, always territorial about his sister, took a deep breath as if he was about to argue. "Dealing with the police is my job," said Jackson, "I'll touch back if I need you to go full lawyer."

"Yeah, OK. Thanks," said Aiden, clearly happy to have the problem off his plate.

Aiden exited the house and got into his vintage Aston Martin convertible. Jackson checked his phone. Aiden's locator app was currently working, as was Dominique's. Strangely, of the three of them, Aiden was the most likely to scrub his phone and disappear. Jackson wasn't sure if that was because Aiden remembered to check his phone and had deleted the software—which seemed unlikely—or if it was because the IT department at his work was actually on top of things. Aiden never mentioned it, but the Deverauxes didn't mention a lot of things.

Jackson watched with a frown as his cousins departed. He'd already suggested to Eleanor that he give them security details and she had shot the idea down because it might appear paranoid. However, they were starting to reach the point where he might need to ignore Eleanor. But bucking an Eleanor directive meant being sneaky or being prepared for a showdown. Eleanor did not take shit from anyone, and she had the kind of lead pipe sensibilities that put loan sharks he knew to shame. There was a reason that half the Senate was afraid of her. The other half of the Senate wasn't scared because they were too stupid to realize that a grandmother could fuck up their lives that badly.

"Problems?" asked Evan, appearing next in line to get his coat. Jackson smiled at his older cousin because he thought not many people smiled at Evan—not that Evan ever tried to give anyone something to smile about. Evan looked pale and tired, but as usual his red hair was in perfect order and clothes were immaculate. When Jackson had first arrived in the family, Evan had been the easiest to get along with. Evan wanted him here. Of course, Evan had been doing a lot more drugs at the time. Now the drugs had tapered off, but that actually seemed to be making matters worse. Lately, Evan had gotten harder and harder to reach.

"I was thinking I might want to assign you all security," said Jackson. He sometimes found that blunt honesty tricked Evan into saying something real.

"No," said Evan firmly. "I do not want that." He paused and shifted his weight. "You can give it to the Aiden and Dominique though. That would probably be good." Was Evan attempting to be helpful? He'd been a dick earlier at brunch about the car, but this comment sounded almost... not dickish. How to respond?

"Evan," said Jackson. "I want *all* of you to be safe." That was honest and left a lot of opportunity for response.

Evan looked haughty. "I don't like being safe," he said and left the house without a backward glance. Jackson thought Evan's response also had the benefit of being completely honest. Unfortunately, it definitely couldn't be categorized as helpful.

Jackson looked at the butler. Theo was pushing sixty and had been in employed at Deveraux House since he was twenty. Theo knew far more about the family than Jackson did, but he rarely handed out advice or commentary. Today was no exception. The man's face remained impassive as he shut the door and went back into whatever clockwork cupboard he stored himself.

Jackson went into Eleanor's office—she was on the phone, as usual. He waited while she talked, trying to formulate the best approach.

"David," said Eleanor in what Jackson considered her soothing mother-knows-best voice. It surprised him how many senators responded to it. "I understand completely. That is so frustrating." She paused. "I know! I know. You deserve it so much more. But these things really have to be hammered out in committee and sometimes the most deserving person doesn't get the position. It's really frustrating." There was another pause. "Mmm-hmm," she said, opening up her laptop and typing in her password. "Completely." She flipped open her email and perused the contents.

Jackson settled into the chair across from the desk. He wondered if David realized he'd been shuffled to a background task. Probably not.

He remembered the first day he'd met Eleanor. It hadn't been a good day. He had been barely twenty-three and fresh off one more fight in the yard, and then he'd been pulled out of his cell and sent into an interview room. Jackson had assumed it would be cops wanting him to snitch on something. He hadn't been prepared for what waited for him. At the table sat a non-descript, middle height, middle weight nobody of a man who Jackson thought would make a great pick-pocket—he introduced himself as Pete Schalding. At the back of the room, leaning against the cinderblock wall, eyeing him with an intense fixation had been Eleanor. She was distinctly not introduced.

Jackson wasn't new to interview rooms. He knew that the person standing at the back was almost always the heavy—the one with the brass knuckles or an equally damaging folder of legalese. Only this woman didn't look like a lawyer.

"Hi Pete," said Jackson, sitting down at the table, deciding to play along.

"Hi," said Pete, scrutinizing his face as if looking for something particular. "Jackson Zane?"

"Yeah," said Jackson.

"Zane isn't a very Ukrainian last name."

"Neither is Schalding," said Jackson.

"But your file says you're Ukrainian," said Pete.

"My mom changed it," said Jackson. "She liked Zane Gray novels." And hated her conservative religious parents, not that Pete needed to know that.

"OK. Um," Pete hesitated, seeming to look for words. Whatever he wanted to talk about was making him uncomfortable. "We've got a couple of questions for you," said Pete.

"Who's we?" asked Jackson, taking out his soft pack and tapping it on the edge of the table. Pete eyed the box of Sobranie cigarettes but didn't comment as Jackson lit up.

"Interested parties," said Pete.

"She's standing right there," said Jackson. "You couldn't just use an alias or something?"

The woman was older and dressed like someone who'd never previously seen the inside of a prison. She was wearing pearls and a sweater with some sort of fancy emerald broach. He didn't even know what to do with that. Women like her, in his experience...

He looked at her again and decided that he had never had any experience with a woman like her. She was obviously pulling the strings of the puppet in front of him, but it was as if she had put on soft clothing to look soft and sweet—like someone's rich grandmother. He didn't think he should make that mistake.

"Like I said, we have questions," said Pete again.

"And like I said: who's asking? You're not cops. Who are you?"

"I'm a private investigator," said Pete, reluctantly.

"So I'm not required to talk to you at all," said Jackson.

"No," said Pete, looking exasperated. "But, if we could just—"

"Yeah, yeah," said Jackson, blowing a smoke ring, and deciding that he'd wrung all the amusement he was going to get out of Pete. Besides, now he was curious. He didn't think he'd ever done anything private investigator worthy. "Ask your questions." Behind Pete, the woman was watching him with a wary expression. As he blew out the smoke ring, she jerked back slightly. He couldn't see why—it was just a stupid party trick.

Pete pushed an orange file folder toward Jackson. "Do you recognize this man?" asked Pete, flipping open the folder. Jackson tried to breathe normally, forcing air in and out of his lungs at a normal rate, masking the suddenly rapid pace of his heart. On the list of questions he'd expected to be asked, that hadn't even cracked the top one thousand.

"Nope," he replied, carefully not fidgeting with his lighter, "don't recognize him. Why, what'd he do?"

Pete glanced nervously at the woman, then back at Jackson. "He didn't do anything," said Pete. "He's dead."

Jackson looked at the photo again. He was about 98 percent sure that the man in the picture was his father. Not that his mother had ever specified. "I didn't kill him."

"No," said the man, seeming distressed, and then he looked to the woman again.

"I'll take it from here, Peter," said the woman, pushing away from the wall and Pete seemed to breathe a sigh of relief.

"I'll be outside, ma'am."

She nodded but didn't make any other comment as he left.

Then she came over to the table and sat down across from him, picking up the picture.

"His name," she said, "was Randall Deveraux. Ten years ago, he died in a plane crash with his brother Owen, their sister Genevieve, and her husband Sam Casella."

"Bad day for the Deveraux family," said Jackson, feeling a sense of vindication. There was a reason his father hadn't come back for him. Not that it mattered.

"Fifty-fifty," said the woman, with a shrug. "Genevieve and Sam were a tragedy, but Randall and Owen were sadists. Their funerals were attended by a great many people who wanted to make sure they were dead."

"Harsh," said Jackson.

"No, not really. What was harsh was abandoning them to their father and letting him turn the boys into monsters."

"Not really a winning parenting move," agreed Jackson.

"No," agreed the woman. "As their mother, I should have done more to protect them."

Jackson felt his heart rate pick up again. He wasn't sure what she wanted from him, but she had to know. There could only be one reason for her to seek him out.

"Why didn't you?" he asked.

"Hard to protect anyone with a broken arm and ribs. Their father was not a very nice man. It took me over a decade to figure out how to protect myself, and by the time I did, it was too late for my sons."

She looked at the picture again. "Are you sure you don't recognize him at all? Even when you look in the mirror?"

He was silent.

"I'm Eleanor Deveraux," she said. "I'm your grandmother."

"What do you want?" he asked.

"What do *you* want?" she parroted back to him.

"You came looking for me," he said. "Not the other way around."

"I've been looking into your past," she said, smiling at him. The smile felt genuine, but he couldn't understand why—his past was nothing worth smiling about. "Not really a groups person are you? Like doing things on your own?"

"I enjoy being independent," hedged Jackson. It was easy to be independent when you didn't have anyone to depend on.

"And how is that going for you?" she asked. She reached over and touched the side of his face where it was still bruised. Her fingers were cool against his skin, but he jerked his head back out of her reach as if it burned. "I had a word with your arresting officer. He offered up the opinion that he hoped you got beaten to death in prison."

Jackson grinned. "I may have instant messaged his wife and casually mentioned that her dipshit husband was having an affair with his partner."

"Well, apparently, he does not appreciate having to pay alimony. I have also spoken to your former social worker."

Jackson tried not to groan. He knew exactly which social worker she was referring to—the tirelessly caring Brandi Oluo. He'd aged out of her program five years ago and she had still sent him a batch of cookies last Christmas.

"I told her we were reviewing you for a special early release program and she called me back six times and emailed me three letters of recommendation. She seems to think that you're off-the-charts smart, sensitive, caring and a prime example of someone who has slipped through the cracks in the system."

Jackson knew Brandi's opinion. And he knew that her opinion didn't do him a damn bit of good when he needed to pay rent. He also knew that words like *sensitive* and *caring* didn't exactly earn him extra points in prison. He wasn't sure why his mysterious grandmother had shown up, but if she wasn't going to help him, then he didn't really need to revisit the past.

"Lady, what do you want?"

"I want you to join my gang. It's not a very big gang. There's only three of them. But I'm getting older and I need someone to help me."

"Help you do what?" Jackson didn't know what the fuck she was talking about. She sounded insane. Was this a job interview? Weren't grandmothers supposed to be sweet and caring? Admittedly, his mother's mother had cursed him to hell and told him that he was possessed of the devil the last time she'd seen him, but theoretically grandmothers were supposed to be nice.

"I believe the position is referred to as an enforcer. I need you to protect the gang from outside threats and enforce my decisions within the gang, as well as keep an eye on whatever it is that they get up to when I'm not looking."

Jackson was familiar with what enforcers did. Her description was accurate. He'd just never heard it put with such an Ivy League accent.

"Just hire out," he said. He wasn't sure what he was supposed to feel, but he decided that he felt insulted that his grandmother would seek him out only to offer him a fucking job.

"That would never do. Your cousins would never permit an outsider to join them."

"My cousins?" There were others?

"Evan, Owen's son, and Aiden and Dominique, Genevieve's children."

"You want me to go home with you and keep an eye on your grandchildren? Do I look like a babysitter? I don't know shit about kids." He buried his momentary interest. It was never going to amount to anything. He was in prison and he was going to stay there for the next five to ten years unless they carried him out in a body bag.

"Evan is a few years older than you. Aiden is about your age. And Dominique is a few years younger. They need a contemporary to help curb them."

Jackson turned the idea over for a moment, wishing it were a possibility.

"You belong with us," said Eleanor, reaching out to touch his hand, this time he didn't pull away. "You should have been with us to begin with. I don't understand how Randall could have been so careless."

Randall had not been careless. Randall had acquiesced to the wishes of Jackson's mother. Most people had.

"But having explored your past, I've come to the conclusion that simply offering you a home is not likely to sway you."

"So this is your way of persuading me?" asked Jackson. "Offering me a job spying on my newfound relatives?"

"No, this is my way of killing two birds with one stone. I'm telling you what I want you to do for me, and I'm telling you what you will get return."

"And what will I get?"

"You will inherit millions."

"I don't need you then," said Jackson. "If I'm really Randall's..." he hesitated, he'd never actually said the word out loud before, "his son, then I'll just sue you and collect my millions."

She smiled. "I have a lot of lawyers and you're not mentioned in his will. Related or not, you'll never see a dime."

"I'm in prison, I have nothing but time and prison lawyers are better than you think."

"And I can get you out. I have a lot of money and a lot of lawyers and I will make it happen."

He had stared at her. She met his eye with a rock-hard look that made him believe more than any words that she meant what she said—she would get him out of jail.

Millions. Cousins. Freedom. Freedom from here, anyway. He thought about his mother, pulling him away from a family wedding. *We don't need them. We just need you and me.* Only she had fucking OD'd and left him on his own. What had being alone ever gotten him? Sleeping with one eye open. No one to watch his back. Always on the losing end. He'd always wanted brothers and sisters. He'd wanted what everyone else seemed to have—a family. This woman had his family.

Eleanor wound up her call and Jackson brought his gaze down from the coffered ceiling and out of the past.

Eleanor hung up the phone. "I suppose at my age it shouldn't be, but I admit that it is a surprise to me how many men constantly need to have their ego assuaged."

"Giant babies," said Jackson.

"In congress, certainly," she agreed. "Where are we on yesterday's incident?"

"The police have dick," said Jackson. "Mostly because the lead detective is one." Eleanor frequently thought the police were idiots—she would instinctively want to side against them, which was what he wanted. "I think we ought to let Dominique try again. I think she's right."

"No," said Eleanor. "The less the children are involved with my messes, the better. I dislike it intensely that Aiden was even partially targeted by these crazy people."

Jackson pursed his lips, trying to figure out how to push

Eleanor down the road he wanted her to travel. "I don't think they're crazy."

"Fine. Persons with mental health challenges."

Jackson laughed. "I'm not the press. You can use all the non-politically correct words you want. No, I meant, I literally don't think they have mental health challenges. I think it's bigger than that."

Eleanor's perfect French manicured nails tip-tapped on the top of the desk as she considered. "You think it's…directed?"

"Yes. I think there's a plan at work."

"You want me to turn you loose, don't you?"

"Yes," said Jackson. "You've been letting the police handle it. All that's gotten us is a car aimed at Aiden."

There was more tapping. "How far along are you?" she asked.

"Nowhere. I've been letting the police handle it," said Jackson innocently. Eleanor raised an eyebrow and Jackson grinned. She liked it when he was impudent. She didn't mind it when he knew things—it was only when he acted that she got antsy. "Pete and I, through our various channels, have sourced the mailbox from which the letters were mailed. It's taken some legwork, but we've found some security cameras that show someone who may or may not be our letter writer. I'm going to take another look and compare it to the footage from the tennis club."

"I thought the police impounded that?" asked Eleanor frowning.

"I was on-site first and had a good half-hour before the cops even made it into the security room. If I can't get a copy made in that time, then we are not paying that place enough money."

Eleanor smiled. "All right, so say we tie the letter writer to the incident. Then what?"

"More leg work," said Jackson. "Hunt down witnesses who

saw the guy, figure out where they came from, figure out where they are now. Go there, shoot them in the head."

"Jackson!" snapped Eleanor.

"What?"

"We do not say such things out loud."

"Fine," said Jackson. "We turn them gently over to the police. But first I'm going to talk to Dominque about her florist."

"I'm sure that is nothing," said Eleanor. "I mean, really—a florist's van that she sees at work? That sounds ridiculous. It's an accounting firm. How many flowers could they possibly be ordering? Why she wants that ridiculous sham of a job, I will never understand." Jackson smiled at the abrupt segue to Dominque's job. No one in the family, even Aiden, really understood why Dominique would go through the trouble of not being a Deveraux.

"She wants to succeed like a regular person," said Jackson.

"She is not a regular person," said Eleanor. "She is a Deveraux. And she is wasting her time. Personally, I blame you for her insistence on doing this."

"She was heading there with or without me," said Jackson. "I just make sure her undercover status stays undercover. Dominique Casella is doing great and none of your snobby friends have to know about it. It's all part of her master plan. Let the girl rock and roll."

"Master plan?" said Eleanor, arching an eyebrow. "She's a baby. She has no plans."

Eleanor was a very smart woman, but she had blind spots about *the children* as she called them. "We'll keep Dominique away from the police," said Jackson, wanting to appear to concede. "You're probably right. I'll check out the florist myself."

"I don't think it's necessary," she complained. But he noted that she didn't say no. "It's awkward to insist the police listen to my grandchild. It smacks of nepotism."

"You know what's going to be even more awkward? If she turns out to be right. It's a loose end," he added and watched her frown. She hated loose ends. "It'll take me two seconds. Let's just do it and then we can tell Nika we take her seriously, but she was wrong."

"Well, that wouldn't hurt," admitted Eleanor. "I don't want her to feel like we don't listen to her. But why don't you wait until we get back from DC? There's no rush and I want you focused on security there."

Jackson did not think she was more likely to be attacked there. Senate security was good and when she wasn't in the Capitol, he had a solid team in place. He thought the weak point was here at home and he'd said as much, but he didn't think Eleanor liked hearing it. He tried to evaluate how far to push.

"I'll wait until after we get back from DC," he said. "But at some point, I'll be running down every lead we've got, whether you think it's stupid or not." He watched for her reaction to his warning flare.

"Well, don't let me tell you how to do your job," said Eleanor with a disapproving sniff. He wasn't worried about disapproval. She could disapprove all she liked as long as she didn't actually attempt to stop him.

"Thanks, Grandma," he said with a laugh. "I'll remember that next time you tell me how to do my job."

# Maxwell - Play Date

Max lay on his bed in his father's guest room and stared at the ceiling. He was giving serious thought to taking a shower so he could think about Dominique and jack-off. Was it something about being under the same roof as his father that made him want to act like a teenager or was it something about Dominique?

By the time he'd returned to his father's condo the previous evening, it had felt like another day at work—all cops, all the time—only it was worse because he couldn't pull his shield and boss the local PD around. Usually, being a U.S. Marshal gave him privileges at a crime scene, but being on vacation and between assignments made him merely inconvenient. At some point, Dominique and her family had been separated from the other guests and moved to another room. He hadn't even had a chance to say goodbye. Not that it mattered. The obvious affection between the Deveraux siblings and Jackson pretty much negated any chance he had with Dominique.

He was stopped by the thought. Did he want a chance with Dominique?

Yes.

Six years were an eye blink as far as his body was concerned. He still wanted her. Only now, he actually liked her too. Watching her obvious panic and willingness to throw herself into the rubble to look for her brother and Jackson, and then seeing her put on a smile to go keep her grandmother's guests calm, he'd realized that she wasn't an ice queen. She never had been. It had always been the armor that she put on to deal with the assholes who wanted a piece of her. Somehow that made it worse that he had been one of the assholes.

He'd spent most of the day avoiding his father. Three days of togetherness was starting to wear on him. He'd used the condo's gym and then sat in the sauna for as long as he thought he could get away with. Now, he felt drained and lethargic and he smelled like whatever herb had been placed on the steam vent.

His phone jingled with a text. He picked it up and saw a message from his father. Apparently his father couldn't bother to walk the twenty feet down the hall to his room. He flipped open the message.

You have a guest.

Max stared at the message. What did that mean?

He got up, slipped into his shoes and walked down the hall to find out. He was almost to the living room when he heard his father bark out a laugh and the distinct sound of a feminine voice. He turned the corner and saw Dominique Deveraux standing on the Persian rug. She was wearing a sensible puffer jacket, jeans and boots and looked as if she had just breezed in from outside. She had a knit hat pulled down and her blonde hair poked out in two ridiculous poofs of cuteness on either side. She didn't look like the sleek, always prepared, always aware of the camera Dominique Deveraux from the society pages. She looked, to be perfectly honest, like someone way more fun.

"Hey," said Grant, looking up from his spot on the couch. "Dominique says you're taking her to dinner?"

"Um," said Max. His heart rate took a sharp spike upward. Was she serious? Had he put on deodorant? What was she doing here? What... Just, what? He looked from Grant to Dominique. She smiled hopefully.

"Yes?"

"Cool," said Grant. "I'll call Smitty and tell him I'm going to his poker night after all."

"Let me get my coat," said Max. He ducked back into his room, pulled on his coat and checked the mirror. His hair was doing that thing he hated, but there never seemed to be much he could do about that. On impulse, he grabbed his gun and tucked the holster into his waistband. If someone was targeting the Deveraux it might be a wise precaution. Dominique waited by the door when he returned. Her energy had a twitchy edge, and she practically bounced down the stairs in front of him as they left the building.

"I'm taking you to out to eat?" he asked when they were at street level. He checked his watch. It was almost four, which seemed early for dinner. He was mystified. He thought that they had parted at least on cordial *I no longer hate you* terms, but he had not predicted that she would reach out to him. He really didn't want to screw this up. She seemed nervous. What was she nervous about? Being with him? He didn't want that to be the case. Now he was nervous. Crap. Why couldn't he be cooler?

"I think I'll probably owe you dinner when we're done," she said, putting on her sunglasses and setting a brisk pace.

"Done with what?" he asked, taking a longing look at her ass before stretching his legs to keep up.

"Well, Jackson says if we're going to go on adventures that we should always have back-up, but I can't have him because he's with Grandma."

"We're going on an adventure?" he asked. He found himself grinning. He couldn't remember the last time anyone had promised him an adventure.

"Yes? Maybe? Maybe I'm wrong. Maybe it's not him."

"Not who?"

In response, she pulled out a printout. He'd seen the images the previous night on the footage from the club security cameras. The first was of the hooded figure who had launched the car through the country club window and the second was of the partially obscured license plate of the van that had picked him up.

"You saw this guy? Call the police!"

"I don't know if it's him," she said. "I might be getting carried away. I want another look, but I thought I should take back-up. You do the thing too, so I thought you could be back-up."

"What thing?" He was thoroughly confused.

"The tough guy thing. Where you talk to cops and know about guns and things. You *can* punch people, right?" She gave him an arched eyebrow over her glasses, clearly taunting him, and he was torn between confusion and amusement.

"I can," he agreed. "But I try not to. Are you planning on punching people?"

"No! Hopefully, they won't even see us. But I do *try* to listen to Jacks about these kinds of things. It's better to believe people who have experience."

He felt his heart sink. Being the boyfriend substitute was not what he wanted. And now he wanted to know just what Jackson had experience in.

She hesitated at the curb, checking the traffic, clearly planning on cutting across.

"Not going for the crosswalk?" he asked. "You rebel."

"I'm lawless and there's no stopping me," she said, craning to see around a parked car. Being taller, he could see over it and realized that the road was clear.

"You'll never make it. You'll be arrested and die," he said, stepping off the curb ahead of her. She laughed and hurried to catch up with him.

"So where did you bump into this guy?" he asked, when they got across the street.

"I didn't bump into him," she said. "I work for an accounting firm."

"You're an accountant?" For some reason that was the strangest thing she'd said to him yet. He supposed that accountants *could* be drop-dead sexy, but it certainly went against their stereotype.

"No, I do marketing for the accounting firm. But we work with all kinds of clients, one of which is a florist, so of course we order our front desk flowers from them. And they deliver in white vans with pink license plate frame holders." She held out the photo again.

"You need to call the police," he said, staring at the blurry but distinctly pink license plate frame.

"I already told them last night," she said, "when I saw the video. But the police detective, in the most condescending way possible, told me to leave the police work to the police. And I really was going to, but..."

"But you decided you wanted to get yourself killed?"

"Don't be ridiculous," she said. "That's why I'm bringing you. So I don't get killed." She hesitated and paused on the sidewalk, causing an annoyed grunt from another pedestrian who was forced to detour around them. "The detective seemed really certain that I was wrong. And Evan seemed really certain. Of course, he is always certain I'm wrong. But, I don't know, I thought I'd just cross this off the list and then I could stop worrying that there were killer florists out there. I didn't think I'd actually find anything."

"But you did?" Max didn't know whether to smile or be alarmed. Dominique looked upset and for some reason a little embarrassed.

"I was going to pretend to check on flowers for the office. But then, before I could even go in, I saw this guy!" She pointed to the picture, then bit her lip. "Or maybe not. He looked like the picture, but I mean, that picture is pretty vague. But he was wearing the same kind of pants. You can see the logo on the back pocket. Carhartt. Whatever that is."

"They're work clothes," said Max, deciding that alarmed was more the emotion to go with. Dominique had pulled straight $A$'s in college. She hadn't ever seemed prone to logic failures. If she was even remotely on the right track, she could be walking into a load of trouble. "You didn't go in, did you?"

"I chickened out," she said, shaking her head. "I did a walk by and there were a bunch of people in the shop, even though it's Sunday. I called Jackson, but like I said, he's with Grandma. And then I remembered that you were staying with your dad and he lived close by, so I came to get you. I thought we could loiter in the park across from the florist and take pictures of anyone who comes out." She stared up at him anxiously. "You don't mind, do you?"

Loiter in a park on a sunny afternoon with a beautiful girl? Why would he mind? Other than that they were looking for someone who might want to kill her. The thought brought him up short.

"I want to, but..."

Her shoulders sagged. "It's fine," she said, hitching her purse up higher on her shoulder. "I mean, if you think it's stupid, you don't have to come."

"No!" Max felt a swell of panic as she took a half step away from him and crossed her arms. "No, I believe you. But I want you to be safe. What if we just go see the lead detective on the case? I think I've got his card somewhere."

She shook her head. "Grandma was super adamant that I not be seen going into a police station. And then she suggested that I let Aiden write a letter." She pointed at him with a little laugh. "Yes, that's the face I made. Basically, if I don't come back with some sort of evidence, I'm pretty sure that I'm going to be ignored as being a hysterical female."

Max frowned, realizing why she was nervous. She thought he was going to brush her off or call her stupid. It was a bullshit position for either her family or an investigator to take—a good investigator sought trust and listened to every witness. Ignoring someone was how details got missed. On the other hand, the police detective had seemed like a territorial asshole, so she was probably right.

"So, basically," she continued, "I'm going to do this. I was just hoping that... you would... you know..."

"Risk life, limb and a Sunday afternoon based on your first-hand observation of a pink license plate holder and knowledgeable understanding of pants styles?" he asked, leaning in with a smile.

"Yes?" She smiled hopefully.

He considered the matter. He was probably being an idiot, but he really didn't want to disappoint her.

"All right, but we are not to approach them. We stick with observing and leaving."

"That's all I want to do," she said, nodding vigorously. "I swear. I'm not crazy. I just don't like people trying to squash my family. Except for Evan. He could be squashed and that would be OK." She paused, eyes narrowing as she contemplated the option. Then sighed. "No, it wouldn't really. I really can't have people squashing *any* Deveraux. It sets a bad precedent."

"Sure, it's precedent you're worried about," he said with a laugh.

They reached the edge of a quiet neighborhood with a mix of shops and narrow row houses centered around a park. The park itself was a scraggle of under-kempt bushes, littering oak trees, and a play area that had seen better days.

"The florist is just down there," she said pointing down the block to where he could see a pink neon sign. He looked around, trying to get his bearings and form a plan. A group of kids were playing on the playground, or at least screaming at each other in something that passed for play. The moms and nannies loitered on nearby benches checking their phones and drinking coffee. Pedestrians cut across the park to their various destinations. He looked back at Dominique who was watching him.

"If you're waiting for me to be brilliant, it'll be a long wait," he said, and she grinned.

"I'm waiting for you to have a strategy. Jackson always has a strategy—which is the Deveraux approved philosophy, but I don't know what the right strategy is here."

He wasn't sure how much he was going to like this afternoon if she was going to spend it comparing him to Jackson. "The strategy with surveillance is always to blend in and not look like you're watching someone. We want to look casual. We want to look like we belong. We want to not attract attention to ourselves," he said.

She nodded and turned around and looked at the park, like he had done. "I should have borrowed a kid," she said. "That would totally blend."

"Not an option," he said. "Rent-a-kid is closed on Sunday."

"Well, next time we'll kidnap one," she said. "I'm sure that will go well."

"Definitely," he agreed.

"OK, so we don't have any kids, but… we should get coffee?"

"Yes," he said. "Now explain why."

She nibbled her fingernail and looked around again. "Adults who loiter in cold weather all bring hot beverages. Adults without hot beverages look like stalkers."

"Bingo," he said, and she beamed.

"Coffee shop is on the other side of the park," she said pointing. "So we go, we get the beverages and come back?"

"No, we amble slowly through the park and drift into position, like we just happen to be stopping."

"I'm so happy I decided to bring you."

He wasn't sure what she was basing her decision on, but he'd take it. He offered her an elbow and she tucked her arm through his, looking pleased.

The tables outside the coffee shop were full, showcasing a handful of bundled chess players and a few grumpy old men drinking tiny cups of espresso and reading what passed for news. Max couldn't help noticing that the Daily News had the Deveraux story on the front page which was now in the hands of a plaid deer-hunter-hat-wearing octogenarian.

Driving At Miss Deveraux.

The Daily News, as usual, thought they were funny. There was an unflattering picture of Eleanor below the headline and a picture of the wreckage.

"You done with the front page?" asked the man's friend—a slightly less wrinkly fellow in a knit hat with a yellow bobble on it—reaching across the table.

"Done before I started," replied the deer hunter. "Don't know why they waste the ink on the Deveraux. Ought to run them all over."

Max fought the inclination to stop in shock. Dominique continued on toward the door and he barely recovered in time to open it for her.

"Do people say that kind of thing a lot?" he asked.

She smiled at him in a sad sort of way and patted his arm. "Try not to let it bother you."

"Try not…" He stared at her, baffled. "They don't even know you. How can they say something like that?"

"Because they don't know me. They don't even know Grandma, and that's usually who they really mean. I try not to think about it."

He suddenly wanted to hug her. It must have shown on his face because she patted him again. "It's really fine. Forget about it." She took a few more steps into the space and he followed her, trying to take her advice and put it out of his head, but still grappling with idea of having an entire group of people passing judgement on her. He wasn't sure he could deal with the monumental unfairness of having people armchair quarterback his appearance and actions every day of his life. He wasn't sure how she managed it.

The coffee shop was a buzz of steaming milk and more chattering adults. An artistically drawn chalkboard sign above the counter proclaimed a ban on Pumpkin Spice with a flourish and a Day of the Dead sugar skull thrown in for good measure. This was not the *order what you want* kind of coffee shop. This was an *artisan* coffee shop and no one should dare to forget it. Customers were packed in tight, and a rumpled looking thirty-something typed furiously in the corner, periodically looking up in annoyance.

"Why do laptop people come to these places?" he asked, struck by the typer's bitter expression. "They never look happy."

"It's the requisite writer that's issued to you when you open a coffee shop," she said as she sorted through her purse. "Writers never look happy, except when they're by themselves, and then who would know?"

"Did you lose something?" he asked as she reached her arm into her purse again. The collection of items in her other hand was growing.

"I think I left my wallet at home," she said, looking plaintively up at him. "I changed purses because of the party last night and I think maybe it didn't make it back into this purse."

"But I just watched you pull out two ChapSticks, a pair of sunglasses, a tape measure, what I think was a set of false eyelashes, a stack of business cards and a one-dollar bill, so you know... You're all set if you want to moisturize and attend an outdoor networking event that requires you to measure and tip a very poor stripper."

"It was one ChapStick," she said with dignity. "The other one was a lip gloss."

He chuckled. "I'll buy you a coffee."

"Yes, but I was going to buy you dinner for helping me."

She looked genuinely distressed. It was probably the cutest thing he'd seen in weeks. Up there with kitten memes. "I can also buy you dinner."

"No! That wasn't the point!"

"The point wasn't to eat dinner? I'm confused."

"You're doing this on purpose."

"Making you forget your wallet? No, I don't think so."

"Maxwell," she said sternly, "I think you are—"

"Can I help you?" asked the barista.

"Yes," he said, promptly. "I'd like a sixteen ounce latte with skim milk and she will have..." he risked a glance at Dominique. She was glaring at him. He grinned unrepentantly and the corner of her mouth twitched. "Whatever she wants."

"The same," she said. "But decaf."

"So, like, not the same, then?" asked the barista, dripping hipster condescension from every beard follicle.

"I don't know," said Max. "It depends on what you want your tip to be."

"Exactly the same it is," said the barista, without blinking.

## Dominique – Max Sass

"Mr. Ames," Dominique said when they were outside, beverages in hand, "I did not know that you were so full of the sass." Full of sass, brains, and utter sweetness. Watching him realize that people said mean things about her and her family had been precious. He'd looked so distressed. It made her want to hug him.

"I have been accused of having maximum sass," he agreed.

"I guess, knowing your father, I should have expected it, but I really didn't. You were always such a jock in school."

"What do you mean, *knowing my dad*?" he asked.

"I don't know," she said, "he's just always very light-hearted. He makes me laugh. It makes sense that you would be equally cheeky."

"If you mean equally full of shit, then, sure. How often do you see my dad?" he demanded.

"Whenever he pops into the office," she said with a shrug.

He stared at her.

"My company does accounting for the school," she added.

He continued to stare.

"We usually chat for a minute. He's funny."

"So, you would say that you... like him?" he asked, looking so skeptical that she laughed.

"Yes! What kind of question is that?"

"I don't know. I've always thought of him as incredibly pushy. But maybe that's funny when you didn't grow up with him."

"It's my impression that your own parents are always more annoying than other people's parents." She did not add that, having lost her parents at ten, she'd never had the chance to test the theory herself, and she'd always envied her friends the ability to be mad at their parents.

She glanced up at Max as they walked. He was frowning thoughtfully. Last night, Max had been calm, professional, and obviously on the same wavelength as Jackson. She had selected him as her safety net based on those factors and his geographic proximity. And also, because later, when Jackson asked her what the hell she'd been thinking, she wanted to have someone else to point to. And, if she was honest with herself—although, she would never admit it to anyone else—she also kind of wanted to see Max naked.

She had spent a great deal of time in college declaring that he wasn't *all* that great looking, but truthfully? He really, really, really was. And she had hated him for it. His apology had come as a jaw-dropping shock, but equally surprising was that he was funny and charming. Why couldn't he have been like that in college?

"Why did you say that to me in school?" she asked, and he went red in the face.

"I'm really sorry," he said.

"Yes, I gathered that. Why did you say it in the first place?"

"I was really drunk, and I didn't plan that. I'd just moved up in the National rankings I was feeling on top of the world. I saw you and I got... I don't know... Then I walked over and I just... that's what came out."

"Yes, that was very disappointing," admitted Dominique.

"Disappointing?"

"Well, I'm at my very first college frat party and oh, look, a cute guy is coming over. What will the cute guy say? Will he introduce himself? No. Cute guy walks up and says, *let's go back to my room so I can watch you wrap your lips around my cock.*"

Max went an even brighter shade of red. "Again, I'm really sorry! I don't... That's not me. I don't say stuff like that!"

"Yes, I heard that from every other girl you dated. It was very infuriating to think that you reserved it just for me. It was like you thought all the other girls should be on a pedestal, but I should be on my knees."

Dominique watched the progression of his blush with interest. "That is not what I thought. That is not remotely what I thought. If I made you feel that way I am so, so sorry."

He was being incredibly sincere, and it was clear he was still embarrassed by the incident. After he had graduated and was no longer around to rub his handsome gallant suitor routine in her face, she had put it out of her head. One man's idiot suggestion was just filed with the rest of the idiot offers she received. But even six years later, it obviously still bothered him. Personally, she thought the statute of limitations on self-flagellation for bad decisions should be limited to three years.

"You did look sort of surprised after you said it," she said reflectively.

"I was!"

"And then I poured my drink all over you and you sort of nodded like, *yup, that's what happens when I say that*."

"Well, it's what *should* happen." His tone was bitter, and she laughed. "I said it," he continued, "and it was as if I was hearing someone else say it and I couldn't believe that had come out of my mouth. Like, in my head, it was totally fine and then it got out in reality and it was… not OK. It was this giant wake-up call that I was three steps toward douchebag city. I'm really sorry."

"Why didn't you just apologize when we were in school?"

"I was going to! I saw you at that Phi Sigma Sigma party and I was going to go over and apologize, and then you gave me that death stare and Becky Kaverton took off her shirt. And then I freaked out because you were standing right next to her and how was I supposed to come over after that without looking extra weird? Which I now realize is not a stellar excuse, but it was sort of a brain short circuit."

"Uh... yeah," she said. "Becky fried more than one person's brain. The way I look at it, sex is a human thing and it's not like guys have cornered the market on being assholes. But when you start adding in power and privilege, things get weird, and guys usually have more of those two items. Plus, in all honesty, those things were huge, right? Like some sort of natural wonder of the world?"

"Yes!" he exclaimed. "And real! I still don't understand how it's physically possible for a girl that tiny to have boobs that big."

"Some sort of genetic fluke," Dominique agreed. "Although, how did you know they were real?" She gave him a raised eyebrow.

"Not for the reason you think," said Max, emphatically. "She was a cheerleader and they were doing the pyramid thing and I was walking by. Behind the pyramid, I should note, where I thought I was out of the way. And I hear this screech and the next thing I know I've got a cheerleader hurtling at my head and I'm wearing Becky Kaverton's boobs on my face."

Dominique burst out laughing. "Yeah, they banned her from being the top of the pyramid at some point. She kept laughing at people below her and then she'd crash the entire thing."

Dominique kicked at a pile of orange leaves for the sheer joy of making leaves go crackle and swoosh and then realize it was a tad childish. But when she looked up at him to gauge his reaction, he was looking thoughtful.

"Wait," he said. "How did you know they were real."

Dominique realized too late that guilt was obvious on her face. His eyes widened in excitement. "Spill," he ordered.

"OK, well, number one, girls can tell. But also, I was at a party and, like you, I was really drunk, and I looked over—you remember the kind of shirts she wore?"

He nodded.

"And I said, *I'm not into girls, but I really want to motorboat your boobs.*"

Max tripped over his feet and stumbled, taking a giant step to stay upright, and his hand clamped around his cup causing a geyser of coffee to shoot out onto the gravel path.

"And then," continued Dominique, "Becky said, *They're real, you know! And when you do it, they jiggle like Jell-O. Like this.*" Dominique bounced up and down to demonstrate Becky's technique.

"What is wrong with you?" he demanded, sucking coffee off his hand. "You have to warn me if you're going to say shit like that."

"Do I?" asked Dominique, taking a sip of her own coffee. "But that would take all the fun out of it." She took a napkin out of her pocket and offered it to him. He took the napkin, shaking his head. Then he schlepped the ten feet back to a trash can to deposit his empty cup.

"OK," he said, coming back, "so we both drunkenly propositioned people in college. Nice to know we have that common."

"I'm still friends with Becky. We had a nice, long wine-fueled chat one night about the objectification of women's bodies and how as women we internalize Western patriarchal ideals and police each other, which super sucks. Particularly since she loves pin-up art and doesn't want to have to feel guilty when she wears heels and a polka-dot bikini."

"I..." said Max. "I don't think I can contribute on that topic."

"Of course not," said Dominique. "Trying to figure out the way forward in a conversation about sexuality, oppression and harassment without sounding like a mansplainer, douchebag, or idiot would be some next level shit. On the other hand, if we don't say this stuff to men, then men don't even know that the conversations exist to be had."

"Thanks? I think?" said Max with a frown. "I don't want to enforce patriarchy at people. I just want to be able to like girls in bikinis. And I have no idea how to talk about it without getting yelled at."

"Girls want to be liked in bikinis mostly," said Dominique with a shrug. "They just don't want to *have* to wear bikinis, or have you think a bikini is a permission slip to anything more than swimming, or that they exist only to wear bikinis."

"I do *not* think any of those things!" exclaimed Max triumphantly. "Hashtag winning at feminism."

Dominique laughed again. "Becky is also winning at feminism. She moved to Tahoe and is a professional wake-boarder with her own line of bathing suits for well-endowed women. I was one of her first investors. She is doing fascinating things with Lycra."

"Well, good for her. I guess that means there's hope for you and me to be friends too." He paused and gave her a look full of both discomfort and hope. "What should I have done? I have tried really hard not to be that guy so I wouldn't have this problem again. But I really don't know how to come back from it."

"You apologize and talk to the person like a human being. At least that's what worked for Becky and me. And you already pretty much covered that with me, so…"

He smiled at her and Dominque felt her heart melt a little bit. He offered her his arm again and she tucked her hand through, still smiling. She wished that the weather was a tad warmer so there was more Max and less jacket.

"So why do you think someone wants to kill your grandmother?" he asked.

"I don't know. The notes are always vague and rant about her liberal snowflake politics. But you would think there would be something… more specific, wouldn't you?"

"You have to really hate someone to want to kill them specifically," he offered. "It's usually personal. I mean, maybe only he perceives it to be personal, but there's usually something."

"The car bugs me," she said.

"It was upsetting," he agreed.

She shook her head and took a sip. "Yes, it's upsetting, but that's not what I meant. The use of the car bothers me and it took me until after brunch to figure out why. It wasn't aimed at Grandma. It was aimed at Aiden."

"More or less. A car is a pretty blunt instrument. Aiming may be a strong word."

"Yeah, but those are big windows. Anyone starting the car would have seen that Grandma wasn't in the vicinity."

"So they want to hurt the Deverauxes, not just her."

"But the notes are all specific to her."

"Killing her grandson would hurt her," he offered.

"Yes," she agreed, nodding. She wasn't sure how to express what she meant, and she chewed her bottom lip, trying to come up with the right words. "But the notes were death threats, not pain threats. It feels…"

"Off?" He suggested, and she nodded. He seemed to consider the matter.

"There's also the van," he said.

"What do you mean?"

"Angry white males that make death threats usually come to kill with guns and don't really have an escape plan. The van, the obscuring hoodie, that all says pre-planning. Which would imply that the threats are pre-planned as well."

"Pre-planned to do what?" she asked.

He seemed to ponder. "Scare her?" he offered. "I'm not sure.

You're right, it feels off. But, I'm not the investigator on this case. We may not know all the details."

She was unsatisfied by that answer. "Aiden is right," she said plaintively. "Everyone is operating under some sort of game theory and I don't know what the rules are."

He laughed. "Because Aiden is a master of predicting human interaction?"

"Oh, no," she said earnestly. "That's literally what he says— that he doesn't know what the rules are. He says he's permanently mystified by sixty-five percent of human activity."

"And the other thirty-five percent?"

"The law and sex. And he says he's got a lock on both of those."

Max shot her a dirty look. "I told you—warning. There needs to be warning. And now I'm going to wonder about how he got his numbers." They had reached the far side of the park and could see the lights on in the florist's shop, but blinds had been drawn across the windows. It seemed safe to go a little closer.

They were almost to the last of the trees before the street when the door opened. Max stopped by a tree and swung her around, putting his back to the shop. "You watch," he said. "Surveillance looks more realistic when a pair of people aren't both staring."

"I am learning so much," she said, feeling impressed. She handed him her coffee and took her phone out of her pocket. He took a giant drink out of her cup, his eyes twinkling above the rim, daring her to say something.

"You finished it, didn't you?" she demanded.

"You made me spill mine," he said, and she shrugged. That was true. He linked his hands around her waist, still holding her now empty cup, careful to not to make too much contact with parts that didn't belong to him. "What do you see?" he asked, leaning against the tree.

"Nothing. Your enormous shoulders are in the way."

"Oh? Sorry. Here." He pretended to squeeze his shoulders smaller. "Nope, sorry, this is as small as they go. You'll just have to try moving your head."

"So much sass."

She leaned slightly, her coat making a rasping noise as it brushed up against him. He smelled like sage, and she restrained the impulse to lean in and huff him.

"There's a group of people," she whispered. "They're standing out front talking. I've seen the owner before. None of them look like him."

"Can you take any pictures?" he asked.

With great concentration, she held her phone against his arm, and pinched to zoom in, snapping photos of the group as they left the florist's shop. She was concentrating so hard on taking photos that it was a moment before she realized they were walking her direction.

"Shit," she muttered. She glanced up at Max, struck by a hilarious thought. "Um, they're coming this way." She shifted her position in his arms. On TV, whenever anyone was trying to stay under cover, the couple always kissed. If her story about Becky's boobs had caused him to trip, what would this do?

# *Maxwell - Trailing*

Max went from trying to ignore the fact that Dominique smelled like she'd been bathing in cinnamon rolls and wondering if she tasted like icing, to having Dominique's lips planted on his. The angle wasn't quite right, and on instinct he adjusted his hold on her and corrected. Her lips were cool from the October air, but her mouth was warm. He was dimly aware of the passing group of people, but more aware of the fact that her body had melted against his, becoming a pliable invitation to go further. As their tongues met, he wrapped his arms around her more tightly, one hand coming to rest on her ass.

He realized, quite suddenly, that he was kissing someone else's girlfriend, and broke away. She was staring up at him with a dazed look and stepped back, touching her lips.

"Um, sorry," he said. "I wasn't quite prepared for that."

Why had he said that? What the fuck did that even mean? He decided to not make it worse by speaking further.

"Really? Because it seemed like you knew what you were doing," she said. She shook herself and looked around for their targets, which were moving away across the park. "Should we follow them?" she asked, doubtfully.

"No," he said.

She flipped open the photos on her phone. "I don't think these are good enough," she said, shaking her head. "They moved and I wasn't ready."

"I'm not sure how much good photos would do. We don't really have anything. Except that one guy was wearing the same kind of pants."

She frowned. "I'm following them."

"Dominique, no. That's a bad plan."

"Just across the park," she said, taking his hand. "They're probably going to dinner or something. Groups don't walk somewhere unless it's close by."

Reluctantly, he let her lead him after the group of six men but forced her to slow down as he tried to observe them—two black guys, three white guys and someone who might have been Asian or Hispanic. It was hard to tell at this distance. Dominique tried to speed up again.

"Walk casual," he whispered, pulling her back against him. "We're out for a romantic stroll, remember?"

"Right," she agreed, snuggling against his arm, keeping her hand tight around his. It gave him the electric thrill of attraction. The only thing that was saving him from an outright hard-on was the fact that he couldn't actually feel the details of her body through her puffer jacket. That, and he might or might not be following killers.

He tried to concentrate on the group in front of him and ignore Dominique. It was a task made more difficult by the fact that he could still taste her on his lips. He focused on the men and tried to cudgel his brain into ignoring his body. The clothing of the men was varied—track suit, jeans, Carhartts, hipster black—it was all different, but there was something about them that seemed homogenous. They were the same shape, he realized. Like Victoria's Secret models, if you popped their heads off, you wouldn't be able to tell which was which. They were all the same age, about the same height, and obviously in shape, and two of them had the same close-cropped, no nonsense hair-cut. Individually, it would have been hard to spot, but as a group, they practically shouted military. They were almost to the edge of the park.

"Dominique," he said, pulling up and bending down to fake tie his shoe. "I've got a bad feeling about this. Let's hang back."

"Um, yes," she agreed, sounding nervous. "One of them is looking at us."

Max stood back up as one of the group approached. Dominique covered her face by taking a drink of her now empty coffee cup.

"Hey man," said the guy, approaching. It was one of the white guys in jeans. "Do you happen to have a lighter? Mine just ran out." He held up a silver Zippo flip-top lighter. It had some sort of inscription or mark on it that Max couldn't read.

"Sorry—non-smokers," said Max with a smile.

The man ignored Max's comment and looked inquisitively at Dominique. Max was very glad she was wearing sunglasses and a hat. She shook her head.

"There's a vape shop around the corner," she offered, pointing.

"I'm not that big of a douchebag," said the man with a smile. "Thanks anyway." He turned and jogged back to his friends.

"Do we leave?" she whispered, looking up at Max.

"No," he said, leaning down to kiss her lightly, knowing for certain this time that they were being watched and depending on that fact to make the kiss acceptable. "We keep walking in the direction we were going." He held out his hand and she took it. "Try to look happy," he added. She didn't look happy. She looked worried. He needed her to change it up quickly. "People who do surveillance are never happy—like writers."

She laughed, which had been his intention.

"Maybe the police department should recruit out of the MFA program," she said, stretching her smile, leaning into the role and to him.

"It sounds good in theory, but the reports would always be in revision."

He took a side-long look up the path—the group ahead of them clustered at the corner.

"Should we keep going?" she whispered, still smiling.

Max considered. Smart move was to walk away, but they didn't actually have anything. He looked Dominique. She had the same steely look he remembered from when she'd poured her drink down his front. She wasn't about to run away. "We walk up to the corner, take one more look, and then go the exact opposite of whichever way they go."

"Got it," said Dominique, with a firm nod.

They walked along the path and Max tried to keep it brisk without being hurried. He was trying to time it so they wouldn't miss the light and their opportunity.

"I don't know," he said, raising his voice enough to be over-heard and taking out his phone, pretending to poke at it. "What time are our reservations?" He went to the crosswalk and punched the button.

Dominique burst out with a startled laugh. "How long were you in California? You know those don't actually work, right?"

"No?" he asked, looking at the button.

"She's right," said one of the group, turning to him. "They're not connected to anything. The crosswalks are on timers. They're goddamn placebo buttons. It's just the government fucking with you to give you the illusion of control."

Holding his phone low down at his side and angled up, Max snapped a photo of the one talking.

"Well, now I want to time them and find out," he said pivoting slightly, pretending to look up at the light. He snapped again. Hoping he caught the whole group. The men laughed.

"We don't have time for you to play public works director," said Dominique, taking another faux drink of her coffee.

"Reservations," Max said. "Right."

"Personally," said one of the group, "I think crosswalks are overrated." Then he proceeded to jaywalk, and his friends followed. They crossed the street and continued to the right. Max waited for the light to change and then led Dominique across the street going straight, trying to make it as obvious as possible that they were going a different direction.

"I really want to look back," she said.

"Yeah, but don't. Is there a restaurant around here somewhere?"

"I think there's an Italian place a few blocks up."

"Great, we'll head that direction."

"Did you get any good pictures?" she asked, keeping her voice low.

"Caught that?"

"Well, knowing your stance on crosswalks, it seemed unlikely that you really felt the need to push the button."

"I could use crosswalks. You don't know. I'm totally a rule follower. Boundaries and rules, I just toe the line."

She chuckled and he looked down at her, wanting to stop and wrap his arms around her and kiss her again like he had in the park.

Boundaries and rules—he toed the line all right, except for the one about her being in a relationship. That one he was stepping right over.

## *Dominique – Dinner*

Dominique sipped her wine and tried not stare at the adorable cowlick on Max's head as he studied the menu. She was fighting a serious urge to drop into his lap and smooth his hair down while he figured out what to do with the rest of her.

She had thought he would be startled and laugh when she kissed him. Instead, she was the one who had been surprised. The kiss was burning, passionate and had left her light-headed. But she didn't know what to do with his comment afterwards.

*I wasn't quite prepared for that.*

What the fuck did that even mean? Did it mean he thought he could do better? Because, she wasn't sure she could handle better. At least not in public. Better might end up with her panties exploding off of her. Did he mean that he hadn't expected that and had gotten carried away? That was her preferred explanation. After his sudden withdrawal it had taken all of her concentration to focus on the task at hand and it hadn't helped that he kept insisting that she snuggle up to him. Way too distracting. And now he was acting all reserved and that wasn't helping either.

"Fly in your wine?" he asked, and she looked up at him and blinked, trying to think of something pertinent.

"I was trying to decide if I just got... If I were telling someone about this, they would say that nothing really happened. We stalked some people. One of them asked us for a light. And then we chatted about crosswalks and they left. I was trying to decide if I was making things up."

"No, you aren't," he said firmly. "I don't know if those guys are connected to what happened at the tennis club, but that wasn't normal."

"How do you know?" she asked.

"No cigarette. Smokers wouldn't hold up the lighter. They would hold up the cigarette, the thing they want lit. They were all military or ex-military, I'm certain of it. And they all looked at your face."

"What's wrong with my face?"

"Your face is perfect. But most men are going to look at... other parts of you. Not just your face."

Dominique found herself pinking up. "OK, but, well, honestly, I was thinking about telling Grandma and Evan. Jackson and Aiden will believe me or at least roll with me. But when I say it in my head it sounds like a lot of... well, Aiden would say circumstantial evidence. And Evan will say I'm being overly emotional and imaginative and probably follow it up with something about woman problems."

Max's expression seemed to express disbelief. "That's stupid," he said bluntly.

Dominique leaned back in her chair, startled. Why had he said that? He been so supportive earlier. Why would he dismiss her feelings like that? "Well, it may be stupid," she said, knowing that her voice had acquired the brittle tone she thought of as distinctly Eleanor, "but I can't really afford to lose any more family members. I need to get them focused on actually being safe and maybe coming up with an actual reason for why someone would want to hurt Grandma."

Realization seemed to dawn on his face. "No, that's not what I meant. I meant that Evan is stupid."

"Oh," said Dominique, relaxing, "all right then." She smiled, feeling silly for having misjudged him. Dominique felt strangely suspended between their past and present. She was used to judging him under a certain light and having him turn out to be kind and supportive, not to mention damn sexy, was throwing her off. She probably shouldn't be suspicious, but when was the last time she'd met someone and not been suspicious?

"Because what does that even mean?" he continued. "Overly emotional? Yeah, because you're so well-known for an excess of emotion."

Dominique found herself blushing for real this time. She was well aware of her ice queen reputation. She didn't need to have it thrust into her face. Why did everyone always think that because she didn't show emotions that she didn't have any?

"It doesn't work any better the other way!" she snapped. "Show a little emotion and people freak out. So I'm either an ice queen or an emotional wreck. Of the two, I'll take the ice queen." She grabbed for the menu again wanting something to look at that wasn't him.

"I'll take the emotional wreck," he said. She blinked at him over the edge of the menu and he smiled, looking a little embarrassed. "I just mean, you shouldn't have to shut down all the time to make other people comfortable or to be taken seriously. That's bullshit and I hate it. You don't have to. At least, not for me."

Unexpectedly, she found her eyes filling with tears and to her horror, the waiter walked up. She buried her nose in the menu.

"Have you made a decision?"

"Um, yes," Max said.

She flashed a quick glance at him, trying to signal that she needed a minute.

"I'll have the *Tortellini all Panna*, and she'll have the *Gnocchi Aglio e Olio*." He rattled off the dish she'd selected ten minutes ago as a random side comment during the middle of another story.

She wasn't sure why his comment touched her that much. Somehow the way he'd said it had been more than a passing line. Max and the waiter debated over salad and soups and then salad dressings and she snuck a look at him. Was he really volunteering for emotional wreck? Not that she was any sort of wreck. But guys always wanted someone with *no drama* and the emotions of women were always drama. It was such a cheat—a way of declaring anything they were uncomfortable with to be drama and therefore absolve themselves of the responsibility to deal with it. Dominique paused and almost laughed at herself. There wasn't a spot on the planet where a car through a window didn't count as drama. She might want to make a feminist stance on emotions, but currently, she really did have enough drama to put together a *Telenovelas Mexicanus.*

"Honey, did you pick out an appetizer?"

She took a deep breath, put her smile back on, and took the first thing on the menu. "Yes, the roasted tomato tart, please."

She handed the menu back without making eye contact and turned to the window as the waiter left, wanting another moment before she looked at Max again. She wasn't sure what to say. *You're adorable—you made me melt right then, and I want to kiss you* was honest, but in dating, honesty rarely ended up being the way to go. Outside and across the street, a man leaned up against a building, ostensibly looking at his phone, and Dominique froze as she recognized him. She reached out and grabbed Max's hand, her eyes going wide.

"He's across the street," she hissed.

He switched the grip of her hand on his, so that it looked more romantic and specifically didn't look out the window.

"Which one?" he asked, stretching his mouth into a smile and leaning in.

"The one who asked about the lighter," she said. "What do we do?"

"Nothing. We sit here and eat dinner and look like a couple. They'll either buy it or they'll make a move. Can you call for a car?"

"Yes," she said. "I can use Grandma's car service."

"OK, give it a few minutes, so you're not reaching directly for your phone."

She stared at him anxiously. She had not intended this at all. She had just wanted to make sure she didn't get in trouble, mostly with Jackson. She hadn't thought anything serious would actually happen. The drama quotient was definitely climbing. At what point would he reach his limit? No one outside the family was going to stick around for this. "This really was supposed to be a go and look kind of thing," she blurted out. "I didn't mean to get you into trouble."

He grinned. "Are you kidding? This is the best day of vacation so far."

Dominique had read the phrase *her heart skipped a beat* in any one of a dozen trashy novels, and up until that moment she'd always thought it was a metaphor. She took a quick breath and then another, trying to make her heart settle down. Why did he have to be so ridiculously good looking?

"You're weird," she said, trying for playful. "But if this is your kind of thing, then stick with me. I know all the best restaurants to get threatened in."

He laughed as if she'd surprised him. "Is that list on Yelp? Should we leave a review?"

She found herself smiling. If he was laughing, then things couldn't be *that* serious. "Probably. But if you want to almost die in a rental hall, then you'll have to stick around because I only do one of those a week."

"I am officially around for the next two weeks," he said. "You can put me down for next Wednesday."

"You're here for the next two weeks?" asked Dominique, trying not to sound overly eager or hopeful. "Are you and your dad going to do anything fun?"

"Besides almost dying at Deveraux parties, you mean? I doubt it. Dad doesn't really take time off work. I don't know why I thought two weeks with him would be a good idea."

"You really don't like your dad?" She felt distressed by that. She liked Grant. He had always been kind to her. And not in the creepy older guy stalking her way, but in the genuine, mentor type way.

He sighed and hung his head a little. "I love my dad. He's smart, and, you're right, he is funny. But in some ways, that's all he is. I had a front row seat to my parent's divorce and what I saw was that my mom had the same problem with him that I do. He never says anything really real and I never ever get his whole attention. Only I don't get to divorce him and go find a Jeff to pay attention to me."

"You could totally get a Jeff," she said, and he chuckled.

"I guess I was kind of hoping that this trip I could get him to actually focus on me for two seconds. Maybe at least give me the same attention he gives his work."

Dominque bit her lip, wishing she had something pithy or helpful or at least soothing to say. She really didn't. He was right. She could see what he meant about Grant. But she hadn't ever considered that it would be frustrating to have him as a parent. "He does always seem to be working," she said. "I'm sorry. That sucks. Somehow it's worse when it's family that lets you down."

He took a deep breath and looked out the window. Dominique

was startled to realize that she had forgotten that outside the window was a stranger who might have tried to kill her brother.

"He's gone," he said looking back at her with a smile that made her stomach flip-flop. She looked down at the table, hoping he couldn't tell and realized that she was still holding his hand. She didn't know what to do about that. After holding it for the last few minutes, it was going to seem conspicuous if she suddenly stopped. And maybe she didn't want to. "Here comes are appetizer," he said.

"Your roasted tomato tart," said the waiter, setting it down in front of them.

"Oh," she said, leaning back in her chair and freeing her hand.

"Right." The waiter left and she looked up at Max. "I don't actually like tomatoes," she whispered, and he began to laugh.

"Drink more wine," he said. "I'll take care of the tart."

"I am not a tart," she said, reaching for the wine and giving him her best flirt face.

"You could be," he said, flashing the smile that made her feel warm all over but specifically in certain lower areas.

"Could be what? Both flaky and crusty?" she asked lifting an eyebrow.

"Delectable and buttery," he said, slicing into the appetizer. She giggled and he smiled, but then his smile faded. "You should probably still call the car service."

"No," she protested, surprised by the turn in the conversation. "Can't you walk me home? I can get a cab at your dad's."

"No," he said firmly. "I want you to take the car."

She frowned and tried to think of an argument that would work against him. She felt like he'd taken an abrupt turn out of fun and flirty to serious. She didn't want serious. Except maybe she needed to be serious. If he was worried, maybe she should be too?

"It's safer," he added, watching her carefully and she let out a snort of disgust.

"You and Jackson! Do you have a play book somewhere that you're following?"

"Didn't you just say that you wanted your family to focus on safety?"

"Yes, them. I want *them* to focus on safety. I'm fine."

He raised an eyebrow and she glared. She was about to argue further when her phone rang.

"Hey Jacks," she said, picking up.

"Where the fuck are you?"

"At dinner," she said faltering. He sounded actually angry. She had figured he'd be mad. She didn't think he'd be really, really mad.

"What the fuck kind of bullshit was that message you left me?"

"It wasn't bullshit," she said. "I was... investigating." There was silence on the other end of the line. "Are you counting to ten?"

"Twenty."

"I'm fine. Nothing happened. Well," she glanced at Max, who was studiously eating the tart, "I mean, not quite nothing."

"I'm sending a car for you."

"We're not done with dinner."

"Who's we? And dinner, seriously? It's barely after five o'clock."

"We were followed, so we had to stay in character, and we said we were getting dinner."

There was another silence.

"Twenty again?"

"Thirty. Who is we?"

"I took Max. Because you said never do anything crazy without back-up and you were with Grandma."

There was a silence again, but this time it seemed less mad. "How long until you finish dinner?"

"I don't know, an hour?" She glanced at Max, who shrugged his agreement. She couldn't tell if he was annoyed. He'd gone very impassive.

"All right, I'll have the car pick you up in an hour. Next time fucking text me an update."

"OK." Dominique felt relieved. The magic of Max was more powerful than she had thought it would be.

"K. Bye. Have fun."

"Don't you need our address?"

"No, I low-jacked all your phones forever ago."

"You low-jacked my phone?"

"None of you ever listen to me."

"I listen," she protested.

"Oh yeah, I can tell by the way that you're safe at home right now that you have heard every word I've ever said. I'm in charge of security for this stupid family. Stop trying to make me suck at my job."

"Well, I figure if I get in trouble you can ride to the rescue and that would make you look good. So really, this is for your benefit." He snorted. "I'm thinking of nothing but you," she added sweetly, because she knew that if he was bothering to complain, he was no longer mad.

"With family like you, who needs enemies," he said.

"Love you too," she chirped.

"Whatever. Bye." He was laughing as he hung up.

"Well, you get your wish," she said, turning back to Max. "He's sending a car."

"He low-jacked your phone?"

Dominique scrutinized his face. She wasn't sure how to interpret his tone. "Not just mine."

"Are you OK with that?"

Dominique considered. Was she OK with it? She probably shouldn't be. But of course Jackson had low-jacked them. That was what she would do if she were in charge of keeping track of Evan and Aiden. Although, God forbid she should ever have to do such a thing. She tried to think of somewhere she'd been that Jackson couldn't know about and couldn't come up with anywhere. Also, she suspected that he didn't spend his every waking minute checking on them. "Well, he *is* in charge of security. And the Deveraux as a whole do kind of suck at following directions."

He opened his mouth as if he was going to argue. "It's none of my business," he said sitting back, pushing his tiny appetizer plate away.

"But?"

"I wouldn't be OK with that invasion of privacy."

Did Jackson invade? "I don't think he invades."

"He's sending the car and he doesn't need an address," said Max, as if that settled the argument.

Dominique didn't like answering questions about Jackson. They always ended up being too much about how her family functioned, or rather, didn't function. Aiden wandered off at the drop of a hat. Evan was secretive and withdrawn and doing God knew what. Eleanor was always on public display. And Jackson made all of that work. And he probably made all of it work by knowing things he wasn't supposed to know—like where she ate dinner. But one of the most beautiful parts about Jackson was that he only he used that information when he needed to. But she didn't want to say any of that to Max. No guy wanted to hear that the cousin of the girl he was dating was always going to know when she was at his place or anywhere else. This was why she didn't ever date seriously. Being a Deveraux came with strings and so did being *with* a Deveraux.

"I did leave him a message saying that I was going to go investigate the florist and then didn't send an update," she said. "I would have checked up on him if he'd done that to me."

He looked displeased with that answer. "None of my business," he said again, with an awkward shrug.

"Are you going to the Friends of the Rainforest fundraiser tomorrow?" she asked, retreating into small-talk. She knew it was the coward's way out, but she didn't know what else to do. "I think Grant said he was going."

"Um," he hesitated. "I hadn't decided. I'd have to, you know, iron my suit. And that sounded like work."

"We're all going," she said. "It would be nice to see you."

He hesitated again, then smiled. "I guess I could probably iron. For you."

## *Jackson – Marks on the Wall*

Jackson parked his car and stared at the latest graffiti on the wall of the run-down Cheery Bail Bonds office through the raindrops on his windshield. Jackson had the wall painted black every few months. Ostensibly, it was to cover up the graffiti and make the business compliant with property laws meant to discourage such itinerant arts. In practice, it just meant a fresh canvas for the local kids. Today someone had started to sketch in the Ukrainian word *Тихше!* It meant *hush*, which Jackson thought was funny. Someone had probably been trying for *peace*, but Google translate had failed them.

He got out of the car and opened the trunk. The rain had stopped for the moment. It would probably pick back up again by the afternoon. He tossed his jacket in the trunk, popped a piece of nicotine gum, and took out a couple of cans of spray paint and a mask. He rolled up his sleeves and finished roughing in the word, switched to green and then added highlights. Then he used his old tag and tossed the spray cans back in the trunk.

"New graffiti?" asked Peter as Jackson entered the office.

"I don't know what you're talking about," said Jackson. Being a Deveraux had come with a straight jacket list of rules, but he had never had more than a nodding acquaintance with most rules anyway, so he didn't think he needed to start now. He just assumed that he had to be sneakier while breaking them. Not that he tried very hard to sneak stuff past Pete. But the quickest way to get in trouble was to admit to something, so he generally didn't.

"I'm talking about the paint fumes," said Pete, sniffing the air around Jackson.

"New cologne," said Jackson.

"Uh-huh." Pete's eyes twinkled.

When he'd first come to live with the Deverauxes, Jackson had been suspicious of Pete. Pete was ex-army intelligence and his client list was limited to a select few. He seemed to enjoy keeping his life simple and had eyed Jackson's arrival doubtfully. It had taken a few missteps for both of them to realize that neither was planning on taking advantage of the Deveraux bank account. Once that had been straightened out, Jackson had enjoyed working with Pete. And he thought Pete liked working with him.

What Pete hadn't liked was Jackson bringing in other operatives. However, while the man could turn up tons and tons of dirt, Eleanor's ability to do anything with that information had been limited. Jackson's arrival changed that. And new faces and new talents meant that the dangling threads all got wound up, tracked down, and snipped. The other operatives weren't around all the time, but the extra staff had meant that Pete could no longer operate out of the spare bedroom in his house. Hence the office with the conference room and the kitchen area and the wall full of graffiti. The only thing Pete insisted on was that nothing in the office should be new. He wanted the building and everything about it to look like a run-down, piece of crap, bail bonds office. He said that felt authentic to the neighborhood. Which was why the sign out front still read CHEERY BAIL BONDS and the kitchenette still had yellow Formica on the countertops. Jackson didn't mind—it felt more authentic to who he was too. Eleanor thought they were both insane. She never actually said it, but he got the impression that she thought a Deveraux shouldn't know what Formica was.

"Where is everyone?" asked Jackson, pausing to hang his coat on the rack by the door.

"Out doing what they're supposed to be doing," said Pete.

"Glad somebody is," said Jackson. "I feel like I'm chasing my tail. What's the run-down?"

"Dominique went to work," said Pete. "Evan kicked out a couple of models and did the same. Different ones from last week, before you ask. And Aiden spent the morning at his *other* gym. Our friend Tailor finally got an invite as of Friday. So we should have a report on that soon."

It had recently come to Jackson's attention through his various efforts at surveillance that Aiden had two gyms. One was the bright, shiny mid-town gym with the sauna and the great view from the treadmill. The other was invitation only and located down near the port in a grimy, converted warehouse with no signs and an ill-lit parking lot. But surprisingly, no one touched the cars in the lot and none of the local junkies loitered there. From his surveillance, the members looked non-descript and a little on the small side. There were none of the mountainous steroid fiends that might be predictably found at a barely-legal-looking gym. The building was owned by an ex-Golden Gloves boxer who had done all right for himself by turning his winnings into real estate, but that was all the information they had on the place.

"Well, then," Jackson said, "I guess on Friday we'll find out if Aiden has secretly joined a gay men's choir or something else."

Pete gave the small bark of an almost laugh but continued to type in one finger hen pecks at his keyboard. Jackson left him to it and headed for the kitchenette to make himself a cup of coffee.

"Hey, I ran that guy," Pete yelled after him.

"Which guy?"

"The U.S. Marshal you said was chatting up Dominique."

"Yeah? Anything good?" Jackson yelled down the hall as he filled his cup.

"Bupkiss," said Pete, arriving to dig into the fridge.

"Nobody has nothing," said Jackson, leaning against the counter.

"Yeah, well, I ran the paperwork, the guy is clean. Solid savings account considering his paycheck. Minimal debt." Pete pulled a leftover burrito out of the fridge and put it in the microwave. "So then I made some calls out to California. His mom lives out there. The sub-contractor I used nosed around. She says that Maxwell Ames AKA Max has an ex-girlfriend who'd like to not be an ex. But apparently, she burned that bridge by cheating on Maxwell with some plastic surgeon and he is not returning her calls. Next up: work. Apparently, his co-workers all like him. Fills out his share of the paperwork and does not shirk at the back on raids. So then my gal dug a little further and turned up a couple of other exes and some college friends. They all gave him high marks for promptness, cleanliness, and the remembering of birthdays, et cetera."

"So we're saying he's squeaky?"

"Seems that way. Do we have reason to think he's not?"

"Apparently he got drunk at a party one time in college and said some inappropriate shit."

"Well, that is unfortunate, but not the first time that alcohol has caused a lapse in judgement."

Jackson raised his mug in a toast of agreement.

"Are we worried about him for some reason?"

"No," said Jackson, taking a cautious sip. Pete believed in making coffee STRONG with extra capital letters. "For the hour he spent helping me sort out the tennis club debacle, I actually liked him. Which, considering that he's law enforcement, made me instantly suspicious."

Pete laughed.

"But Dominique says that the first thing he did when he got two seconds alone with her was apologize for the college thing, and then yesterday he went with her on her not-so-wild goose chase. And, from what I can tell, he managed to keep her from doing anything ridiculous and got us those pictures."

"Those pictures were good," said Pete. "He got them? That guy in black matches our guy at the mailbox and the guy in the brown Carhartts looked like our guy at the tennis club."

"I'm aware," said Jackson. "So anyway, what I'm saying is that I'm not worried about him as a player on the field. It's more that I'd like to know who's stepping up to the plate with Dominique."

Jackson tried not to make a habit of checking out his cousin's dates unless the person showed up more than a couple of times. None of the Deveraux were serious daters. But Dominique was the only one who seemed troubled about it. Not that she ever said anything—more that she seemed sort of wistful as her girlfriends paired off and shackled up. Jackson generally liked his cousins not have significant others, although, he tried not to think about what it said about him as a person. But it was hard enough getting them to like him without adding extra people to the family. But Max was different. Jackson liked Max. And he liked the way that Dominique had come home sparkling like champagne and just about as fizzy. He really wanted Max to be the good guy he seemed to be—and Pete's background check made that seem like a solid bet.

"He'd better be ready for some curve balls," said Pete. "She does not play softball."

"I think yesterday's trip to the florist shows he knows how to read the pitch."

"Probably true. But speaking of those guys—" Pete paused in the middle of his own thought and then frowned at Jackson.

"You're not supposed to be here today, are you? I thought you and Eleanor were out to DC?"

"We were, but then she found out that Ralph Taggert is going to be at some sort of party thing here in town." Pete groaned. "And of course, Eleanor will be damned if that bastard is going to fundraise in her territory. So now we're all going to the Friends of the Rainforest dinner."

Pete chuckled. "I shouldn't laugh. You clean up good. But every time I picture you at one of those things it cracks me up."

"Because you know I stick gum under the tables?"

"Yes, exactly. But as I was saying, about those guys—from the pics it looks like the letter writer and the guy at the tennis club are part of the same crew. Which lead me to do some deep thinking last night about who has the time, energy, or funding to operate a six man crew to threaten a senator."

"I did notice the time stamp on the email," said Jackson. "That *was* some deep thinking."

"It's easier to write an email than to remember what I was thinking in the morning. What do you think?"

"I like your theory," said Jackson. "It's not the first time I've had the thought. Absolex certainly has the most to gain by having Eleanor pull out or delay the hearings. But we have zero proof."

"OK, but here's my thing. If we assume that this is a paid gig," said Pete, searching through the drawers for a fork, "then that means that we're dealing with a higher level of players than your random redneck whack-job."

"Random redneck whack-jobs don't make sense for this anyway," said Jackson. "They never have. The conspiracy theorists are all against Big Pharma. Sure, no letter writing nut-ball likes the government, but Eleanor's checking all the right boxes on this one—it's pro-veterans, its anti-Big Pharma, and it's the uncovering of a conspiracy. She ought to be getting love notes."

"This is what I'm saying. So we assume that Absolex is paying for it in some way. We need to be looking at the key players—who has the most to lose if Absolex gets fined. That's J.P. Granger, the CEO. Or what's-his-face, Rashim, the head of research. Or any of the fucking board members. They all have stock up the yin-yang. If Absolex goes down, so does their net worth."

"Well, if Eleanor's right, it's not just a fine. Someone knew that the PTSD medication was based on fraudulent research. Someone signed off on it. That someone is responsible for those suicides. That's jail time."

"We'll see," said Pete, finally giving up and washing a fork in the sink. "Suits don't go to jail."

"Isn't that my line?" asked Jackson. "Are you allowed to be the cynical one in this partnership?"

"Cynicism is issued when you get your PI license. Didn't I warn you?"

Jackson laughed. "All right, so basically we think that someone is covering up their crimes with a fresh crime?"

"Yes. And that means," said Pete, shoveling a bite of burrito in his mouth, "that the guys from the picture aren't going to turn up on random chat boards. I need to be looking at a bigger, meaner, more professional pool of fish. That's my theory." Jackson nodded—it made sense to him. "The only question is can we run with it?"

Jackson considered the question.

"I guess, to be more clear," said Pete, "what I'm asking is whether or not Eleanor is going to let us run with it?"

"No," said Jackson, "the second we bring up Absolex she's going to tell us to hand it the police or the Feds. These hearings are a political coup for her. She's not going to risk endangering that. She'll want everything to be as squeaky clean as Max's background check." Pete chuckled. "Unfortunately, I think we've now reached the point where I don't think that's safe."

Pete grunted and Jackson tried to assess if it was in agreement or not.

"I think we need to move ahead without telling her," said Jackson, watching for a response.

Pete chewed through another bite of burrito.

"Are you going to be comfortable with that?" asked Jackson.

"What would you do if I wasn't?" asked Pete.

"I have a big checkbook and I've been in this town long enough to have a few resources. I think I can move ahead without you. But I would prefer not to."

"Damn right you would prefer not to," said Pete and Jackson grinned. "Yeah, don't sweat it. I'm in. I'll start asking a few questions and running some leads."

"Run, rabbit, run," said Jackson. His phone tinged in his back pocket and he pulled it out and checked the message.

Pete clicked his tongue, seeing the sender's picture. "Mrs. Ambassador is going to get you burned one day, kid."

"I keep a fire extinguisher handy," said Jackson. He texted back a quick answer that he was indeed available in an hour. Mrs. Ambassador was married, hot, and loved her husband. She also happened to love sex, which her husband apparently did not, or at least not to the level and enthusiasm that she did. It was the perfect arrangement as far as Jackson was concerned. Since becoming a Deveraux, he'd felt inundated by debutantes. He liked sex as much as the next guy, but debutante sex was never really free, and he wasn't about to get himself tied up or tied down. That was Evan's thing. Or at least it had been.

He flipped to the locator app and checked on his cousins. Dominique was at her shitty job at the accounting company. Evan was at the high-rise investment firm. And... Aiden was at a comic book shop. He wondered if Aiden and Evan knew they frequented the same comics establishment. He doubted it. He also wondered if Aiden's high-priced corporate lawyer employers realized how much time Aiden spent out of the office during the day. Jackson doubted that too.

Eleanor hadn't been wrong when she'd shown up at the prison—his cousins needed a minder, but Jackson didn't think they needed the kind Eleanor meant. Eleanor viewed her family with suspicion and kept them all at arm's length, particularly Evan. Which was unfortunate because, in Jackson's opinion, Evan needed the most help.

Dominique was easy. She had brains and plans—all she needed was for the boys to fall in line and do what she told them. Eleanor didn't see it because Eleanor didn't think the children could have ideas and had somehow convinced herself that Dominique was a delicate child. Aiden was always recalcitrant even when it seemed like he was going with the flow. It was his way of getting out from under everyone's thumb—play the dumb blond and no one would expect much from him. It had been a rough first year with him, but Jackson thought he had Aiden mostly solved. Not *all* of his mysteries by a far stretch—Aiden disappeared too routinely and took too many mystery trips out of town to be considered a completely known quantity. But Jackson thought he had a pretty good bead on what made Aiden tick, and once they had resolved the initial jealousy of having a new quasi-sibling around, the rest of the Deveraux and Jackson got along well. But Evan... Evan made life miserable for everyone because he was miserable.

Once Jackson had realized that Evan was visiting a very

exclusive, very expensive BDSM sex club called Fetish, the picture of Evan had gotten a lot clearer. Jackson understood that world. His mother had given him a front row view of it. It worked for some people. But Jackson didn't think it worked for Evan. And the morning that Evan had ended up in the hospital, Jackson had thrown caution to the wind. Evan avoided talking about real things and real pain, but it was damn hard to avoid someone who was in your hospital room.

Evan was sitting on the hospital table when Jackson walked in. He went directly over and looked at the x-ray on the light up box in the wall.

"How'd you get in here?" demanded Evan.

"I bully people," said Jackson. "And I said you were my brother. Radial fracture."

"Yeah."

"How'd that happen?"

Evan stared at Jackson mutely; he obviously had no intention of answering the question. Jackson sighed.

"Did I ever tell you about my mom?"

"No?" Evan looked off-balance. Which was why Jackson usually started in a strange place. If he could keep Evan out of control of the conversation, Evan would talk, or at least listen.

"She liked S&M. It was one of the reasons my grandparents booted us out of the family. They said she was a whore and they thought she… defiled herself. I believe that was the term my grandfather used."

Evan swallowed hard. "Defiled?" he repeated.

"I punched him in the face," said Jackson. "Not that it did much good. I was twelve. He threw me out of the house. It doesn't matter anyway. I've told you before—they abandoned Mama and me. They are not my family. *This* is my family."

Evan remained silent, watching Jackson warily.

"What I haven't wanted to mention previously is that I met Randall. A bunch of times. Not that I ever knew his name. He used to visit my mom every three or four months. She usually sent me to my aunt's, but after I ran into him one time when I was eight, she let him see me."

"She *let* him…" Evan seemed shocked.

"That doesn't make sense to you, does it?"

"No," said Evan shaking his head. "I can't really picture Uncle Randall having a long-term relationship with someone, let alone that Randall needing permission for anything."

"Yeah, I know. The rest of you think that he was unstoppable, but Mom had his balls in a vice. Possibly literally for all I know."

"Did he… Was he nice?" Evan looked worried.

"I don't know. Sort of? He usually asked me what I was doing and sort of looked at me like I was some sort of bug that he couldn't decide whether to swat or not. Mostly I think he was confused that I existed."

"Oh," said Evan. "That sounds… right?"

Jackson thought Evan looked like he was taking this information relatively well.

"Anyway, my point is that when you grow up with that, it can warp how you think about sex and relationships. Or at least it did for me. I thought that's what it was supposed to be. And then one day this guy I was staying with, George—he and his partner let me crash on their couch after Mama died—he caught me being an asshole to this girl I was seeing and he slapped me upside the head and said, *hey moron, not everyone likes that.* And he meant girls, but it was like it hit some sort of light switch for me. Not everyone likes that. I'm an everyone. And it turns out that I don't like it."

Evan stared at him.

"My question to you is, are you sure that *you* like it?"

"What?" Evan looked at the x-ray and then back at Jackson. "I... I don't think... I'm supposed..."

Evan looked terrified. His good hand was clamped on the edge of the hospital table in a white-knuckled grip.

"I see you," said Jackson. "I see that you don't like being told what to do. I see that you like controlling things. But there's a big difference between control and pain. And if you don't like it, why are you doing it?"

"It's better," whispered Evan, his voice hoarse.

"For who? It's not better for you."

"It's safer."

"Again, for who? Not for you."

"We don't need any more Randalls and Owens in the family," said Evan in the brittle sneering tone that always managed to make the listener feel stupid.

"We don't have any," said Jackson. "We just have an Evan and an Aiden and a Dominique."

Evan gave him a withering stare. "Why do you bother? None of this matters. Why are you even here?"

"Because I don't want you going to a place where you get hurt. I'm not going to sit back and let people hurt you."

"And what about the rest of the family? What about them?" demanded Evan. Jackson frowned, uncertain what Evan was asking.

"I won't let anyone hurt them either," said Jackson, hoping it was the right response. "Who would hurt them?"

Evan stared at him angrily. "Why don't you ask Dominique?"

"Or you could just tell me what you mean."

Evan was stubbornly silent.

"I want you to stop going to that place," said Jackson, letting it lie for a moment. "Whoever did this to you doesn't care about you or they would be here now."

"I did it to myself," said Evan. "I'm stubborn."

"Well, I can't argue with that, but it doesn't mean that you should go back there."

Evan's shoulders sagged tiredly. "I want..."

"What? Tell me what you want, and we can make it happen."

Evan looked up at him hopelessly. "I don't want anyone to hurt the family."

"I won't let anyone hurt them."

Evan eyed Jackson carefully. "*Anyone?* Do you promise?"

"I promise," said Jackson, looking him in the eye.

And just like that, Evan had stopped going to Fetish. But Evan hadn't gotten better. There was more drinking and even less smiling and he'd stopped talking to Jackson, even when he was drunk. Jackson had given it some time, hoping that Evan would come around, but as far as he could tell, Evan was only getting worse. Jackson was going to have to move him up on the priority list. Except the priority list kept including things like death threats and cars through tennis club windows. It was getting hard to keep up.

# Maxwell – Echoes of the Past

Max straightened his tie and looked at himself in the mirror. The suit was practically at James Bond level suave. His hair, with the help of some styling gel wax shit stolen from his father's bathroom, actually looked good. All in all, he looked fucking *GQ*. He wondered what Dominique would be wearing and then realized that it didn't matter—he was only going to spend half the evening thinking about taking it off anyway.

Fuck Jackson. There was no such thing as stealing a person—people went to the bed they wanted. If Dominique showed so much as an ounce of interest, he was going to take her up on it. It's not like she was married or anything. Yesterday had been the best date of his life. Why should he have to give up a connection like that? And he could swear—swear—that Dominique had felt it too. Right up until Jackson had called.

Which brought him back to his original thought: fuck Jackson.

What kind of guy low-jacked his girlfriend's phone? So what if he was head of security for Eleanor? That didn't make it OK to keep tabs on his girlfriend.

Max's father came out of his bedroom and looked Max over, a smile quirking up one side of his mouth.

"I have never understood how you ended up being so big. I mean, I'm not exactly breaking any size records and your grandfather was five-foot-five-and-a-half on a good day."

"Didn't I tell you? Mom's genealogy obsession finally paid off. She found her bio-dad's military record. The guy was like six foot five."

Grant burst out laughing. "That explains you, anyway. Frankly,

I would have accused her of having a back-door man, except with that nose, there's no doubt that you're mine."

"And also, she's not like that?" snapped Max, annoyed. It didn't feel like the right response, but he didn't know how to fight that kind of casually callous comment.

Grant shrugged. "All women are like that. Some just more so than others. It's not personal."

"Yeah," said Max, "it *is* personal. You're talking about Mom. Also, no, all women are not like that."

"Really, so your last girlfriend didn't step out on you with a guy who could fix her nose, thus helping her career?"

"Stacia had problems. But my three girlfriends before that didn't cheat. And Mom and Jeff are happily and *faithfully* married, which is more than you've ever managed."

Grant laughed. "Don't get mad. Like I said, it's not personal. In the end we're all just looking for a genetic advantage. I'm not talking any individual person—although, obviously there are plenty of examples—but in general, when you're talking about the human race, it's what we do."

Max felt the familiar upwelling of frustration. His father would never engage. It was always *in theory* and *in general*. Grant could never see that his theories and generalities had real repercussions.

Max thought about yelling at Grant to stop being a dick, but he knew exactly how that would go. All his life, Grant had managed to make him furious and whenever he gave in and yelled, Grant would accuse him of getting too emotional and oversensitive. Max was the problem—never Grant. Anymore, Max just resorted to direct insults. Although his father never seemed to take them as seriously as Max meant them.

"You are such a cynical bastard," said Max with a tight smile.

"Yes," agreed Grant with a laugh. "Anyway, you ready? Do you have your Dominique approved underwear on?"

"I don't know what you're talking about," said Max, feeling annoyed that Grant had pegged his crush on Dominique so easily.

"Liar," said Grant. "And if you're not lying, then you should get your head out of your ass and figure out what I'm talking about. Dominique's a good kid. You two would be a good fit."

Max stared at his father trying to find the hidden meaning. "She said she thinks you're funny," he said at last, looking to see Grant's response.

Grant grinned. "I am funny."

"Why do you bother?" demanded Max.

"I like to entertain?"

"I mean, why do you talk to her? What's in it for you? Don't they donate enough through the Deveraux Fund or whatever?"

"I talk to everyone," said Grant. "Never dismiss anyone. You never know when someone will come in handy. But I actually knew Dominique's dad—Sam Casella. We worked together my first job. He was…" For a moment, Grant looked sad. "He was really smart. Way smarter than me. He and Genevieve never wanted the kids to be Deveraux. They didn't want the kids to turn out like her brothers. Randall, the oldest, was—well, from what I hear, no woman wanted to be in a meeting alone with him. And Owen, the middle one, he was just about as bad. When they died… Well, I worried about Dominique and Aiden, especially when Eleanor changed their names to Deveraux. I always thought that was weird, particularly considering that she's not even a Deveraux."

"What do you mean?" asked Max.

"Henry Evan Deveraux was Eleanor's husband and an asshole of the first order. But Eleanor makes a thing of *being Deveraux*. Always seemed weird. I don't know, maybe she was trying to get the kids to feel like one family. It would probably be easier with the same last name. Although half the population manages without, so I don't know what the big deal is. Anyway, yeah, I was worried about Dominique and Aiden. And when I saw the name Dominique Casella on the directory at Ace Accounting, I got curious and popped in. It's nice to see that she escaped turning into an asshole. She really turned out OK. Not that you care what I think, but I like her." Grant shook his head as if contemplating the past. "Oh! Forgot my phone." Grant turned around and walked out of the room, leaving Max staring. He didn't know what to think about his father displaying actual emotion and forming attachments to people.

"All right, let's go," said Grant coming back. "We're not going to get any better-looking with time."

"Speak for yourself," said Max, checking the mirror again, and Grant laughed.

# *Dominique – Getting Dressed*

Dominique sprinted down the hall and unlocked the door to her unit. She threw her purse on the kitchen counter and dashed into her bedroom, yanking off her shirt as she went. Her meeting with Eleanor's campaign strategist had taken too damn long. Which was to be expected. Too damn long was exactly how long it always took. But she really wanted to look off-the-charts hot tonight. She had a dress she'd been hoarding for just such an occasion, but utterly magical hair did not do itself. She was almost to the shower when her phone buzzed with a call from Aiden. She sent it to voicemail and turned on the water. She was halfway through shaving one leg when the phone rang again. She ignored it and tried to shave faster.

When she finally got out of the shower, she hit play on her voicemail and put it on speaker as she began the moisturization and hair goop process.

"Hey, it's me. Jackson says we're doing the Friends of the Rainforest thing. Are we doing that? Did I know we were doing that?"

Dominique paused to dash off a text to her brother.

YES, WE'RE DOING FRIENDS OF THE RAINFOREST. YES, YOU KNEW. I'M NOT YOUR MOTHER OR YOUR SECRETARY. USE YOUR CALENDAR LIKE A NORMAL HUMAN BEING.

His reply was almost instantaneous.

BUT THEN HOW WOULD I TORTURE YOU?

ALL THE NORMAL WAYS, I ASSUME.

He spent back a laughing emoji.

She hit play on the next voice mail.

"Nika, Pete says you sent him an email?" Jackson sounded

uncertain of how he felt about her email to Pete. "Anyway, give me a call."

Dominique grimaced. She'd meant to call him. But that was before Eleanor's graphics person had called to walk through the problems with the upcoming video release.

SORRY, I FORGOT TO CALL YOU, BUT GOT SIDE-TRACKED...

She hesitated. She always felt weird about talking about all the stuff she did for Grandma. Jackson probably knew, but no matter how she phrased it, in her head it sounded like complaining. And Jackson didn't need to hear any more of her complaining. He was already her sounding board for other stuff. Dumping Grandma shit on him seemed excessive. Particularly since he dealt with way more of Eleanor's bullshit than she did.

... BY WORK STUFF. I PULLED ALL THE BUSINESS INFO ON THE FLORIST AND EMAILED IT TO PETE. I THOUGHT YOU GUYS MIGHT NEED IT.

IS THERE GOING TO BE ANYONE I LIKE THERE? IS IT REALLY FANCY? OR JUST KIND OF FANCY? WHAT SHOULD I WEAR?

That was Aiden outsourcing his decision making.

GET A GIRLFRIEND.

I'VE TRIED THAT, BUT IT TURNS OUT THEY REQUIRE MAINTE-NANCE AND CARE IF YOU WANT THEM TO STICK AROUND.

Dominique laughed as she began to blow dry her hair.

DON'T MAKE ME ASK EVAN.

ASK EVAN.

There was a pause and Dominique managed to get her hair to the right level of dry and then switched to a curling iron. It was a constant mystery to her that Aiden could get Evan to respond to him on random questions like what to wear to an event. She remembered vaguely that when they were younger, Evan had policed Aiden's clothing choices for all of Grandma's functions. She had always assumed it was just Evan being controlling and that Aiden hated it. And maybe he had. But she had to admit that, left to his own devices, Aiden was likely to show up in something ridiculous like a purple velvet suit and not the trendy, fashionable kind—the horrible vintage seventies kind. Evan at least had good taste and would ensure that Aiden showed up in something respectable.

GOT IT. PETE SAYS THANKS. WHAT AM I SUPPOSED TO WEAR TO THIS EVENT THING?

Dominique hung her head in defeat. She wondered if other women were responsible for dressing all their single male relatives.

WEAR THE BLACK HUGO BOSS SUIT.

She almost texted Evan to ask if he wanted advice on what to wear but knew that would only result in sarcastic texts back if it resulted in anything at all.

EVAN SAYS I CAN PULL OFF A WHITE JACKET. THAT'S NOT TOO RETRO IS IT?

Since Aiden's entire design aesthetic seemed to be centered on 1964, she could sense that he really wanted her to say that the white jacket was fine.

YEAH, GO FOR IT.

She carefully applied a coat of lipstick and paused to stare into the mirror. She had just done a quick search of the florist's information at work. It wasn't anything she, or Pete for that matter, couldn't have gotten from a public records search. But since Ace Accounting had it on file, she'd thought it might at least save Jackson and Pete the legwork.

"Why the florist?" she asked her reflection. She frowned; that wasn't quite the right question. "Why *that* florist?"

Ace Accounting would have a lot more information on the company in their files. But prying into client files was wildly illegal, and in order to do it, she'd have to break into her emergency kit.

When she had first set out on her campaign of shitty jobs, she had been flopping around looking at job postings and wishing that she could have the kind of job that would give her actual work experience. All the silver spoon kids she'd gone to school with who had moved straight to the top of a pyramid seemed to flounder at their jobs and had to be back-managed by their staff. She didn't want that. Dominique wanted not just the knowledge that came from working her way up, but the respect that went with it.

Getting a shitty job as Dominique Casella had been relatively easy, but she had quickly realized how difficult what she was proposing really was. Moving into management as an under-thirty person was difficult enough, but being a woman seemed to double the difficulty. It was Jackson who had showed her that she needed to hack the system.

Whenever she started a new job—and this was her third since starting her shitty job mission—she did what Jackson termed *passive information collection*. Each company had a handbook of how they claimed to operate and then they had the reality. Dominique spent the first two weeks at new place figuring out the reality. Inside of a month, sometimes with Jackson's help, she had a file that contained an assortment of other people's passwords, personality assessments, and systems analysis. It was her emergency kit for when she wanted to do something that flexed the system too hard. Like when she had wanted to deal with the misogynistic boss who couldn't stop banging his mistress—who happened to work in HR—long enough to promote appropriately. But mostly she tried not to fall back on the emergency kit too often. It was a little too much like cheating and defeated the purpose of succeeding like a normal person.

But if there was something in the files at Ace Accounting to help her family then didn't that constitute an emergency? There had to be a reason those men had selected that particular florist. She would look at the files tomorrow.

Dominique finished applying her lipstick and checked the time. If she wanted to go in the limo with everyone else, then she had exactly two minutes before she needed to be in a car headed over to Deveraux House—just enough time to put on the dress that she hoped was going to make Max lose his damn mind.

# Maxwell - Friends of the Rainforest

The Friends of the Rainforest was the kind of event that Max avoided when he'd been younger. There was a cocktail hour with a silent auction, then dinner with a live auction, and more cocktails, and then dancing and done. His dad, of course, was off to the races, circling the room like a shark. A happy shark.

Max collected a drink and ambled down the line of silent auctions items staged on long tables, looking at the gift baskets, expensive jewelry, golf clubs, artwork, and other random items. The only thing that looked particularly interesting was a hundred-year-old bottle of Scotch that he thought his father would actually be enthusiastic about. He was putting his name down on the sheet when one of the women further down the row gave a practically orgasmic moan. He looked up startled.

"Oh, God," said the woman, looking toward the door.

He followed the direction of her gaze and saw that the Deveraux family had arrived. Aiden was wearing a cream dinner jacket that made his hair look like a burnished gold piece. Jackson was wearing a black suit with a skinny tie and seemed to radiate a tense energy. Evan, as pale as Dominique but with red hair, was also in a dark suit, and escorted Eleanor, elegant in a white tuxedo-cut pantsuit. But it was Dominique that held his attention. She was wearing a red dress in silk that was skintight over her ass and showed her mile-long legs to the best possible advantage, draping in loose folds over her cleavage. He found it suddenly hard to breathe.

"I would give my Lexus for a piece of that," continued the woman next to him.

"Which one?" asked her friend with a laugh.

"Who cares? The girl. Any of the guys. All of the guys. Seriously, they are all so fucking hot, I would do any of them."

"I like Jackson," said her friend, pointing. "He looks like he works out. Also, I heard he grew up on the wrong side of the tracks in Chicago. I bet he can get freaky."

"I like the blondie-bear one. He looks like he could be talked into a few fantastically bad ideas. The ginger, though, he looks like he'd want to be on top. And I'm not, like, super gay, but I'd definitely take the girl. Seriously, what's her name?"

"Dominique," supplied the friend.

"Dominatrix? Yeah, she could dominate my ass all night long."

Max took a hard swallow of his drink and moved away from the pair. He didn't need help from the peanut gallery. He had enough naked fantasies about Dominique on his own. He also really hadn't realized how often Dominique's life seemed to be considered public property. What a weird way to grow up. No wonder she and Aiden had always been walls-up in college.

He headed for the bar. He wanted a refill, but mostly he didn't want it to look like he'd been waiting for Dominique. This wasn't a date or anything. They were just accidentally bumping into each other.

He was almost to the bar when he saw a familiar face and ducked down low, trying to hide in the crowd.

"Are you hiding?" asked Aiden, and Max looked up to see Aiden and Jackson looking at him as if he had lost his mind.

"Sasha Beckstale," whispered Max, hoping Aiden remembered her and would understand. Instead, both Aiden and Jackson looked sympathetic, although Aiden's expression almost immediately changed to subversive glee.

"What? You're not anxious to meet a dear old college chum?" he asked, grinning malevolently.

"Don't start," said Max. "I once left a party through a window to avoid her."

Jackson burst out laughing. "Completely understandable. The woman does not know how to take no for an answer." He shoved a fresh drink at Max and Max took it without thinking, still worried about Sasha.

"I think you're safe with us though," said Aiden, craning to look across the sea of faces. "She hates Jacks, so she won't come over here."

"I'm easy to hate," said Jackson. "Meanwhile, I hear Dominique's figuring out ways to get you in trouble."

"It wasn't any trouble. She was actually pretty careful." Max felt the stab of a guilty conscience.

"Careful? Are you sure you were out with our Dominique?" asked Aiden.

"She's careful," said Jackson, laughing at Aiden. "In her own way."

Aiden looked unconvinced. "Sounds like crap. It's far more likely that Max managed to keep her from going off the deep end."

"Yes," agreed Jackson. "But the question is how did he convince her to do that?"

Both men turned to stare at him, and Max felt himself start to sweat. "I didn't convince her of anything. We checked out the florist and found some weird shit going on, so we left," said Max defensively. "I'm going to run the pictures we got through facial recognition. I don't know if the florist is connected to what happened at the tennis club, but something was off."

Aiden was looking over the crowd again, his attention obviously not on the conversation, but Jackson nodded. "Hey, is that Alicia Storm?" asked Aiden, pointing.

"What *is* your obsession with the Channel Four weather girl?" demanded Jackson.

"It is not an obsession. I happen to think she's really amazing at the weather."

"Her name is Alicia Storm," said Jackson. "She should have just named herself Sunny Weatherman. The only thing she's amazing at is pointing at things that aren't there."

"You underestimate her talent," argued Aiden. "I totally understand cumulus clouds thanks to her."

"You should go tell her that," said Jackson.

"I'm going to," said Aiden.

"Better go then," said Jackson.

"Watch me," said Aiden and pushed his way through the crowd. Max wanted to laugh but didn't know if he was on good enough terms with either of them to do it publicly. Jackson met his eye and Max couldn't help letting out a little snort of laughter.

"He really likes the weather," said Jackson, chewing on an icecube from his drink, his eyes twinkling.

Max found himself reluctantly smiling. He wanted to hate Jackson. He wanted to not feel a twinge of guilt every time he was with Dominique, but the truth was that Jackson made that difficult. Jackson was exactly the sort of guy Max liked working with: smart, tough, and clearly on top of his job. If it weren't for Dominique, Max would be convincing Jackson and Aiden to forget the monkey-suit event and go for beers.

But there was Dominique.

"Hey!" said Dominique, appearing out of the crowd and looking Max over from head to toe. "Nice ironing!" Then she looked quizzically at both of them. "What are we talking about?"

"Aiden's obsession with the Channel Four weather girl," said Jackson.

"Oh God," said Dominique, looking around. "She's not here, is she?"

"Oh yes," said Jackson. "Here she is, and there he went."

"I'm not saying she's not cute—that damn nimbostratus could distract anyone," said Dominique. "But really, don't we think she's just a little to cirrus for him?"

"You are such a nerd," said Jackson affectionately.

"What? Cloud puns are all I have to fall back on when he starts blathering on about her really intelligent use of forecasting models. You don't know. You're not home. Seriously, I appreciate that he's interested in her mind and everything, but I wish he could take an interest, you know... elsewhere. It's not like he's going to be serious about her."

"What do you mean?" asked Jackson, frowning, and Dominique seemed at a loss for words.

"He's never serious about anyone," she said at last. "I think he almost was with Kennedy last year, but she kept pushing him to be something he wasn't."

"A vegetarian?" suggested Jackson, and Max couldn't tell if that had been sarcasm or not.

"Yes, but also... I don't know. She wanted him to buckle down, be a grown-up, get serious. She didn't like that he's kind of a dreamer."

Jackson grunted as if recognizing the truth.

"But he's always been like that, right?" asked Max. "I mean, when he used to wrestle with the guys, he..." Max trailed off as Dominique and Jackson turned toward him with wide eyes. "What?"

"I'm sorry, my brother used to do what with *the guys*?" She made air quotes around the phrase.

"He came to the wrestling club. With his roommate Harry. You remember Harrison Gordon? Or was it Gordon Harrison? I don't remember. Whatever. We all called him Harry. He was on JV and they used to hit the off-season wrestling club together."

Jackson began to laugh.

"No," said Dominque. "You must be thinking of a different Aiden. My brother does not *do* sports. I tried to play tennis with him last summer and I beaned him in the head twice with the ball because he was looking at birds."

"He was looking at the doubles team on the next court," said Jackson into his glass.

"Either way," said Dominique. "My point is: the most sporty thing he does is golf and I'm pretty sure that's just because he gets to wear plaid pants. He says that there aren't enough opportunities in life to wear plaid."

"I don't know," said Max. "He seemed pretty good for someone who hadn't been on a team. But it was hard to wake him up enough to be aggressive. He was always really laid back."

"Well, *that* at least sounds right," said Dominique.

Jackson chuckled again, and then frowned at something or someone behind Dominique. "Here," he said, handing Dominique his drink. "I have to go extricate Eleanor. Ralph Taggert is trying to maneuver her for a photo op."

Dominique wrinkled her nose in dislike. "I hate him."

"Doesn't everyone?" asked Jackson before beginning to worm his way through the crowd.

"Is he away a lot?" asked Max. That facet of their relationship hadn't occurred to him.

"Lately, he's been going with Grandma whenever she's in DC. I wish he didn't have to, but," she shrugged. "I'd rather Grandma was safe."

"But that must leave you feeling a bit neglected," said Max. He felt like he was edging into dangerous territory, but he wanted her to make a definitive statement of some kind.

"Grandma has to come first. You know, like always." The bitterness was clear on that statement, and Max nodded. He got that message. Someone ought to be putting her first, and Max thought maybe he should volunteer for the job.

"Come, tell me if I should bid on any of this crap," he said, offering her his arm.

"OK," she agreed, tucking her hand in, like she had on their walk. "But if I make you bid on it, you are forbidden from describing it as crap."

"I don't know," he said, shaking his head. "They're saying it's worth money and I guess I'll believe them, but... honestly, it looks like crap."

They walked down the row of auction items and she sipped Jackson's drink.

"Like this," he paused in front of a chunky bracelet thing. "I don't even know what to think about that."

"You think that it's crap," she said, as she scanned the rest of the table. "But this," she took him two steps to the right, "this is lovely." It was a necklace with a pearl placed with improbable balance on a twist of gold. It was small and subtle, and he'd completely missed it on his first walk-through.

"Oh," he said. "That actually is pretty. Mom would like that." He checked the bid sheet; there were only two names and the number was still within his reach. He put down a bid.

"You're easy," she said. "Every time I walk through with one of the boys, they quibble about how everything is not quite what they had in mind."

"I'm just here for Christmas presents," he said. "Plus, all of you probably go to more of these things than I do. When you see more, you get pickier. I have nothing to compare against."

"That's probably true," she agreed. "And you're right—I should look for Christmas presents! That's a great idea. You can help me pick out guy stuff!"

He complied and they spent the next half-hour dithering over whether or not Evan would want the enormous framed original artwork poster of Dark Phoenix or if Aiden would like golf clubs.

"At this point," said Max, looking over the crowd to where Aiden was very much in Ms. Storm's atmosphere, "we may need to find out if the weather girl golfs."

"I wonder if she does," said Dominique, looking thoughtful.

"Yes," said Evan, arriving unexpectedly out of the crowd. "And she's hosting a charity golf event in the spring. Aiden could brush up his game over the winter. Here, drink this for me, it's disgusting." Dominique accepted the glass of wine with an eye roll. "Seriously, why do I ever think the wine is going to be good at these events?" He focused Max. "I'm outbidding you on the Scotch."

Max shrugged. "I thought someone probably would."

"Grandma is still talking to Ralph Taggert," continued Evan as if Max hadn't replied. "That guy pisses me off. I swear he gets extra-Southern whenever I'm around."

"Me too!" exclaimed Dominique and she and Evan eyed each other in surprise. "But he probably doesn't call you *Little Miss*," she added.

"Pretty sure he's been thinking it though," said Evan. "I'm going to go talk to someone I'm not related to." He walked off, leaving them by the golf clubs.

"I don't know why he's not your favorite relative," said Max drily.

"That was actually him being civil," said Dominique, sipping the wine. She made a face and then downed most of it in one go. "It's not hideous," she said, to his questioning expression. "It's just not worth savoring, and I want to get a cocktail before we go into dinner."

She was putting a bid down on the golf clubs when Max turned to find himself confronted by Sasha Beckstale in a dress that seemed a little overly exciting for a charity event.

"Maxwell Ames! I heard you were in town. It's been an age. We should catch up." She leaned forward and caressed his arm, sending her bosoms shuddering toward the precipice of her gown.

Max felt like his tongue was stuck to the roof of his mouth. He felt embarrassed to have Sasha hitting on him in front of Dominique, but he didn't know how to respond that wasn't *I'm with some-one*. Because the someone he wanted was right there, but she wasn't with him.

"Why, Sasha," said Dominique, standing up and turning around. "Aren't you looking well? It's so nice to see you've recovered from your liposuction. It's such a shame how those procedures make you swell so unattractively."

Max blinked uncertain whether to laugh or simply gasp in shock.

Sasha looked frozen and then pissed. "I didn't have lipo," she said icily.

"You didn't?" Dominique mimed confusion. "Well, then your new diet must be working. But be careful, if you lose any more, people will think you're getting down to your fighting weight in time for another divorce. Max, did you want to take another look at the Scotch?"

She smiled up at him, the picture of innocence. "Mm-hm," he murmured, not trusting himself to not laugh if he actually opened his mouth.

"Holy shit," he said when they were far enough away, "And thank you. I was trying to figure out how to get away from her. Straight wig snatching never occurred to me."

Dominique giggled.

"She really hasn't gotten better since college, has she?" Max continued. "I don't think I could have been clearer about not being interested back then. I never understood why she wouldn't just leave me alone."

"Really?" demanded Dominique, her eyebrows going up dangerously high. "Not even a clue."

"No?" He wasn't sure what the eyebrows meant. It seemed like sarcasm, but based on what?

"That's adorable," she said. "Just like you." Max felt himself start to blush, but Dominique continued as though she hadn't said anything. "Although, now I feel guilty."

He looked at her in surprise. "For what?"

"Body shaming is so not cool. It's such an easy target. Society spends about twenty-some years installing weight anxiety in girls and it's like when women get mad, we reach for the easiest slam we can find, and it's always weight."

"Huh," said Max, relieved to turn the conversation away from himself. "I feel like when men get mad at women they go with *slut*."

"Speaking for all women everywhere—yeah, we've noticed."

"Sorry," said Max, laughing. "I don't mean that's what I say. I was just saying… trends."

"Yeah, I know," said Dominique. "But trends don't help anyone. Although, all things considered, Sasha is lucky she got me instead of Grandma. Grandma is far more creative than I am and probably would have said something absolutely devastating. I mean, she would have said it so it sounded nice, but she also probably would have said it louder so everyone could hear. Ever since Sasha practically tried to blackmail Jackson into having sex with her, Grandma hates her. Grandma does not approve of people trying to leverage us."

Max didn't know what to make of that comment. The Deveraux were notoriously clannish, but he hadn't realized that Jackson was that much in Eleanor's favor. Perhaps that explained Dominique's reluctance to break up with him or her willingness to spend time with another guy on the side.

"But never mind that," said Dominique leaning into him with a smile. "We should talk about something more fun."

"Crazy florists trying to kill your grandmother?"

Dominique giggled. "Yes, but I really, really don't think they were florists."

"No, probably not," he agreed, sliding an arm around her waist to move her out of the way of a passing buffalo of a man. She moved even closer, her thigh rubbing against his. He felt like the temperature in the room had gone up ten degrees.

"It's a very successful evening," she said, sounding a little breathless. "They really filled the space."

"Good news for the rain forest," he said, clearing his throat. "Um, were we going somewhere?"

She stared blankly at him. "The Scotch?" she finally offered.

"Right," he said.

Dominique stopped in front of the Scotch and she took a look at the bid sheet. He watched with glazed desire as she bent over the table to write her name down, her dress stretching tight over her ass, leaving no doubt as to her shape. She shifted her weight from one foot to the other, pen poised above the sheet. He wanted to reach out and run his hand over the curve up to her waist and nibble her ear while he inched the skirt up. Her weight shifted back as she made a decision and committed to a bid. He tried to pull his eyes away because if he continued to think along those lines, he was going to end up needing to spend a few minutes sitting down and thinking about beige, boring things that were not at all curvy, and not at all Dominique.

"Well, that will annoy Evan," she said sounding pleased as she stood up. "He shouldn't get away with blocking you," she said to his questioning look. And he felt like it was a tiny win. She was going to be taking his side on at least one thing against her family.

There was a shift in the noise of the crowd, and he looked around trying figure out what had happened.

"The doors to the dinner room opened," said Dominique. "Quick! To the bar!" She held her arm out as if calling the troops to battle, but the gesture made her wobble a little on her heels.

"Maybe not quite so quick to the bar," he said with a laugh. "Between Jackson and Evan's leftovers I'm not sure you need another one."

"I don't need it," she said, taking his arm again and leaning on him. He could smell her perfume which was a little bit spicy, and her body was warm even through his suit jacket. "But, and as much as it pains me to admit it, Evan really is terribly educated about wine. If he recommends something, don't ask questions, just buy it. And if you spend any time with him, not that I would wish that on you, you'll start to get picky as well. I really would prefer to have a cocktail rather than wine that probably isn't appropriately paired."

They procured Dominique's drink and headed for the dining room. "Can you sit with us?" asked Dominique. "I don't mind sitting with you, but the whole point of all of us coming to these things is that we're seen being *all of us*."

"I have no idea if I can or not," said Max. "I don't know the rules of musical chairs and who sits where at these things. That's Dad's department."

"Let's go find him," said Dominique. "I'll do the negotiating."

"Why do I feel like I'm about to be purchased like a pound of beef?"

"Oh no, you're worth way more than a pound," said Dominique. "I'll probably have to promise something extravagant like donating to his next capital campaign."

Max pulled up short. "No."

She looked up at him in confusion.

"I don't... Don't give Dad anything. He is always roping people into doing shit they don't want to do."

"I usually donate though. That school isn't going to put up a new gym on their own and I've seen the stats on their scholarship levels. They help a lot of people get a preparatory school education that couldn't afford it otherwise. What's wrong with donating?"

"It's not the donating. It's Dad. I feel like my entire life has been Dad pressuring people."

"He's in Development. That's his job. To squeeze funds out of us rich bastards for noble causes. I really respect his work choices. I don't think he's ever worked for a place that I haven't whole-heartedly agreed with their cause."

"I don't want him to think that he can apply extra pressure to you, because we..." He didn't know how to finish that sentence either.

"Oh." She smiled up at him. "Has anyone mentioned recently that you're adorable?"

"Just you," he replied. "Has anyone mentioned that you're the sexiest woman in the room?"

That made her smile extra wide and she leaned in, then stopped, seeming to hover on the point of touching him. "You and three drinks are not at all good for my self-control," she said. "Let's go fix this seating thing."

Dominique did indeed fix the seating and he found himself seated between Evan and Dominique and facing Eleanor. Eleanor eyed him with an expression that implied he was a new and curious form of insect.

"So, Maxwell," said Evan. "You're sitting here."

"Yes," agreed Max. He scrutinized Evan and then checked the table in front of him. Evan had not replaced the wine with anything but water, but he had a slightly glassy-eyed look, and his pupils seemed overly dilated. Max glanced at Dominique, but she was leaning across Jackson to talk to Aiden.

"Why is Dominique talking to you? Didn't you proposition her in college?"

Max took a deep breath and smiled tightly. "Yes. And I have apologized."

"Huh," said Evan. "That actually worked?"

"A sincere apology generally goes a long way," said Max.

"I wouldn't know," said Evan. "I've never tried it."

Max didn't know what to say to that. He wasn't sure that Evan was going to remember this conversation tomorrow. "Might want to think about starting," he said, and Evan blinked at him.

"It's a bit late for that," he said and turned away to speak with the female half of the couple on his other side.

Jackson leaned back to look around Dominique and talk to Max. "Do you think that—"

Whatever he had been about to say was cut off as the MC began to speak. After that it was almost impossible to talk to anyone, even Dominique. Dinner was served, the auction was called, and Jackson seemed oblivious to the fact that his girlfriend was resting her hand on Max's knee. They had just been served the main course when Dominique leaned over, looking flushed.

"You may have been right on the subject of cocktails. Now that the room has heated up, I kind of don't feel so good."

"Do you want to go out in the hall for a minute?"

"Um, maybe... Can you get me a water from the bar?"

"Yeah, of course." He managed to get up without accidentally bidding on something and went to the bar. He waited through the small line, got a water and turned around to see if there would be a break in the action that would allow him to unobtrusively return to the table.

He looked back at the table and saw Dominique stand up. As he watched, she leaned over the back of Jackson's chair and hugged him. Her face was so full of genuine affection that he felt like he'd been kicked in the stomach. Max could tell himself that Dominique was into him all he wanted, but it wasn't going to change the fact that she loved Jackson.

He walked quickly out to the hall. The cocktail area was empty. The silent auction had been torn down and even the coat check area was unmanned. Max needed to get out of the damn place before he did something that he'd regret. He opened a ride-share app and took the closest ride to him—a mini-van that was one minute away.

"Hey," hissed Dominique, slipping out into the hallway, shutting the door to the ballroom carefully. "What's the matter? Where are you going?"

"Home," he said, tersely, backing up. "I can't do this. I shouldn't have come."

"Wait a minute," she said walking after him, her strides short in her tight dress.

"No," he said and turned around and left.

# Dominque – The After Party

Dominique hiked up her skirt to climb the stairs up to the Ames condo, then smoothed it down again as she approached the door. It took a minute because that last drink was kicking in and she felt a little unsteady on her shoes. Did she really want to do this?

Yes.

Maybe it was the four drinks and not enough dinner, maybe it was pride, or maybe it was the memory of Max's kiss, but she really did want this. She hoped her text to Jackson would be enough for him to cover her abrupt exit out to the cabstand. But she really hadn't wanted to go back into the ballroom and explain what had happened to Max. Because, for one thing, she didn't know what had happened. She thought the evening had been going well—like really, really well, and then poof—he was gone. And she wanted an explanation. She wanted to make-out. She wanted to make-out and get an explanation.

She knocked on the front door. It took a few moments, but the door opened. Max was in his stocking feet and he'd untucked and partially unbuttoned his shirt, giving her a tantalizing glimpse of chest.

"Hi," she said, breezing past him, stripping off her wrap and dropping it on the couch. She liked Grant's living room. It was cozy and manly without being weird.

"What are you doing here?" he asked, shutting the door and crossing his arms over his chest.

"I came to see you," she said.

"Why?"

"To find out why you left. I thought we were having a good time. I stopped to talk to my family and then you were gone."

"Your family, yeah." He looked annoyed. "Why were you talking to me in the first place?"

She frowned. He made no sense. Had he not looked in the mirror this evening?

"Well, if nothing else, because I was going to have to stab Sasha Beckstale if she flashed her boobs at you one more time."

"You're jealous? That's rich."

"Well, why shouldn't I be?" she demanded, stepping closer to him and staring up into his face, trying to interpret his expression. She leaned in, allowing her breasts to gently press against his folded arms. "Unless you kiss everyone that way." She went up on tip-toe and let her lips graze over his. He grabbed her by the arms and shoved her away, breathing heavily.

"You misunderstood," he said.

"You son of a bitch," she blurted out and slapped him. For a moment she stared at him in horror and then she put her hand over mouth. She felt like she was going to be sick. She turned and fled down the hall. She grabbed the first door she came to and flung it open. She had only gone a few steps before she stumbled and tripped onto a bed.

She sprawled across the bed and closed her eyes against the spinning in her head. It didn't seem to help. God, what had she been thinking? Why had she thought this was a good idea? She should have known better than to think he actually liked her.

"Hey!" Max entered the room, his voice a sharp crack in the dark, and she winced. "What the hell was that?"

"I'm drunk," she said. "Go away and leave me alone."

"No, I will not. I don't care how drunk you are." She felt his weight bounce the bed. She rolled back over and found him leaning over her, a dark solid form illuminated by the light from the hallway. God, he smelled good. If he leaned down a little further, she could kiss him. If he moved his hand over a few inches, he could put his hands on her... whatever he wanted, honestly. Ever since that kiss in the park the idea of him putting his hands anywhere had sounded great.

Only right now, he didn't look like he wanted to. He looked angry.

"When I was twelve, Evan threw a dart at me," she blurted out. "Pegged me in the back. I still have a little scar."

"What?"

"He said it was because I ran in the way. But I swear I didn't. And when I was fourteen, he held me under water at a pool party. Then he claimed to have saved me from drowning."

Max's expression softened.

"And when I was fifteen, he slapped me so hard I got a nosebleed. He said it was my fault for being a bitch and that it was just a slap. It's never anything big. It's never where other people see. But it's always demeaning and afterwards everything he says makes me question if I interpreted it right. Maybe I'm the one who got it wrong."

"No," he said. "Evan is an abusive asshole. But that doesn't mean you can come in here, kiss me, and then call me names and slap me."

"I'm sorry." She meant it. "But you said..." She looked away, embarrassed.

"I said, what?" he asked, leaning down closer, trying to make eye contact. He had tasted like he'd been eating peppermints. She reached up and straightened the collar on his shirt, not wanting to say it. She risked a glance upward from his collar. His expression was sweet and concerned. "You said I misunderstood and that's what he always says."

"I'm not trying to gaslight you," he said, looking frustrated. "I want you, but it's not that simple."

She looked up at him, trying to decide if she cared about simple. Did he have a wife or girlfriend back in California? She was supposed to care about that kind of thing. But she could feel the warmth of his body on hers and she found that she really... just... didn't... care.

She wrapped her arms around his neck, pulling him down, kissing him again. This time he didn't resist. This time, his hands slid up the length of her body. She felt the world spin again as she broke free of his lips, angling to let him kiss along her neck. Somewhere his shirt was untucked, and she worked one hand down until she found a piece of exposed skin, running her hand inside his shirt, feeling the soft but hard expanse of his back. He pulled her dress down off her shoulders and crooked a finger into her bra, bending down the cup and freeing her breast of confinement. He continued kissing her, letting his mouth trail over her nipple, flicking it with his tongue.

She gave a gasp of pleasure and tried to wrap a leg around his. She wanted him between her thighs, to feel the weight and heat and hardness of him. But instead she found herself blocked by the tightness of her own skirt.

"Fucking skirt," she muttered, and he laughed softly.

"Looks good standing up," he said. "Not so convenient lying down." He put his hand on her thigh, searching out the edge of her skirt, even has he continued to lick and kiss her cleavage. His hand slid gently up her skin and the skirt fabric shifted upwards. She wriggled against his hand happily. He was going to fix the situation for her.

Then they both heard it. The sound of the front door opening. She stared up at him in a panic.

"It's my dad," he said.

"Can you get rid of him?" she demanded in a whisper.

"Not really," he whispered back. "We're in his room."

"Shit!"

He pulled her off the bed and out into the hall. He opened a second door and shoved her inside and shut the door behind her. She tried to right the mess he'd made of her top and correct the bra situation. She could hear Grant and Max talking out in the living room. She slipped out of her heels, trying to get steadier on her feet, and looked around the room.

It was clearly the guest room, but Max's possessions were starting to take over. His wardrobe from the evening was distributed around the room. His jacket and tie were hanging on the doorknob to the closet. His shoes had been abandoned on the floor. But the rest of his belongings were laid out with military precision along the dresser. She found herself staring at the pistol on the dresser top. It said *Glock, Inc.* on the side and the holster looked well used. When she talked to Grant, they generally avoided the subject of Max. She hadn't wanted to tell him that she thought his son was an asshole, and the one time Max had come up Grant had shaken his head and simply said that he hated his son's job and didn't want to talk about it. But now she was wondering if maybe she should have covered the topic at least a little bit.

Up until Jackson had come to live with them, she'd never known anyone who carried a gun regularly. Jackson wore his with a conscious sense of ritual that had at first seemed mockable. Aiden, in his grumpy phase, had certainly derided him—calling him a paranoid thug with delusions of persecution and a substitute dick. Aiden had spent the first year after Jackson's arrival being a jerk. Dominique had never fully discussed the reasons, but drugs, low-level depression and jealousy of the time Dominique spent with Jackson seemed to be the main causes. Jackson had won him over eventually, but it had been a hard year. And in that year, Dominique had discovered that Jackson was the most reliable, and possibly smartest, family member she had. Aiden, when he wasn't over-partying and being an asshole, was a darling, but easily distracted. Evan was always an asshole, whether he was over-partying or not. And her grandmother was rarely available, emotionally or otherwise. Jackson, on the other hand, turned up when he said he would, gave good advice, and over the last few years had helped her out of several messes.

More than one of her girlfriends had hinted that Dominique might have a crush on her cousin, and although she hadn't admitted it to them, she had given the matter some thought. It wasn't as though she had grown up with Jackson, and he was certainly crushable, but she really didn't. Mostly, because every once in a while, he would smile and she would remember what her mother had looked like. Photos never captured that vivid little way her mother's mouth had crooked up at the corner. Having Jackson around was like recapturing a little bit of Genevieve. She knew Aiden saw it too, although they never talked about it. No, she didn't have a crush on Jackson, but he had illuminated for her what she did want in a partner. And after her afternoon with Max, she had thought that he was definitely in the right category. But she hadn't quite connected the dots that Max would be quite so much like Jackson in the gun department.

She wasn't sure how she felt about that. Jackson's past was checkered, but that didn't mean that Max was similarly engaged in illegal activities. It had only been six years since she'd last seen him. How much trouble could he really have gotten into? Maybe he just liked carrying a gun? People did that. Not generally people she knew, but Jackson said people did.

The bedroom door opened, and she whirled to face it, then blinked as the world kept turning. Max was across the room in a second, propping her upright.

"Come on," he whispered.

They tip-toed down the hallway and out to the living room. Dominique grabbed her wrap off the couch and Max pulled her out into the hallway. She shivered in the sudden draft of cold air and fumbled for her wrap. Max took it out of her hands and tucked it around her in the least fashionable, probably warmest manner possible.

"Your Lyft is on the way," he said checking his phone. "You should probably put your shoes back on."

"Max," she said, then stopped, not really certain where to take things.

His phone pinged. "Car is here," he said. He took her shoes out of her unresisting hand and knelt down, helping her slide them on.

"I'm not sure this how the Cinderella thing is supposed to work," she said, looking down at the cowlick on his head.

"Your shoes weren't lost, you don't clean anything, and you don't need to be rescued, so no, it's not," Max said standing up.

"I clean up lots of things," she said. She was a lot closer to his face in heels. "And just because I don't *need* rescuing doesn't mean I don't *want* to be rescued."

He leaned in and kissed her with an intensity that left her wobbly in her shoes.

"Car is here," he said and stepped away.

## Jackson – Morning Visits

Jackson answered the knock on his bedroom door in his box-
ers and stared at the fully dressed and cheerful looking Aiden. He
was aware that his cousins, despite owning their own homes, viewed
Deveraux House as their permanent home base, but he had never
quite gotten over the idea that they could turn up randomly outside
his bedroom door without warning.

"What fucking time is it?" he demanded.

"Like six?"

"What the fuck?" demanded Jackson. He had also never quite
gotten over the idea of six in the morning.

"Alicia had to be up early to do weather for the morning com-
mute," said Aiden looking smug.

"Fuck you," said Jackson. "I hate you."

"I brought coffee," said Aiden, holding up a Dunkin' cup with
steam leaking from the tiny hole at the top.

"Fine," said Jackson, "I won't kill you." He took the coffee and
went back into his room. Aiden followed him.

"You redecorated," said Aiden, looking around the suite at the
modern, streamlined furniture, blue-gray walls and sleek light fix-
tures. Jackson's 'room' was divided into a sitting area, bedroom and
bathroom. Jackson liked that the furniture all felt restrained, but all
the fabrics were explosions of luxurious softness.

"Theo did it," said Jackson, feeling self-conscious. "I came
home one day and he started showing me fabric samples. Next thing
you know, my room looks like I know what the word *décor* means."

He looked around again, trying to see if anything truly embarrassing was hanging out. As a habit from prison, he kept things fairly tidy. He didn't think there was anything that Aiden could judge him too badly on.

"It looks good," protested Aiden, with a laugh. "More like you, anyway."

"That's not hard. The last stuff looked like it belonged to Wyatt Earp or something." Jackson took a cautious sip from the cup Aiden had brought him. It was so much better than Pete's coffee that his mouth didn't know how to react.

"It's a Victorian mansion," said Aiden. "I'm pretty sure the furniture was authentic to the house."

"I'm pretty sure it was *original* to the house," said Jackson. "What's up?"

"Last night seemed to go OK," said Aiden, cautiously.

"Yeah," agreed Jackson, still not clear on Aiden's purpose for turning up at this hour.

"You ran a background check on Max, right?" Aiden asked.

"Yeah, of course," said Jackson, sipping the coffee as Aiden flopped down on the couch and flipped on the TV. "You're staying?"

"I didn't come over here just to wake you up, piss you off and give you coffee. I wanted some of Theo's pancakes. And, also, to talk to you."

"Uh-huh. Theo's making pancakes?"

"Yeah, he said he'd bring them up. You should probably put on pants. Although, Jesus how far does that thing go?"

"What?" asked Jackson blinking at his cousin.

"Your tattoo!" Aiden waved at Jackson's naked torso. Jackson looked down at himself. He'd skipped the jailhouse tattoos and decided to scratch the itch for ink by going big. He had a graphic black-ink dragon that started at about his lowest rib and traversed his side.

"Top of my thigh more or less."

"You couldn't just get some sort cartoon character and call it good?"

"No," said Jackson. "I read a book about samurai when I was a kid and how they would only have tattoos under their clothing where no one could see. I thought it was cool. I wanted to do something like that. I also liked dragons. And cartoon characters are dumb."

Aiden glared at him. "I was going to watch Powerpuff Girls."

Jackson laughed. "I meant that cartoons are dumb when stamped on someone's ass."

"Well, that is a reasonable position," admitted Aiden, although he still looked suspicious.

"What did you want to talk about?" Jackson asked, going to his dresser and rummaging around for sweats. He heard the TV flip on and the artificial click sound as Aiden slid through the TV guide.

"Well, the background check thingie."

"Max is single, gainfully employed, non-smoking, and problem free," said Jackson pulling on his most ratty pair of sweats. They were the only article of clothing that had made it through the Deveraux cleanse and restock of his wardrobe. He looked up and realized that Aiden had been entirely serious and had landed on the Cartoon Network. Leave it to Aiden to know when the Powerpuff Girls were on.

"Honestly, he always seemed OK in college," said Aiden, with a shrug. "I could never figure out what the hell he'd been thinking saying that to Dominique. But I figured it would be better to check him out."

Jackson didn't respond as he pulled on a t-shirt. Aiden wore carelessness and a smile like a suit of armor. If he was going to the trouble of actually asking, then he thought it was important to him, no matter what he said.

"Grandma seemed to be giving him the evil eye," said Aiden, eyes fixed on the TV. Bubbles was fighting Mojo Jojo.

"Yeah, I got the feeling she didn't like that he's a Marshal," said Jackson.

"What's wrong with that?" asked Aiden, looking up in surprise.

"I don't know," said Jackson, taking his coffee to the couch and sitting down. "Just the feeling I got." He took another sip as Aiden seemed to ruminate on that. "What else is on your mind?"

"Nothing. I mean..."

Aiden flipped the remote around in his hand. Jackson waited. It didn't pay to try and rush Aiden—he'd clam up and disappear if pushed. Everyone hated Randall and Owen for their abusive ways, violent tempers and utter lack of empathy. And everyone knew Aiden wasn't like that. *Aiden was so nice! So easy-going! So...nothing like his uncles!*

But Jackson knew better.

He had learned it while still in prison. It had been clear from the minute that Aiden had walked into the interview room that Eleanor was forcing him to be there. Aiden did not want to get Jackson out of prison. Aiden didn't want Jackson to exist at all. He had smiled and made jokes, but Jackson had seen the clenched jaw and buried anger. But it was the day that Jackson had been taken to the visitor room instead of an interview room that he'd seen where Aiden truly stood on the subject of family.

Jackson had scanned the visitor's room and felt a cold prickle of fear. He knew he shouldn't have been there. The visitor room was not for private conversations. All his other meetings with Aiden had been in a private interview room.

He could see Aiden standing by a table with a large book in one hand, looking uncomfortable in a way that read to the assembled prisoners as fresh meat. Visitation, as it was properly termed, was a large open space with scattered tables and bare walls painted in institutional cream. It always reminded him of his junior high lunchroom. Jackson also saw Bubba Sweets two tables over, talking to someone who looked enough like a clone that they must have been related. Bubba was an asshole and a hired gun. Jackson had knocked out Bubba's front tooth three months ago, a fact that Bubba had not forgotten.

The CO pushed him through the doorway and Jackson dug in his heels.

"Cuffs?" he said.

"Fuck you," said the officer. "You stay in the cuffs 'til we get to your lawyer."

"That's not how it's supposed to work," said Jackson. "I get turned loose once I get to the visitor room."

"You get turned loose when I say you get turned loose," responded the officer, pushing him. Jackson started to sweat and went through the list of people who might want him dead—aside from Bubba. Top of the list was the local Ukrainian mob, a branch of the Solntsevskaya Bratva. They were pissed that Jackson turned down their offer, but they wouldn't be stupid enough to use any of their own people. Bubba's toe was tapping nervously and he was looking anywhere but at Jackson.

The CO walked Jackson across the room, guiding their path. Jackson stalled, dragging his feet as the CO pushed him. They passed Bubba's table and Jackson relaxed a fraction when nothing happened.

They reached Aiden's table, and the CO shoved him so that he was positioned with his back to Bubba and Aiden. Jackson heard the rustle of movement and spun, yanking his still-cuffed hands out of the CO's grasp.

There was a solid thud as Bubba's shiv slammed into Aiden's book. Aiden yanked the book upward, wrenching the shiv out of the man's hand. Then he brought the book down again on the back of Bubba's head. Jackson moved to the side to let Bubba fall to the floor. As the entire room watched, Aiden stepped forward and brought his foot deliberately down on Bubba's hand, grinding it into the linoleum. They all heard the crack of bone, and Bubba screamed.

Aiden's expression was one of cold fury. "From now on," said Aiden turning to the CO, "I expect a room when I fucking ask for it."

At the time, Jackson had been shaken. Aiden hated him, so why not let him get shanked? Jackson had never met anyone who acted against their own self-interests in his defense. It was perhaps that moment more than any other that had convinced Jackson that the Deverauxes were the right family for him. But it had taken Jackson another year and a fist-fight to convince Aiden to truly let him in. Aiden had been drunk off his ass and literally falling over, but he had still been a handful. Everyone who thought that Aiden didn't care about anything and didn't have a violent bone in his body had no idea about who Aiden really was.

"I'm worried about Evan," said Aiden, quietly, eyes locked on the Powerpuff Girls.

That was Aiden. Family to the core.

"So am I," said Jackson.

Aiden was silent. "I thought he was getting better there for a bit. But last night... He didn't look good. And I feel like I can't say anything."

"Yeah, I know," said Jackson. Aiden had drawn the line in

the sand, clear for all to see—Dominique came first. So Evan had always targeted Dominique. And Aiden had always rushed to the rescue. Prince Charming to the end.

"You said you were working on it," said Aiden, looking at him angrily.

"I *am* working on it," said Jackson. "I'm also working on not having any of you get killed. And I'm also flying to DC with Eleanor in a couple of hours."

Aiden made a disgusted noise.

"I just want the old Evan back," he complained. Jackson had heard him say that before, but he wasn't sure what it meant. Dominique didn't have many memories of Evan from childhood, but Jackson thought that Aiden and Evan had been close. But Aiden wouldn't talk about it in front of Dominique.

"What does that mean?" asked Jackson. "How was he different?"

Aiden looked annoyed to be having to explain. "When we were kids, he wasn't like this. He used to take care of me and Dominique. If I had a problem, I would go to Evan. And he always figured it out. Or took the blame. He was the smartest older cousin ever with all the best comic books. And then it was like he hit puberty and things started to go sideways. Owen kept making him do more adult things and he couldn't come play with me. And then our parents died. I was twelve. Dominique was ten. So Evan would have been…fifteen? And we all moved in with Grandma and then… it all went in the shitter."

There was a knock on the door.

"Come in," yelled Jackson.

"Where shall I serve the pancakes?" asked Theo. Theo always looked disapproving, but he seemed to have a soft spot for Aiden's ridiculous food requests.

"Coffee table," said Aiden, grinning and patting the table in front of him.

Theo set down the tray with two plates under covers and gestured to the syrup pitchers. "Maple and blackberry."

"Ah, yes," said Aiden. "This is what I'm talking about. You do realize that I had to move out to prevent becoming a giant fatty."

"I've gained fifteen pounds since moving in," said Jackson.

"You needed it," said Aiden dismissively. "You were too skinny."

"Is there anything else?" asked Theo, and Jackson thought he looked almost pleased. Although, whether it was at Jackson's weight gain or at Aiden for bossing Jackson around, Jackson couldn't tell.

"Nope. Thank you," said Aiden, shoving a giant forkful of flapjack into his mouth.

"Buzz me when Eleanor is ready?" suggested Jackson, and Theo nodded.

"She's gonna pop a screw if she catches you calling her Eleanor," said Aiden as Theo left the room.

"I call her Grandma to her face," said Jackson. "But it feels weird to call her that to other people."

"Uh-huh," said Aiden around a mouthful of pancake.

"Aiden?" asked Jackson, pouring out a measure of both syrups.

"You're going to ruin your pancakes," said Aiden. "You can't mix your syrups."

"I like it this way," said Jackson. "The maple is stiff. The blackberry cuts it down."

"Sugars it up you mean," objected Aiden. "You need to develop your syrup palette."

"My syrup palette?" demanded Jackson, looking up. "Really?"

Aiden grinned impudently. "It could be a thing."

"Or you could be yanking my chain."

"Yeah, maybe," agreed Aiden. "What'd you wanna know?"

"Did you see the news coverage of the car incident?"

"Yeah," said Aiden with a shrug. "Depending on which story you go with, we were resilient and resolute in the face of danger. Or panic stricken ninnies who willfully endangered our guests. Whatever." He made a sarcastic finger whirl.

"Do you think that…" Jackson hesitated, unsure of how he wanted to ask what he wanted to know. Aiden looked at him questioningly. "I wonder about our parents sometimes. How they would have handled things."

"Mm," said Aiden. "They wouldn't have had to handle it because they wouldn't have been there."

"What do you mean?"

"Randall and Owen would never have bothered to attend and probably would have given money to her opponent just because, and Mom… Mom hated public stuff. I know Grandma kind of thinks of us as The Children 2.0, but honestly we're nothing like them."

"We're not?"

"Well," Aiden continued. "Maybe you and Evan are, in the occasionally punching people department. But I'm definitely not. I am a very peaceful person."

Jackson tried not to roll his eyes.

"And Dominique certainly isn't. It's weird, but the older she gets, the more I see how she *isn't* like Mom."

"What do you mean?"

Aiden hesitated. "You can never repeat this to Grandma, but the older I get the more I see how fragile Mom was. Dad treated her like a princess and Grandma coddled her. And I'm not saying she didn't have strength, but none of them ever really stood up to Randall and Owen. They could have taken Evan away from Owen.

They *should* have taken Evan. But they didn't. And that makes me mad."

"I don't think they knew how," said Jackson.

"Bullshit," said Aiden. "Grandma knew how, but she didn't because she didn't want to cause a public scandal."

"Randall would have contested her claim on the trust," said Jackson. "If she'd made a move against them."

"Probably true," agreed Aiden. "But it shouldn't have come down to money. The narrative you'll always hear from Grandma and everyone else was that Randall and Owen were horrible, and that Dad and Mom were saints. But what they were was weak."

Jackson looked at his cousin in surprise. The last sentence was delivered with a surprising amount of venom. Aiden blushed and looked at the TV.

"Sorry. I'm just... I get mad. Why did they get on that stupid plane? Mom hated Randall and Owen. She would never have wanted-ed to fly with them. You know Randall bullied them into it. They should have been stronger. They should have been stronger all the way around."

"My mom overdosed," said Jackson. "She always claimed to be in control of everything. She said we never needed anyone else. Then she OD'd and left me on my own. I am also quite... angry at my mother."

Aiden looked down at his pancakes. "Sorry, this turned into a downer of a breakfast," he said pushing away his plate.

"FYI, prison provides therapy. Which is where I discovered that being angry doesn't mean I loved her less," said Jackson.

Aiden made an unhappy noise. "I love them. I miss them. But... You know what bothers me about being called Prince Charming?" Jackson shook his head. "Prince Charming is a useless dickweed. He doesn't actually do anything. He's the dipshit that shows up at the end to kiss the unconscious girl. Like it's OK to just go around kissing dead slash sleeping chicks. Can you imagine waking up after a hundred years to some jackass who probably never brushed his teeth once in his entire life? Also, in some of those stories it wasn't just a kiss. Pretty sure Briar Rose woke up after giving birth to twins or some shit like that. That won't give you PTSD or anything."

"What?" Sometimes with Aiden, Jackson felt like conversations that were going one place ended up taking a back-road to a random gas station that existed only in the topographical map of Aiden's brain.

"I took a historical literature class one time. Fairy tales will fuck you up. Don't read 'em."

"I admit I have not read many fairy tales," said Jackson, trying to drag the conversation back to the main highway, "but I thought Prince Charming showed up in time to slay the dragon and save the day."

"Yeah, that's what people mean when they say it. And that's what Mom always expected out of Dad. But I don't want to be like Mom—always needing to be rescued and afraid to face life. I think I've done OK at that. But here's the other part, I don't want to be Dad either. I can't spend my life constantly being in charge of someone else's happiness and decisions. I want someone awesome and tough who doesn't mind a helping hand, but who's not going to take crap from anyone. And believe me, that girl is incredibly hard to find."

Jackson had the odd feeling that Aiden was speaking about someone specific, but he had no way to justify the intuition.

"Stick to the weather girl?" he asked.

"Weather girls are not half bad," agreed Aiden, with a laugh.

"I'll talk to Evan when we get back from DC," Jackson promised.

"Thanks," said Aiden. "I'm really worried."

# Maxwell – Working Out

Max stared at the ceiling and thought about Dominique. Her lips, the way they had brushed over his. The softness of her breasts and the way she had moaned when he put his tongue on them. Her thighs... He had been so close to having those legs wrapped around him. He could imagine working the tight fabric up, feeling the supple skin of her thighs, feeling the way her legs would part for him. He groaned and rolled over onto his stomach. He had never been so close to patricide as the night before.

"Hey!" yelled his father through the door. "I'm going to work. Swing by if you want to grab lunch!"

Max considered yelling back that his father should go to hell. "OK," he yelled back instead.

He waited until he heard the front door slam before rolling back over and reaching for the lotion on the bedside table. His Dominique fantasies were not going away. Not that it mattered. Because fantasies were all they were going to be.

He couldn't decide who he was more mad at—Dominique or himself. He'd gone to that damn fundraiser with the single purpose of connecting with her. And he so very clearly had. The way she had kissed him, the way she had touched him, had all left very little doubt that she wanted him. But he was a little bit shocked to discover that he wasn't that kind of boy. He didn't want to be the reason someone broke up. He didn't want to help anyone cheat.

Still, when he closed his eyes, she was right there, her blonde hair spilled out in a pool on the bed, while her hands slid inside his shirt and she looked up at him with those blue eyes...

When his head was finally clear enough to focus on something besides his dick, he got up and got dressed. He pulled on a button-up with his jeans, then a suit jacket so that he at least looked somewhat work appropriate and left the condo heading for the local U.S. Marshal's office.

Although he was having some serious qualms about Dominique and whatever the fuck was going on between them, he hadn't changed his mind about what had happened at the florist. He still wanted to run them through the system. And maybe, if he figured out who they were, he could drop off Dominique's list of who to call in case of danger.

Max flashed his badge at the front desk and headed straight for the nerd department to where Harris worked. He stopped to ask directions a few times, but eventually found himself leaning over the cubicle wall of Patricia Harris, certified nerd, and one of the reasons he'd listed this branch as his top pick for his next assignment.

"How many Starbucks is it going to cost me for some off-the-books facial rec?" he asked, and she jumped in her chair.

"Ames, you asshole," she said, grinning. Patricia Harris was a decade plus older than him, with short-clipped hair that could have either gone toward soccer mom or lesbian, but that he happened to know really meant that she cut her own hair with a pair of beard clippers. She said she wasn't trying to make a statement; she was just cheap. She pulled out her ear buds and stood up to hug him. "What's this about facial rec?" she asked, leaning back to look at him. At five foot one, she was always looking up at him. "I thought you were visiting with your dad."

"I was. I am. But a friend of mine is in a little bit of trouble."

"What kind of trouble?" she asked skeptically.

"Did you read about the car through the window at the Deveraux fundraiser?" he asked.

"Saw it on the Channel Four news," she said nodding.

"My friend is Dominique Deveraux."

"Ooh la la. Hotness."

"You have no idea," he said. "But more to the point, she's not an idiot. And she thought she recognized the van the suspect used as belonging to a local florist, but the cops gave her the brush-off. So she decided to go take a look-see herself."

"Are we sure she's not an idiot?"

"I went with her," he said.

"And we do know that *you're* an idiot," said Harris with a grin.

"Yes, we do. Anyway, there were some suspicious characters loitering around the florist. I took some pictures. I was hoping you could run them and see if anything popped."

Harris checked her watch. "It's going to cost you more than Starbucks. It's lunch time."

"I am your delivery guy. You name it, I buy it."

"Tacos," said Harris. "From the truck three blocks down. Plus, the horchata and some churros."

"Mexican Death Truck, it is. Your wish is my command."

"Damn straight it is."

"Emailing you the photos now," he said, backing away, hitting send on the message from his phone.

He was picking up her order plus a lunch combo for himself when his phone rang.

"Hey Dad," he said, pinching the phone between his shoulder and his ear and tossing napkins and tomatillo salsa into the bag.

"Hey," said Grant. "I thought you were going to swing by for lunch."

Max frowned. He hadn't thought that was a serious invitation. He'd thought Grant was saying that because it was the sort of thing you were supposed to say to your kid to make it sound like you wanted to spend time with him.

"Yeah, I meant to," he lied, "but I had to go into work for something."

"You're supposed to be on vacation," said Grant, sounding uncharacteristically frustrated.

"It's just some paperwork stuff," said Max. "I want to make sure that I've got the best shot at being assigned here."

Grant was silent on the other end of the phone. "You said... Do you really think they'll assign here?"

"Yeah, it's down to here or Virginia," said Max, tying the bag shut and picking up the drinks carrier, before going back to holding his phone in his hand. What part of the story had Grant missed when he'd told it the first time? Why did his father always tune out everything about his job? "That's why I said I wanted to look at apartments."

"I didn't think you were serious," said Grant and Max made a frustrated flailing gesture that jostled the bag of food.

"I'm not serious right this second, but if I get assigned here, then I will be. I just wanted to look at the kind of price tag I'm likely to be paying."

"I know agents that can help."

"Yes, Dad. That's why I asked you." Max felt like he was stuck in a loop. Maybe this time it would stick in Grant's brain.

"OK, OK, don't be snippy. You sound like your mother." Max restrained the urge to face-palm himself with the taco bag. "I'll make a few calls."

"Great. Thanks," said Max. He didn't think he lost the snippy tone. "I'll see you when I get home."

"Great!" said Grant cheerfully. "We can grab some beers with Smitty."

Max hung up and made his way back into the building. The entire point of getting reassigned... Well, it was bump on the pay scale for one. But the other point was to build a somewhat functional relationship with his dad. So far it was a complete non-starter. Grant didn't seem to think their relationship had any problems.

Getting into the building was easier the second time around. Carrying food made security more friendly.

"As commanded," he said rounding the corner of the cubicle, "One horchata, three tacos, and—" He stopped mid-sentence as he saw that Harris wasn't alone.

"Ames, is it?" asked the woman with brunette bob and the serious pant suit. He recognized her as Director Gail Cabello, his potential boss. "So nice to meet you in person. Want to explain to me why you're working out of my division without actually being assigned here?"

He cleared his throat and glanced at Harris.

"I was trying to help a friend out," he said. "I wasn't trying to step on anyone's toes."

"Yes, Dominique Deveraux, I heard. The Deverauxes have a lot of reach and a lot of damn nerve trying to use my resources."

"Wait, no," he said. "That is not what this is. Dominique and I went to college together. She did not ask me to do this. Running the photos was my idea. Dominique thought she had a lead on the suspect that drove a car through the tennis club window, but the police blew her off. So when she called me up and asked me to watch her back while she did a walk-by of the business I figured it wouldn't amount to anything. But things were definitely off. I don't know what's going on with that group, but I thought someone ought to tag them."

"So basically, you're trying to get into some girls pants and you just happened to bump into two of INTERPOL's most wanted."

He opened his mouth to protest then heard the rest of the sentence. "What?"

Harris shifted position and gestured to the screen. "We got two hits within five minutes. We're still running the others. They're ex-French Foreign Legion, wanted for war crimes in Iraq."

"I knew it," said Max, leaning into the screen.

"If these guys are after the Deveraux family," said the director, "your girlfriend's in real trouble."

"She's not my girlfriend," said Max, "but yes, it definitely looks that way. We're going to need to interface with the detective on the case. I've got his card." Max patted his pocket, but the director was shaking her head.

"*We* nothing. *You* are still on vacation and *I* haven't decided I even want you here." She held out her hand for the card. "I'm not having you shortcut the process just because you have a messed up idea of what constitutes dating. We'll take it from here."

Max reluctantly handed over the card. "I'll call Dominique and tell her you're handling it," he said.

"No," said the director, "We will handle it. I repeat: you're out. And if you want a shot at being assigned here, you'll stay out of it."

"Understood," he said, clenching his teeth.

"That means you don't get to stay," she said pointedly.

"Fine," he said, and then glanced down at the bag of Mexican food in his hand. "But I'm taking my lunch."

# Dominique – Emergency Contact

Dominique woke up and stared at the ceiling of her apartment. She had returned home last night and collapsed into bed, barely taking the time to strip out of her dress and wipe off her makeup. She was still wearing her bra and underwear. With a groan, she flailed around and managed to unsnap her bra, flinging it out of the bed. Her arm collapsed back down and landed on her breast. With a sigh, she ran her fingers over her nipple, remembering the way Max had caressed it, the way his tongue had brought it to attention. The way his hands had curved over her body. She slid her hands down to her thighs. Would he have been gentle as he pushed her skirt up, sliding it with torturously slow hands? Or would he have yanked it hard, ruining the fabric, but leaving her gasping in excitement? She moved her hands inward, imagining how it would feel if they were Max's hands. She arched under the pressure of her fingers, pushing where she had wanted him to touch her.

Her alarm went off with a jangle of music and Dominique jerked in surprise, rolled over and glared at her phone. Then she realized that it was her leave-the-house alarm. She should have been out of bed an hour ago. Groaning, she dismissed the alarm and sat up. This morning was going to suck so hard.

Once at work, Dominique sat at her desk with her head in one hand and tried to concentrate on the pile of papers in front of her. Her train had been late, and she'd had to run the last few blocks to skate through the door at only ten minutes late. And of course, Sandra, the CFO's Assistant, had spotted her. Sandra hated her with a passion. Dominique suspected that it was because Sandra had somehow figured out that Dominique was a Deveraux.

Dominique had downed ibuprofen before leaving her apartment, but it had clearly not been enough. Her head throbbed, and worse, no matter how many times she checked her phone, Max still hadn't called.

When she left the condo the night before, she had been absolutely certain that things were fine between them. But in the cold light of a rainy October morning and the dull pounding of a hangover, she was far less certain. Max had said that he wanted her, but that things weren't simple. In the rankings of vague non-statement statements, that was up at least in the top ten.

She tried, again, to read the sponsor agreement in front of her. It seemed like gibberish. She wondered if she could sneak away somewhere over lunch and get a nap. Probably not.

Her cell phone rang and she checked the number. It was a hospital. She felt her heart rate pick up.

"Hello?"

"Hi, this Good Samaritan Hospital. We're looking for Dominique Deveraux."

"This is she."

It was a sign of how stressed she was that she fell back on her grandmother's grammatically correct phone response.

"You're the emergency contact for Evan Deveraux."

Dominique tried to process the meaning of those words and couldn't get the past the fact that Evan would have had to write that down somewhere. On purpose.

"Yes?"

"Earlier today, Evan was attacked and suffered a concussion. We would like to send him home with a family member."

"What do you mean, attacked?"

"I'm not allowed to discuss that," said the woman. "You'll have to talk to him about it. Can you pick him up?"

"Of course," said Dominique. "I'll be there in twenty minutes."

"Great!" said the woman, clearly relieved to have a to-do item checked off. "Go to the emergency room and ask at the desk."

"Thanks," said Dominique.

"Have a nice day," said the woman incongruously and hung up the phone.

Dominique stared at the phone in disbelief. Then she dialed her grandmother's car service and directed them to meet her at the hospital. Once she had talked to her boss and was in a cab, she dialed Jackson.

"Hey," he said, picking up. "What's up? Did you and Max go on another date? Do I need to come bail you out of jail?"

She could hear the air quotes around *date* but couldn't clear the head space to respond to them appropriately.

"Evan was attacked," she blurted out.

"What?"

"I'm going to pick him up at the hospital. They said he had a concussion."

"Who attacked him?" demanded Jackson.

"I don't know. They said he had a concussion but wouldn't say more on the phone. I'm taking a cab, but I ordered a car to meet us there. What should I do once I get him?"

"Take him back to the house," said Jackson.

"He'll want to go back to his place."

"I know, but don't let him. I'll send Aiden to grab some clothes for him."

"OK," she said, taking a deep breath. "I can't believe someone..." She trailed off. "What if this is connected to Grandma and what happened at the club?"

"I'm sure that it is," said Jackson.

Dominique sighed. That meant that she was going to have to

think about that instead of thinking about Max. Jackson seemed to think that she could be done, but clearly if Evan was getting attacked then she wasn't.

Dominique checked in at the front desk and was directed back to a nurse's station, but when she got there the desk was unmanned. She pivoted around, trying not to feel like a peeping tom as she caught glimpses of patients around the edges of curtains. She finally saw Evan and found herself stopped in unexpected shock. For as long as she had known Evan, he had always been carefully and correctly dressed for the occasion. Unlike Aiden and Dominique, he had never embarrassed their grandmother by arriving at a party in mud-splattered clothes, or said the wrong thing, or in one infamous incident, dropped the f-bomb in front of a duchess like Dominique. But the Evan on the other side of the curtain was slumped on the edge of a bed. He had his shirt off, his ribs had been wrapped, and there was a butterfly bandage on his cheek. His eye was clearly black, and the left side of his face was puffy from what Dominique suspected were multiple punches.

But it wasn't just the injuries that startled her, it was his slumped posture and the startling paleness of his skin. All of the Deveraux cousins were pale and Evan, a natural red head, wasn't any different. But under the harsh fluorescents of the hospital, his skin had taken on a sickly cast, as if he hadn't been outside in months. As she watched, he picked up his shirt, and with careful movements, began to pull it on. The shirt was bloody and torn. At the half-way point he gave up buttoning it, either in exhaustion or because the buttons were ripped out. He dropped his hands back to the edge of the bed and sat simply staring at the floor. She'd never seen Evan look so fragile and absolutely devoid of spark.

The nurse came back and looked suspiciously at Dominique.

"I'm here for Evan Deveraux," she murmured, and the nurse smiled.

"Great. Here are his release forms and records." She flopped a pile of papers down on the countertop and pointed to where she could sign. Dominque scrawled her signature where indicated and accepted the bulldog-clipped sheaf of paperwork.

"I'll take you in," said the nurse and led her through the curtain to Evan.

He looked up at her and his face froze.

"You said you were calling someone to come get me," he said.

"Yes," said the nurse. "And here's your sister. You're ready to go."

"She's not—" began Evan, but the nurse was already walking away. "I thought she meant a car," he said, looking at Dominique. It was painful to watch him try and put his dignity back on.

"The car is out front," said Dominique, picking up the plastic bag with Evan's personal effects. Jackson had once told her that she was the Deveraux Creative Director—if she chose the course, the boys would do as she commanded. She had laughed because even if she could talk Aiden into doing what she wanted, Evan would never do as he was told. But as she stared at Evan, it occurred to her that she hadn't actually *tried* giving Evan orders before. How did Grandma get him to do what she wanted? Eleanor simply stated what Evan was going to do and then left him to do it. She did that to all of them, really. To Dominique, it seemed a concession to pride. Eleanor knew they would knuckle-under, but she let them do it without being watched. Dominque considered for a moment and then decided that if Grandma could do it then so could she.

"Come along," Dominique said, making her voice as much like Eleanor's as possible, and pushed through the curtain. Evan hesitated, and then followed Dominique. Which was a relief since she didn't have a back-up plan. A black sedan waited for them and Evan got in as she held the door open.

"I don't know why they called you," he said, when they were inside. He sat as far away from her as possible, or maybe he was just leaning against the door for support.

"I'm listed as your emergency contact," said Dominique lifting the front page of the pile of paperwork. The next sheet was a drawing of a human body with circles indicating the location of Evan's wounds. The circle next to his ribs also had a note next to it.

FIFTH AND SIXTH RIBS BROKEN ALONG PREVIOUS BREAK POINT. SEVENTH RIB CRACKED.

As far as she knew Evan had never broken his ribs. She flipped further into the stack and finally found a note suggesting that the previous rib break was a pre-teen injury.

Dominique stared out the window. She had been ten when her parents died. Evan was five years older. A pre-teen injury would have been when Uncle Owen was alive. Her parents had never left them alone with Uncle Owen. They had said, in tight-lipped disapproval, that he was *not a good parent*. Dominique had always assumed that meant that Owen let Evan drink while still in high school.

"I had to fill that out for insurance at work," said Evan.

"They wanted to check you out to some who would care for you," said Dominique, still looking at the pile in her lap.

"Then they should have called my lawyer," he snapped.

"Wouldn't have worked," said Dominique. "Aiden's in court all afternoon." She glanced up and found Evan staring at her. "What?"

"Nothing," he said. His face seemed strained and she couldn't tell if he was trying to say something or to keep it in, then he turned to look out the window. "We need to call Jackson," he said a few blocks later.

"We can when we get home," she said.

"No," he said tiredly. "We should call now. I think you have my phone in the bag."

"It can wait," she said.

"No," he said. "The men who… attacked me. They said to tell Grandma not to go to work tomorrow."

Dominique bit her lip as she tried to judge the effect that message would have on either Jackson or Eleanor. "Tomorrow is the first day of the hearings. I'm not sure Grandma will do what they want," she said at last.

"You misunderstand," he said impatiently. "I want Jackson to make sure she fucking goes to work tomorrow."

For once Dominique didn't mind his condescending tone. She grinned and took out her phone and hit the speed dial for Jackson.

"Did you get him?" asked Jackson.

"Yes," said Dominique, putting him on speaker. "We're on our way home. But he wanted to talk to you."

"The assholes who attacked me wanted to keep Grandma away from work," said Evan leaning toward the phone. "You need to make sure she goes."

"I will," said Jackson. "Did you talk to the cops?"

"Yes, but I didn't have much to tell them."

"Look at the photos Dominique has on her phone. Let me know if you recognize any of them."

"Oh! Shit. Yes, I have those." Evan looked in surprise at Dominique as she flipped the app open on her phone, working around the in-progress call button. "Swipe to the right," she said, handing the phone to the Evan. He did as instructed and she saw his eyes widen when he got to the pics that Max had taken.

"These ones," he said. "These are the guys. Where did you get these photos?"

"We took them when I went to investigate the florist on Sunday," said Dominique.

Evan was silent and then shoved the phone back at her. "You could have been hurt," he said.

"I took Max with me," said Dominique with a shrug.

"That isn't acceptable," said Evan, sounding stiff and awkward.

"We've already discussed it," said Jackson.

"It's so cute that either of you think you're my boss," said Dominique. "But let's move on. Jacks, what do you want to do with the photos?"

"Have Evan mark the ones he recognizes somehow and send me the picture. Aiden and I will deal with the cops."

Dominique nodded, then realized Jackson couldn't see her. "Sounds good," she said. "When are you and Grandma coming home?"

"We aren't scheduled to fly back until tomorrow after the hearing," said Jackson. "We've got the Richland fundraiser on Thursday. I'll see what she says when I tell her about Evan."

"Don't," said Evan, his voice harsh. "I'm fine."

Dominique looked at Evan who glared at her, as if daring her to speak.

"Nika said you had a concussion," said Jackson.

"Every fucking bump on the head is a concussion to the doctors. What the fuck do they know?"

Jackson was silent for a moment. "Nika, you're there. I'm not. What do you think?"

"I think if Evan stays home from work tomorrow to rest up that he'll probably be fine."

Evan's shoulders relaxed.

"OK," said Jackson. "I'll keep Eleanor on the original schedule then."

"Good," agreed Evan.

"Nika, I'll call you later tonight after I talk to Aiden. We may need you to wrangle Max."

Dominique wanted to squirm in her seat. She wasn't sure she could wrangle Max into anything. Instead, she put on the Deveraux smile and agreed.

"Sure, no problem."

"K. Bye."

"Bye."

She hung up and eyed Evan. "You have two broken ribs."

"It doesn't matter," said Evan, staring out the window.

"As soon as Jackson sees you, he is going to know you lied."

"He's not going to know," said Evan tugging his shirt ineffectually closed. "Just take me to my place and I'll rest up there."

Dominique was silent. They all had their own homes, but Deveraux House was where they went in case of emergency. This really seemed like it constituted an emergency. Also, Evan clearly hadn't realized that she'd already told the driver to take them to Deveraux House.

"Besides, you lied too," said Evan before she could correct his misunderstanding. "I'll skip Sunday dinners for a few weeks," he said, as if they were still arguing. "They won't know. It's not like Jackson or Grandma are likely to drop in on me."

Dominique wanted to respond to any of that—all of it—but wasn't sure how. The partition between them and the driver slid down.

"We're here, Miss Deveraux. Did you need any help up to the house?"

"No, goddamn it, we don't!" snarled Evan. He yanked open the door and then doubled over gasping in pain.

Dominique didn't move. She was incredibly unsure of how

to treat a weak Evan. He straightened, apparently through pure strength of will and exited the car. Dominique got out of the car and went around the front, giving a nod to the driver before joining Evan on the curb.

"You were supposed to take me home," he said, staring at their grandmother's house.

"No," said Dominique. "Jackson has more security here and there are people to take care of you. Aiden will bring you clothes."

"I just want to go home," he said, but Dominique ignored him.

"You will stay here at least through tomorrow. And you will tell Grandma and Jackson about everything when they get home."

"No!" he said, clutching at his shirt again.

She ignored him and walked up the front stairs to Deveraux House. The door was opened by Theo.

"Hello, Theo. Evan is going to need his room made up."

"Yes, Miss," said Theo with a nod and held the door wide for them. Dominique went inside and after a long moment, Evan came inside as well.

"Mr. Deveraux, perhaps you would care to have a drink in the study while your room is made up?"

"A drink," said Evan. "Yes."

Dominique thought that alcohol on top of whatever pain medication he'd been given might not be the best idea, but he was already walking past Theo, heading for the study without a second look. Dominique took a little longer to chat with Theo about what kind of help Evan was likely to need and then went to join her cousin in the study. It was the first time she'd intentionally been alone with him in years.

"Your outfit is hideous," he said as she entered. "Why are you dressed as the definition of boring?"

He had collapsed onto the couch and was clutching a Scotch in one hand, resting it carefully in his thigh.

"I was at work," said Dominique, sitting down and texting Aiden.

ARE YOU COMING WITH CLOTHES FOR EVAN SOON? I WOULD LIKE TO NOT HAVE TO BE HERE.

"Your job is stupid and pointless."

"Occasionally stupid, yes," she agreed. Somehow Evan being an asshole while hurt took most of the sting out of his comments. It was like watching the dying thrashing of an injured animal. "But far from pointless. It's not a great job, but it does bump me up to Marketing Manager."

"Oooh. Who are you managing, one person?"

"Two," said Dominique. "Once I've been there a year, I'll leverage it into being Marketing Manager of a firm with a bigger marketing department. Five years from now I'll be at Perteet or ADI."

"I know people at Perteet. You could have a job there now."

Dominique considered Evan with interest. He'd never offered to assist with anything in her life before. He probably found her job embarrassing to him personally, but it was still something new. She looked back down at her phone.

"The goal is not to have a job at Perteet," she said, scrolling blindly through her social media without reading. "The goal is to be Director of Marketing. Five years from now, when I have the resume to support that, I'll be more than happy to have you tell your friends that your crazy cousin has been working under her birth name."

Her phone pinged with a message from Aiden.

NEED ANOTHER HOUR. SORRY. ASK THEO TO STICK CLOSE BY?
IT'S FINE. I'M JUST SUPPOSED TO BE AT WORK.

She looked up from her phone to find Evan watching her. She didn't know what to make of his expression. He seemed strangely defeated.

"I'm really tired," he said. "Is my room ready yet?"

"I'll go check," she said.

She and Theo helped Evan up to his room and Theo took care of the actual getting him into bed. Dominique went back downstairs and came back up with his bag of possessions from the hospital. It contained a wallet, keys, phone, and now ruined suit jacket.

"Already asleep," said Theo, coming out with Evan's clothes over one arm. "I'll take the jacket. Might as well dispose of it along with the rest."

"Aiden's coming with new clothes," she said.

"I believe we have some on hand."

"I'll put his stuff on the bedside table," said Dominique taking the personal effects and handing the bag to Theo.

She crept into the room and gently set the items on the bedside table. Evan was sound asleep, but, on his shoulder, she could see three faint, circular scars. He'd had them for as long as she could remember, but for the first time it occurred to her that they were the same size as a cigarette. Her memories of Uncle Owen were vague, but she did remember that he had never been without a long filter-tipped cigarette in one hand.

# *Dominique – Past Revisited*

Dominique went downstairs and back into the study. She stared out at the back yard with the stiffly trimmed roses and the vegetable garden that seemed to be Theo's extracurricular activity. She tried to decide what she felt.

Angry, she decided at last.

Confused.

Evan was horrible and abusive. It wasn't like she'd arrived at that conclusion on her own. She had independent verification from people he'd worked with. He was condescending and verbally abusive and generally mean. He was someone that other people tip-toed around and she had always resented that. Why did someone mean get all the... everything? She wasn't sure what she even meant by that. Except that having Evan around always pulled everything out of balance. She had to pay attention to him and then she had to pay attention to herself. What was she doing? Would it upset Evan? With Evan present she had to expend a huge portion of her brain-power second guessing everything. Life was so much easier when he wasn't around.

She turned that thought over in her head. She was used to thinking that thought. It was a thought she'd had when they'd first had to move in with Grandma and she'd stuck with it for years. She'd even said to Evan's face once or twice.

She paced the length of the room in agitation, picking up Evan's drink, intending to pour it down the bar sink or hand it to Theo. Instead, she took a healthy gulp and let the warm whiskey burn down her throat.

She didn't want to think about Evan. She resented thinking

about Evan. She never wanted to think about what he thought or felt or did. Evan wasn't her job. Grandma had always made it perfectly clear that dealing with Evan was never to be Dominique's responsibility. Grandma and Aiden, and now Jackson, had always protected her from Evan.

*Fifth and sixth ribs broken along previous break point.*

The words popped into her head unbidden. Who had been protecting Evan? The answer seemed to have been no one. Did everyone else in the family know about this? Was she the dumb younger sister who had never figured it out?

She shut the door and dialed the one person she could trust to be honest with her.

"Hey," Jackson said, picking up, "everything OK?"

"No. I just put Evan to bed. We lied earlier. He has broken ribs."

"Hm," said Jackson.

"He didn't want to tell you. I think because he didn't want Grandma to come home early."

"Sounds right," he agreed.

"Jackson," she said hesitantly, not quite sure where to begin, "there's something wrong with him."

"What do you mean?" His voice registered tension.

"He's not... I'm worried. He seems depressed?"

Jackson was silent. That usually meant that he didn't want to voice an opinion because he already knew more than she did.

"Also, I think, maybe... I saw some of his medical records. They said his ribs had been broken before. Like when he was a kid. Jackson, I think... I think Uncle Owen hurt him."

"Yes," said Jackson.

"What do you mean, yes?" she snapped.

"I mean, yes, your uncle abused him. I'm not sure about

Randall, but Owen absolutely beat him. Why do you think Eleanor tried to keep him at her house all the time when he was a kid?"

"I thought Owen was a lazy parent. I mean, everyone knows he practically paid Evan's mom, I forget her name, the Russian model, to have the baby."

"Ukrainian."

"Ukrainian model doesn't have the same ring."

"They're two entirely different countries. And Owen didn't *practically* pay her. He *did* pay her. And then when Evan was two, he sent her away. I found the paperwork. Owen wasn't lazy. He was a fucking cold-hearted bastard."

Dominique found her eyes filling with tears. Evan had to know. He had to know that his mother had been bought, paid for, and then sent packing. How badly would that fuck up a child?

"But, but, why?"

"I have no idea. Eleanor seems to think he wanted something that was only his. And that possibly he wanted to beat Genevieve to having kids."

Dominique stared out the window into the back garden. "My parents had to have known. How could they leave him with Owen?"

"Randall, I think," said Jackson. "Owen and Randall were always a pair. By all accounts, they always backed each other against everyone else and Randall was the executor of Henry's will. Eleanor got the bulk of the estate, but Randall was the executor. I think with him in charge, they didn't feel like they had the leverage to do anything."

"But Evan is mean and he has always... I don't like being alone with him. He... He hit me once."

"Just once?"

"Isn't that enough?" she demanded.

"More than enough. I'm trying to figure out the extent of his problems. According to Eleanor, he treats you like Owen treated Genevieve."

"Oh." That simple sentence filled in a great deal of information about her mother's behavior.

"But if Eleanor is to be believed, Owen was much, much worse."

"Oh," said Dominique again. And that explained some of Eleanor's. "I didn't know that. Why didn't anyone tell me that?"

"Eleanor doesn't like to talk about her failings as a mother."

"That's not... I can't even. These things are better if you talk about them!"

"Agreed," he said.

"Well, fine, but why didn't Aiden tell me?"

"I believe he thought it would sound like he was taking Evan's side over yours and he would never do that."

Dominique sighed and rubbed her forehead. "That's very sweet, but I would have appreciated the information."

"Well, now you have it. And here's my question to you, has Evan done anything recently? He's been rude, and an asshole, but has he actually done anything to you? Be honest."

"It's hard," she said. "I'm used to thinking of him a certain way." She tried to examine her relationship with Evan. She started with her most recent experiences.

"He's been... Nicer? Since you've been here. He's also nicer when he's drunk. Which sounds weird now that I say it. Usually, people are meaner when they drink—the filters come off and everyone says what they've been thinking. And Christmases. He's definitely made efforts at Christmas recently. He's actually been enjoyable at Christmas. Before that, I was in college. When I was home then he didn't talk to me hardly at all. I think today was the first time I've been alone with him in five years."

"Yes," said Jackson, "he's careful about that."

"I don't understand. He's a jerk to me. If he's so careful not to be alone with me, why not be nice?"

"I doubt he knows how."

"We've got to get him a therapist."

"I would love that. I've been trying. I thought I almost had him last year. And I had, well, I had some luck in one area and I thought that would sort of put him on the right path."

"You're being purposefully cagey, so I'll assume you don't want me to know. That's fine, but whatever it was, it didn't work, did it?"

"No," said Jackson. "In fact, he's gotten worse."

"Well, what does he say when you talk to him?"

"That's what I mean by worse. He's stopped talking to me," said Jackson.

"But Jackson, you're the only one he does talk to! He's your *brat moya* or whatever you call him!"

"Why do you think I'm worried?"

"Why didn't you tell me?"

"You generally do not want to hear about Evan."

Dominique was silent. He was right. But now that she knew about his childhood, was she obligated to forgive him? What did this mean in the big picture of their lives? Why was it always women who had to forgive and forget? When was she allowed to be selfish and tell him to fuck off? Angrily, she picked up a pillow and threw it across the room. She didn't want to deal with this. She wanted...

*I just want to go home.*

Evan's words came back to her. But Deveraux House was home. He always called his condo *my place*, or *my house*. Where did he think he was going to go? Someplace where he could shut down and stop hurting? Where was that? Did that actually exist for him anywhere?

That made her heart and her head hurt. She suddenly realized that no one had been caring for Evan. They had been managing him. But he wasn't a fucking zoo animal—he was a person. A person that she was angry with, but still a person. That seemed like some sort of epiphany. Aiden and Grandma and Jackson were people. But she'd never really thought of Evan as a human being.

And what if it had been Aiden that Uncle Owen had used as an ashtray? She found her fingers curling into fists. What *wouldn't* she do to help Aiden? If it had been Aiden, she would have found a way to run over Owen with a car. Did Evan deserve less? But how was she supposed to help someone who didn't necessarily want help and that she frequently hated?

"Can we commit him?"

Jackson laughed. "Ruthless and efficient. But no, that would be too public. Eleanor would never allow it."

"We're going to have to do something," she said. "We can't leave him like this."

"We'll work on it when I get home. We'll talk to Aiden. Sometimes Aiden can reach him when I can't."

"Aiden remembers him as being kind when we were all kids," she said. "I never believed him. Maybe that helps somehow."

"Maybe," he said. "Whatever it is though, I think we need to do it soon."

"Well, I told him he had to stay here tonight. And you and Grandma will be home tomorrow. Hopefully, you can talk to him then?"

"I'll try," he said. "We'll just have to see."

Dominique bit her lip as she hung up the phone. She had become used to Jackson being able to fix everything. If he was worried about Evan, then she had better be very, very worried.

# Jackson – Deveraux House

Jackson waited for Evan to wake up and wished he had a cigarette. This morning had been full of meetings that no one needed to know about and now he was about to have one more. Well, Evan most likely wouldn't want to have the conversation in the first place, but Jackson had decided that Evan no longer got a vote. He'd been hoping that somehow Evan would manage to pull himself out of his tailspin, but it was becoming apparent that this was not the case. Evan had managed to bump himself to the top of the priority list. And of course, it had to happen now, while he was trying to deal with physical threats to the family.

Evan's childhood room hadn't been redecorated, probably since his late teens. It had a half-lived in, one-foot-out-the-door feeling. Remnants of Evan's younger self lingered in corners, stood on trophy shelves, and hid in the closet—once loved items that had no place in an adult home. Jackson had already prowled around and perused the bookshelves. He was happy to note that he'd read most of Evan's teenage collection of novels and the ones he hadn't sounded depressing as fuck. The most interesting item was a photo on the desk showing Owen holding Evan as a baby, wisps of red curls attempting escape from a knit hat with a bobble on it. Owen looked smug with a cigarette in one hand and Evan in the other arm.

Jackson wondered if he should have talked to Dominique about Evan earlier. She'd rolled surprisingly quickly to figuring out help for Evan. Jackson felt like he'd underestimated her. Dominique could be incredibly stubborn, and he'd been guessing that was the track she'd follow for Evan. Instead, she'd displayed the other parts of her personality—flexibility and graciousness. He didn't understand how the youngest member of the family could somehow manage to be the most grown up.

For the fiftieth time, Jackson reached for the cigarette pack that should have been in his pocket, then shook his head at his own stupidity. He'd stopped smoking to please his cousins who hated his Russian-brand cigarettes with a passion that ran far deeper than simply a dislike of cigarettes. Of all the things he'd changed to become a Deveraux, smoking was the hardest. Instead he allowed himself to pull out his pocketknife and fidget with it while staring into the Deveraux back garden and trying not to think about cigarettes.

He'd spent a great deal of time training for violent kinds of threats against the family, but he was starting to worry that he'd overestimated his own talents. He had also assumed that he would be able to manage his cousin's emotional problems. As a kid, the emotional lives of adults had never been a mystery to him. It was his estimation that most people were unhappy because they lied to themselves about what they really wanted and then tried to believe their own lies. It was one of the reasons he'd never gotten along well in groups. The bubbling friction of internal discontent, unwitting hypocrisy, and power dynamics drove him nuts. His cousins didn't have those problems. They all seemed to be spectacularly honest with themselves about what they wanted, but Dominique was the only one who voluntarily told him what that was. He was three years into this life, and he felt like he'd only managed to make the smallest dent in Aiden and Evan. And beyond being pissed off that he was failing, he was annoyed because he goddamn wanted them to like him.

"The view doesn't change," said Evan from the bed. "You can stop looking at it."

"I love Deveraux House," said Jackson. "I love the way Theo always overdoes Christmas. I love the way we have a vegetable garden for no apparent reason. I love that there's a secret passageway between the solarium and the office."

"Great-granddad ran liquor," said Evan, his voice flat and disinterested, as if secret passages were boring. "He used to take it out through the solarium."

"And I love that," said Jackson. "Hell, I love that there's a solarium. Who has a solarium? We do. Why? Because we're fucking Deveraux and we can rock a solarium if we want to."

"Do you even know what a solarium is?" asked Evan, easing himself upright.

"I looked it up, so yes I do. It's a greenhouse for people."

Evan snorted and then winced at the movement of his body.

"They banged you up pretty good," said Jackson.

"It's fine," said Evan, leaning back against the pillows and closing his eyes. "I'm just tired and I want to go home."

"Uh-huh," said Jackson, letting the silence linger. This was when cigarettes were good. They gave him something to do while playing conversational chicken.

"Dominique was right, wasn't she?" asked Evan, without opening his eyes. "About the florist's shop?"

"Yes, of course," said Jackson. "I'm feeling only marginally less stupid than the police for not acting on it. I believed her, but I put it too far down the priority list. And I didn't think she'd move that fast."

"You told her to text you," said Evan. "Why didn't she do that?"

"Because, like the rest of my cousins, she does not like to be safe."

Evan cracked an eyelid and gave him a sour look.

"She believes that safety is for you and Aiden and Eleanor."

Evan's hand flicked on the comforter, a restless gesture of discomfort.

"She's an idiot," he said.

"Really? What you would do if someone else said she was stupid?"

"I'd punch them in the face," said Evan, but tiredly, as if he didn't understand why he was being asked kindergarten questions.

"So you don't really think she's dumb then?"

"I don't understand her," he complained. "What is she thinking? Why did she..."

"Why did she what?"

Evan was silent.

"What?" prodded Jackson.

"She should have asked you for help," said Evan.

"That isn't what you were going to say."

"I don't want you here," said Evan, harshly. "Why are you here?"

"Christmases have been working, haven't they?" asked Jackson, changing course.

"What?"

"You, me, Aiden, and Dominique—it's fun, right?"

"Yeah, I guess," said Evan sullenly.

"I like that all of you stay here at Christmas," said Jackson.

"Dominique says we have to because..." Evan glanced up at Jackson and then looked away, rubbing his ribs.

"Dominique says you have to because I never got proper Christmases when I was kid," said Jackson with a chuckle.

Evan shrugged uncomfortably. Jackson's mother had been agnostic at best and her family had been from a conservative religious sect that didn't celebrate Christmas until January and certainly didn't indulge in pagan commercialism.

"Thank you," said Jackson. "I love it."

"Thank Dominique."

"But that's my point," said Jackson. "You're here, Dominique's here, Aiden's here. We all get along. We all have fun. All of us. You and Aiden *and* Dominique."

"Things are different at Christmas," said Evan quietly.

"I think the only thing that's different at Christmas is you," said Jackson.

"Why are you here?" demanded Evan again.

"What if things could be more like Christmas all the time?"

"I don't want you here," said Evan. "Why do you never ask? Why do you have to barge in?"

"I'd be waiting until the rapture for an invite," said Jackson.

"What?"

"Sorry. Wrong metaphor for this crowd. I'd be waiting for the next ice age if I waited for an invite. Evan Deveraux does not invite people in."

"Because I don't want people *in*," snarled Evan. "Why don't you get that through your head?"

"Why aren't you ever alone with Dominique?" asked Jackson.

"Go away."

"Because what I think is that you want to make sure that she's safe. Of course, that raises the question that if it's just you and Dominique in a room, where is the danger coming from?"

"You're not really a Deveraux," said Evan. "You don't even look like us."

Jackson was startled. Evan hadn't ever made a direct attack against him. And had certainly never questioned that Jackson was a Deveraux. He tried to pick his next move—advance or defend? "Maybe I'm not a Deveraux," he said at last. "I never hit Dominique."

Evan snatched up a glass from the bedside table and flung it at him. Jackson ducked and it shattered against the wall.

"Go away," said Evan, breathing heavily and clutching his ribs.

"No," said Jackson. "No, *brat moya*, I'm not going anywhere."

"You are *not* my brother," said Evan, through clenched teeth, and Jackson took a deep breath trying to maintain his own temper.

"It doesn't have to be like this," said Jackson. "We can make it more like Christmas. We can get help. We can talk to Dominique."

"Why would I want to do that?" snapped Evan.

Jackson growled in frustration. "Because talking makes it better."

"Talking has never, in the entire history of this family, made anything better. Now go away."

There was a polite knock on the door before it swung open. "Mrs. Deveraux is asking for you Mr. Jackson," said Theo. "Also, the Peter person is on the phone in the hall, claiming an urgent matter."

Jackson took a deep breath.

"Better go," sneered Evan. "The family needs you."

"We will talk about this when I get back," said Jackson.

"Go fuck yourself," said Evan.

"*Potselui meni v sraku,*" snapped Jackson.

"*Chollooy me huey,*" barked Evan.

Jackson slammed the door, took a deep breath, then chuckled. "If he's bothering to swear at me in Ukrainian, I can still get him," he said to Theo.

"Of course, sir," said Theo, without changing expression.

"Evan broke a glass," said Jackson.

"Tsk," said Theo. "I'll get the broom."

"Right," said Jackson. "Good chat. I'll just go get the phone, shall I?"

"Up to you, sir."

"Right," said Jackson again, shaking his head.

He went down to the first floor and picked up the hall phone. "Hey Pete. You forget my cell number?"

"I called like eight times. I figured you were ducking me or you left it somewhere."

"No, it's…" Jackson patted his back pocket and then realized it was in his jacket. Which was in the closet where Theo had put it. "Yeah, sorry. Left it in my jacket. What's up?"

"I have a hit on one of our guys, but it's down in Mexico and they won't send via the internet because they only take cash."

"Mexico?" asked Jackson skeptically.

"Yeah, it sounds like bullshit, but it's not. Our customs are a lot harder to get around, and if these guys are wanted, then they either have to have damn good fake passports and a way around any facial recognition or they have to come in through one of our more porous borders."

"Got it," said Jackson. "OK, so what are you asking?"

"Well, I was going to ask you before I left, but now I'm asking that you approve my reimbursables when you see the invoice with a plane ticket to Mexico and a fat wad of cash for a bribe."

"No problem. But what are we getting out of this?"

"A name, maybe more than one, a definitive point of entry. From there we can start connecting the dots."

"Got it," said Jackson, nodding. "Happy hunting."

"Yeah. I'll keep you posted."

Pete hung up and Jackson went into the closet to retrieve his phone. As noted, there were a stack of missed calls from Pete and one from Dominique.

"There you are," said Eleanor, coming into the hall. "We need to go now."

"Go where?"

"I need you with me while I go have a private chat with Ralph Taggert."

"What's he got to do with anything?" The blustering, big-bellied Republican hailed from Georgia and had clashed with Eleanor on more than one occasion.

"Maybe nothing, but he's going to be on the panel for the Absolex hearing and he says he wants to talk about it."

"What does that mean?"

"Reading between his Southernisms, I think he's hinting that there's additional insider trading charges that could be brought. Which probably means he's offering to burn someone he's friendly with, but he wants something in return. At a guess, he wants to share the spotlight on the take-down. It would play well in his state."

"Well, that explains what he's doing up here, but we don't need him," said Jackson.

"No, we don't, but we want to know what he has. It's worth taking the meeting."

"I'll get the car," said Jackson.

He dialed up his voicemail on the way out to the garage.

"Jackson," said Dominique, sounding plaintive. "I hate your voicemail. I've been thinking about Evan, but I don't think I can think about Evan until I fix up this problem with the people in the hideous jeans. But I had a brainwave about that, so I pulled their file. And you will never guess what I found! It makes total sense when you see the lawyer angle. Anyway, call me back. Don't worry, I'm not doing anything dangerous—I'm at the office! Call me."

Jackson looked at his phone in disbelief. He looked at the car and then back at Deveraux House. He had too many priorities and not enough of himself to go around. He needed back-up. Impatiently, he got in the car and started the engine, but as he pulled out into the drive, he grinned. Dominique had already drafted a pinch-hitter.

# Maxwell - The Closet

Max checked his phone again and got mad at himself. Dominique hadn't called. Of course she wasn't going to call. She hadn't called yesterday. Why would she call today?

He specifically hadn't called her yesterday. He had decided to be good. He'd made the decision. He stood by it. If her relationship status wasn't enough of a red flag, Director Cabello's orders had been perfectly clear.

But why hadn't Dominique called *him*?

He checked his phone again and then clunked it against his forehead for being stupid. He needed to stop. If Dominique *did* call him then he was going to simply say that he didn't like cheaters and he didn't want to be part of that equation. I mean, if he could, he'd leave it open to the possibility that she could break up with Jackson. But he felt like he deserved an explanation or at least some sort of statement about what the hell she thought she was doing.

In frustration, he got up off the couch and looked around for Grant's keys. Grant's car was in the parking garage beneath the condo and since his dad usually took the subway to work, it was available for him to use. Maybe he could go somewhere, anywhere, and think about something, anything, else.

He pulled the keys off the hook by the door and grabbed his gun and badge from the bedroom. He walked back by the couch and reached to scoop up the phone, but as his hand made contact, it rang and he jumped in surprise.

The caller ID said Jackson Zane. He hadn't actually gotten Jackson's last name, but that could be right. And the area code was for Illinois.

"Hello?" he answered cautiously.

"Max? It's Jackson." Max frowned. He was pretty sure he'd never given Jackson his number. "Dominique's leaving me fucked up messages again."

"What do you mean?"

"I mean, I love that girl, but she can't leave a coherent message to save her life. Something about files and jeans and lawyers. I seriously do not know what she's saying."

"OK," said Max, trying not to sound bitter. "And you were, what, hoping I could translate?"

"No, I doubt that's humanly possible. But the last time she left some garbage message she ended up investigating the florists on her own."

"Right," said Max, feeling uncertain. He didn't want to help Dominique cheat on Jackson, but he also didn't want Dominique to end up dead. On the other hand, if Jackson was really worried, he could just reach out to the people actually on the case. Unless, of course, no one from the Marshals had actually contacted him. "They did call you, right?" he asked.

"Who called me?" asked Jackson.

"I ran the photos at work. Two of them came back as wanted by INTERPOL. They're ex-French Foreign Legion."

"And you couldn't pick up the goddamn phone?"

"I got busted by the director. She said I was specifically not to work the case. She thought the Deveraux were trying to use her departmental resources. I'm officially out."

Jackson grunted in dissatisfaction. "Not good."

"Particularly since I'm trying to get assigned here, and I don't want to piss her off," said Max.

"Understood."

"But she said that they would be contacting you. If you haven't heard from them, then it probably means that they're getting the interdepartmental *who has jurisdiction* crap."

"Well, it doesn't matter to me what their problem is, the fact is, they're withholding information vital to the safety of my family."

"They're never going to see things that way. They won't think you're a partner," blurted out Max, and then wished he could take it back. He didn't need to piss Jackson off, even if it was true. Private security was at the bottom of the list when came to law enforcement pecking order, above security guards and bounty hunters, but not by much.

"No, they never do," agreed Jackson, apparently well aware of the stats. "Unfortunately, that also means if I call them for assistance, I'm not going to get anywhere. And I'm with Eleanor for the next few hours, Aiden's in court, and Evan is...unavailable. I know you're not supposed to work the case, but does giving Dominique a ride home from work really constitute working?"

Max hesitated. Jackson's assessment was right, and if Dominique really was up to something and he didn't show up, how was he going to feel later if she got hurt?

"Assuming that's all I do, it's probably fine," said Max reluctantly, looking at the keys in his hand. "Yeah, I can do that."

"Great. I'll text you the address."

"OK," agreed Max.

"It's almost five," said Jackson. "You'll have to call her when you get there so she can unlock the door."

"Got it," said Max.

"Thanks," said Jackson. "Bring her back to Deveraux House when she's done getting you in trouble and we'll figure out whatever she was talking about."

"Sure," said Max, once again tamping down on his bitterness. He felt like he was being set up for something, but he couldn't see

Jackson's angle. Whatever it was, when he saw Dominique, he was going to make it clear once and for all where he stood. There was not going to be any making out, no touching, nothing inappropriate—he was just going to go and make sure she wasn't getting herself killed and call it a day.

He spent the drive to Ace Accounting drafting statements and scripts in his head. By the time he arrived at the drab four-story office building, he felt confident that he could say what he needed to say.

He stood outside the front door and dialed her number. She picked up almost instantly.

"Max?" She sounded excited.

"Yes," he said, trying to sound more formal. "I'm out front. Can you let me in?"

"Out front?" Confusion registered clearly through the phone connection. She was silent for a long moment and he could hear the sound of her walking, her footsteps echoing slightly on the line. He waited and saw her come into the darkened lobby area, her body only a silhouette in shadows. Dominique peered out through the glass door of the office into the vestibule. She spotted him and her face lit up.

"You *are* here!" she exclaimed into the phone. Then shook her head at the phone and hung up. He did the same, dropping his phone into jeans pocket. Unlocking the door, she pulled it open and smiled at him. "You're here!"

"Yes," he said.

She was dressed in a pencil skirt and flats with a button-up blouse. Unlike at the tennis club with her certified fuck-me pumps, she actually did look conservative today and unexpectedly sweet.

She beckoned him in and re-locked the door.

"I think it's just Sandra and Monica here. But they're up on three doing whatever. Sandra claims it's quarterly taxes, but it's my guess that they're really snooping through the CFO's office."

She tossed the door keys onto the front desk and walked back into the office. He followed her through the maze of cubicles and offices until they were in a break-room.

"Yes, I'm here," he said, reaching out and grabbing her arm, trying to slow her down. "I'm here because Jackson called me."

She responded to his touch by stopping instantly and he found himself colliding with her. Stumbling slightly, he ended up with his arms wrapped around her. She turned around and put her arms around his neck, smiling up at him.

"Why is Jackson calling me?" he demanded trying to stick with his script. It was hard to do when she was pressed up against him so tight that he could feel her bra through his t-shirt.

"I don't know," she said. "Why is Jackson calling you?"

"That's not a riddle," he said. "That's an actual question."

Her eyes twinkled and she kissed his chin. "Probably because he's stuck with Grandma and he didn't pick up my call." She kissed up along his jaw. "And probably because my message wasn't very clear, and he couldn't tell if I was doing something dangerous or not." She bit his earlobe lightly, which made him shiver, but then she pulled back and looked up at him seriously. "Which I'm really not. I'm in the office. How dangerous could that be?"

"Pretty dangerous," he said and kissed her mouth. Just as in the park, he felt the intense rush of desire and the kiss went from intimate, but appropriate in a public setting, to over the line in a matter of moments. Her arms pulled tight around his neck and she responded with equal heat.

"I'll be right there. I forgot to grab my stuff out of the break-room," a woman's voice trilled voice from the hallway.

Dominique sprang back and looked around in a panic. She

pulled open a janitorial closet, shoved him inside and stepped in after, softly shutting the door as the woman entered the room. Then they heard her cell phone ring.

"Hello," said the woman, her voice muffled by the door. They could also hear her running water from the sink.

"That's Sandra. She hates me," whispered Dominique. "She cannot catch us here or there will be nothing but digs about making out on company time and then she'll start complaining to everyone that I don't bring donuts for Donut Friday and that I'm a stuck-up bitch."

"Just buy some donuts," he whispered back. Light filtered in from a crack under the door illuminating the closet in a soft glow. The broom closet was a tight fit and Dominique was snuggled up against him as they both tried to keep from knocking over the stack of toilet paper and brooms. She really did smell like cinnamon and he wanted to run his face along her skin to inhale the scent. He knew he should stop. This was exactly what he'd been telling himself he wouldn't do. Instead, he pulled down the collar of her blouse to kiss along her neck.

"There's already too many... um... donuts. I bring fruit." She exhaled and leaned back into him, arching a little as his hands slid over her breasts.

"No wonder she hates you," he whispered. She almost laughed but seemed to lose her breath as he nibbled her earlobe and popped the top two buttons on her blouse. Whatever his problems with infidelity were, she didn't seem to share them. She made no move to make him stop. Instead, she twisted a little in his arms, so she could kiss him, as he popped another button. As they kissed, he did what he'd been fantasizing about for the last two days and slid one hand along her thigh. She was soft, but with muscles under her curves and he felt himself start to get hard as he pushed the skirt upward. She let out a little moan as he ran his fingers over her panties.

"Shhh," he whispered, sliding his fingers underneath the edge of the lace. "You don't want to get caught, remember?" He used his knee to nudge her legs into a wider stance and slid his fingers under the edge of her panties and downward, looking for the softness that he knew was waiting for him. She rocked back into him as he found it and he began to press in small circles while he continued to kiss along her neck. She bit her lip as he undid another button on her blouse and slid his hand inside, cupping her breast. She let out a little gasp but was clearly trying to stay quiet. From the other side of the door they could hear the drone of Sandra's voice and the buzz of the microwave. He ignored her, concentrating on Dominique and the smell and taste of her skin, the silky feeling of her in his hand.

Dominique reached out and grabbed the edge of the door frame with another gasp. She was writhing against him now and he knew in another few moments he'd be rock hard. He pressed harder but kept to tight circles. She was slippery wet, and he took a deep breath in anticipation. God, he wanted to fuck her.

The minutes ticked by, and Dominique was alternately holding her breath and biting her lip as he pushed harder and faster. Out in the break-room, Sandra finished her phone call with a chirpy goodbye, and they could hear her heels click across the floor toward the door.

"Oh God, Max," Dominique moaned. She pressed back against him as he worked his fingers. Her breath was coming in ragged gasps. He knew she was close. He felt her body tighten, going rigid with the first wave of her orgasm and he pulled his hand away from her breasts and clamped it over her mouth. She came, mouthing words into his hand and throwing out her other hand to grasp the doorframe with both hands.

He looked down at her, pressed against him, her ass peeking out from the edge of the skirt that he'd yanked up around her waist, and felt himself groan with desire.

# Dominique – The File

Dominique stared at the wood grain of the broom closet door and tried to catch her breath. She had never played Seven Minutes in Heaven in junior high or high school, but she was beginning to see the attraction.

Behind her, Max's cock was hard and pressed *almost* where she needed it to be. If they were going to be standing up for this kind of activity, she really should be wearing heels—he was too damn tall. She went up on her toes and gave a little wriggle and he groaned, the fingers of his free hand digging into her hip.

"God, I want to fuck you right now."

"So why aren't you?" she demanded, panting a little.

"You want me to go through the reasons?" She rubbed against him again and he groaned. "For starters," he said withdrawing his hand, "this place is filthy, there's not enough room, and," he stepped back and she sucked in her breath at the sudden lack of contact. She turned around as he ineffectually pushed down her skirt, then he stepped in to kiss her, pressing her against the door, "aside from the other obvious problems, I'm pretty sure that by the time I finished, you'd be screaming my name loud enough for the entire building to hear."

"Very salient points," she said, although she hadn't really been listening to them, and kissing along his neck. His hands were wandering again, back up went her skirt. She slid her hand under his t-shirt and wrapped one leg around his hips, pulling him tight to her. He slid one hand under ass, boosting her up into just the right position, and she moaned as she felt his cock press against her now wet panties. He left hot kisses along her neck and she tried to figure out how she was going to get him out of his pants in the tight confines of the closet. She realized that space had been on his list of reasons why not to fuck in the broom closet. Some part of her also registered that it was also probably an HR violation.

"OK, um," she took a deep breath and tried to put her feet back on the floor. "Um, if you're serious about not doing it in the broom closet, you need to um, not…" He murmured something, but she wasn't sure what. Then abruptly he stepped back, his hands going up in the air and then locking behind his head.

"Right, right," he said. "I said no to the broom closet." She pushed her skirt down and he watched in apparent fascination. "God, I'm an idiot."

She giggled, then buttoned a few buttons on her blouse, and he took an unwilling step forward. "You can put your hands down," she said.

"No, I really can't," he said watching the re-buttoning process.

"Suit yourself," she said finishing and then, to be cruel, plumped her breasts, readjusting her bra. He groaned and she laughed. She opened the door and peered out into the breakroom. She settled her skirt more firmly and edged out, listening for Sandra. Hearing nothing, she waved at Max to follow her into the break-room.

He stumbled out after her and stood clutching the back of one of the chairs. She wanted to go over and make it more difficult for him. She pictured unbuckling his belt, unzipping the pants slowly…

"So," she said, trying to interrupt her own train of thought, "let me grab the file and then we can go back to my place, which, while possibly not spotless, is far cleaner and more expansive than a broom closet."

He opened his mouth, as if to speak and then stopped. "Wait, what file? Why am I here?"

She frowned at him. She thought he had been being

purposefully obtuse earlier, but now she wasn't so sure. "Jackson really didn't tell you?"

"Jackson didn't know either. What is going on?"

"Well, I told you that florist is one of our firm's clients."

"Yes, which I have been thinking about. Why, if someone was targeting the Deveraux, would they pick a florist connected to you?"

"Most people don't know I work here," she said. "I use Casella for my professional life. Deveraux is too recognizable and sets up some weird expectations." He nodded thoughtfully. His pants situation seemed to be calming down, so she jerked her head toward her desk. "Anyway, it occurred to me the other night that there might be something in the file. And I was going to look yesterday, but the whole thing with Evan and those guys happened."

"Evan and what guys?" he asked, trailing after her.

"The guys. Evan got attacked by those guys we took pictures of." She glanced over her shoulder at him, and saw his expression change to horrified. "I had to go pick him up at the hospital yesterday. Jackson didn't tell you?"

"No! He called. He said you left him a weird message and that Aiden was in court and Evan was unavailable and could I go check on you. Evan got attacked by the guys we followed?"

"Yes, and they told him to make sure Grandma didn't go to work."

"Why the fuck didn't you call me?"

She stopped at her desk and began shoving things in her purse. "Oh. Well, it was a family thing. And I didn't think Evan would want a lot of people to know. And I didn't know if I was supposed to…." She trailed off. She didn't want to say that Max's mixed signals had left her reluctant to call.

"OK," he said, looking as if he were swallowing something bitter. "So then what happened?"

She grabbed her bag and led the way toward the back door. "Well, like I said, we do their accounting, so I pulled their file."

"That's illegal."

She looked over her shoulder, caught by his disapproving tone. "They broke my cousin's ribs and punched him repeatedly in the face. I don't really care about illegal. Anyway, I pulled their file. Look at this." She pulled the list out of her purse and held up the high-lighted piece of paper.

"What am I looking at?" He took the piece of paper, frowning at the tiny type.

"It's a client list. One of the florist's clients is Richland Law. Frank Richland is hosting a fundraiser for Grandma tomorrow night." Max was looking serious. She wasn't sure if that was a good sign. "But considering that they found Evan and tried to run Aiden over, I figure that it was bad sign that they have access to Richland Law. So I called the florist."

She pushed through the back door that was clearly marked: DO NOT EXIT. ALARM WILL SOUND.

"You did what?"

She looked back. Max looked freaked. "I called the florist. We do their taxes. I figured I would pretend to be Tina and ask for some sort of document."

"Dominique!"

"What? I can't have people trying to kill us! Anyway, it doesn't matter because I didn't talk to anyone. I just got the answer message and it says that they're closed for three weeks."

"Closed?"

"Yes!" said Dominique excitedly. "But then I called over to Richland, you know, as myself, and as far as they know, the florist is still planning on delivering their flowers for the event. So now I need to go tell Jackson and Aiden."

"Again, why the fuck didn't you call me?"

"Well, they're handling contact with the police."

"So, you're going to have *them* call me?"

"What do you mean?" She stopped at the mouth of the alley and turned around, looking at him in confusion. Out of the corner of her eye she caught a blur of movement and turned just in time to see a fist coming at her.

# Maxwell – Stand-Off

Max was only a few steps behind her, but it was a too far to reach her before the punch landed. The next events seemed to happen in slow motion. Dominique fell, unconscious or stunned at the very least. Max reached out grabbed her attacker and swung him into the building, slamming his face against the brick. He recognized the man as the one who had been wearing Carhartts at the florists. The man pushed off the wall and tried to spin around, but Max punched him as he did. The man swung a punch back and Max grabbed it, stepped in, spun, and levered the other man's arm over his shoulder, yanking it down as he stood up. The man screamed as his elbow was forced in the wrong direction. Using the broken arm, Max was about to swing the man to the ground when he was tackled.

Max and his attacker went down, but an entire lifetime of training had Max pivoting, spinning, and grabbing before they even hit the ground. He sprawled, hips and feet out, hands shoving his attackers head downward into the pavement. Max's first instinct was to flip him and pin him, but he chose to go with his more relevant second instinct, which was to grab him by the hair and bounce his face off the cement.

There was movement behind them, and Max grabbed the man beneath him and hauled him forward with one hand, grabbing for his gun with the other.

Dominique was up, sort of. She had made it to her knees, but the first man had pulled out a gun and pointed it at her head. He looked pale and the broken arm dangled awkwardly, but his gun was steady in his hand. Max yanked his attacker, now dripping blood from a broken nose, upright and hid behind him, keeping his gun covering the man with the broken arm.

"Let him go," the man said.

"Her first," said Max.

"No."

"She walks into the building," said Max. "And you two walk away."

"Start him walking," said the man. "I'll do the same."

"Dominique, stay low and go directly toward the door."

"It automatically locks," gasped Dominique. "I can't open it from the outside."

Under his hand, Max could feel the man's neck getting tense. "Nothing's changed," said the man with the broken nose, eyeing his friend and Dominique. "We walk away, you stay here. Everyone goes home."

The man with the broken arm nodded and Dominique scrambled to her feet. She made her way down the alley, swinging wide to avoid Max and the man with the broken nose.

"Got you!" exclaimed a triumphant female voice, banging open the back door. "I've told you to stop using the fire—"

The man with the broken arm swung his gun toward Sandra, a shot popping off with an echoing report. Sandra screamed, and Max grabbed Dominique by the arm and threw her physically through the door and into Sandra. Backing up he kept his gun trained on the two men as they fled down the alley. Max slammed the fire door shut and stepped to the side, breathing hard.

Sandra was on the floor screaming as Dominique tried to disentangle herself and get up. Max grabbed her around the waist and picked her up, setting her on her feet. She clutched at his jacket, her eyes wide.

"Are you OK?" he demanded, but she stared into his chest,

seemingly oblivious to the question. He put a hand under her chin and pulled it up. "Are you OK?"

She nodded, then seemed to jerk in an all-over shudder. "Yes, I'm OK." He crushed her to him in a hug and she gave a sob and buried her face in his chest.

"You are under arrest!" shrieked Sandra, using a desk to pull herself upright. "I am calling the cops!"

"Ma'am," said Max, "I am a U.S. Marshal in pursuit of suspects and I would appreciate it very much if you would shut the hell up."

"You're a what?" asked Dominique, looking up at him.

"A U.S. Marshal," he repeated.

She looked shocked. "Oh. I… That's not good."

"Sandra! Sandra!" screamed another woman, rushing into the hallway.

"Monica, call the cops! We're being shot at!" screamed Sandra.

"Both of you be quiet," snapped Max, taking out his phone. He dialed 911.

"This is 911, what is your emergency?"

"This is U.S. Marshal Maxwell Ames, shield number 4921. There's been an officer involved shooting. No one is seriously injured, but I do need paramedics. I also need to alert Detective Morris of the twelfth precinct as it involves an open case. Two suspects have fled on foot. How fast can I get ground support?"

"Are you at Ace Accounting?" asked the operator.

"Yes," he said. Dominique walked away from him to sit down in the nearest desk chair. Her face looked white and shell-shocked. Monica helped Sandra up and into another chair.

*That's not good.* What did that mean? Why wasn't being a Marshal good? Hadn't she known? She talked to his dad all the time. Had it really not come up? And hadn't she been in the room at the tennis club when he had flashed his ID at the detective? He ran through the events of that evening and realized that no, she hadn't been. It had just been Jackson.

"I'm routing you to my supervisor," she said. "An ambulance is on the way and I have two patrol cars en route. ETA is four minutes." Max sighed. Four minutes was too slow.

"I don't need your supervisor. I need to call my director," he said, and hung up.

He dialed the branch office and stared at Monica and Sandra. They looked equal parts annoyed and scared.

"As the person in charge here, I'm going to be relying on you for help, ma'am," he said to Sandra. Might as well smooth over some of Dominique's problems. Sandra's spine straightened. "And Monica, if you could go grab an ice bag for Ms. Casella from the breakroom, that would be very helpful."

"We took the ice bags out to make room for the ice cream for this month's birthday celebrations," whispered Monica.

"Right," he said. "Of course you did." Because that was the way his day was going.

An hour later, Monica was having heart palpitations and getting checked out by the EMTs he'd brought in for Dominique. He suspected that she really just wanted to be felt up by the EMT, but it seemed rude to point that out. Dominique sat on the far side of the room holding an EMT supplied ice-bag to her face, listening to Detective Morris chew her out with a pissed-off look on her face. Max thought Morris had picked Dominique to yell at because he didn't think he could get away with yelling at Max. Max thought about trying to go rescue her, but considering that she'd gone to sit as far away from him as possible, he didn't think she wanted him to.

"You know," said Jackson, arriving quietly at his elbow, making

Max jump, "if you're going to date my cousin, I'm going to strongly recommend some body armor."

"What?" Max found that his mouth was suddenly dry.

*Cousin.*

"Kevlar," said Jackson, as if that were the stumbling point for Max in his last sentence. "With the track record you two are developing, you both should get some. But unless Versace has got a new line out, I don't think I can talk Dominique into it, so it had better be you."

*Cousin.*

"I have some through work. Or at least, I will once I'm assigned to a new post." Max felt like his mouth was the only thing on him that knew what it was doing. It was well ahead of his brain.

"Yeah, how soon is that happening?" said Jackson, looking around the break-room.

Max wanted to blurt out the thoughts in the forefront of his mind: Jackson equals cousin, Maxwell equals idiot, Dominique equals available. She probably thought he was totally insane. He was totally insane. Why hadn't he asked her about her relationship status up front? What the hell was wrong with him? Fortunately, his mouth was ignoring him.

"I don't know yet. It's down to here or Virginia," he said calmly.

Jackson made a face. "Well, let's hope it's here. I don't want to have to figure out logistics on security if she's spending half her time in Virginia."

"She doesn't really need security, does she?" Max asked.

Jackson stared at him, as if he were a moron.

"I mean, generally. Clearly, currently she needs security."

"No, not generally," agreed Jackson. "But I like to think

ahead. And for my purposes, you getting assigned here would be more convenient."

"Never mind our opinions on the subject?" asked Max.

"Your opinions on the subject are relatively clear," said Jackson, grinning.

"Yeah, well, unfortunately, my future boss doesn't seem to share those opinions."

"You're going to have to work on your suck-up game," said Jackson.

"Yes, because that will help," said Max bitterly and Jackson laughed.

"Ames!" barked Director Cabello, striding through the door.

"Good luck," murmured Jackson and began to pick his way across the room to Dominique.

"Ames," snapped the director, gesturing with an emphatic finger that he should follow her. He did as ordered and went out to the hallway.

"Was I less than clear yesterday?" she demanded, keeping her voice low.

"I was *not* working the case," said Max.

"Really? You weren't working the case? Never mind that I've got security footage of you breaking a man's arm out in the alley."

"I was trying to drive Dominique home," said Max, clinging to his patience. "Due to the fact that no one had alerted the Deveraux family that they were being targeted by mercenaries, she didn't have a security detail."

The director made a sour expression. "The police are giving us shit."

"Detective Morris seems like a misogynistic asshole," said Max with a shrug. "Doesn't change the fact that my friend is in danger."

She scrutinized him carefully. "Did you just use *misogynistic* in a completely un-ironic way?"

"Uh…" Max stalled. "I used it in a way meaning sexist and bullshit?" he offered. The director narrowed her eyes at him and he smiled awkwardly. What was he supposed to be doing right now?

"You really haven't been trying to glory hog on this case?" she asked.

"I really haven't," he said.

"So you're seriously telling me that you are trying to date this girl and INTERPOL's Most Wanted keeps cock-blocking you?"

Max lost his patience. "Yes! Goddamn it! They are!" The policeman down the hall stared at him in disapproval, but the director's face twisted in a mocking laugh.

"Your love life sucks. Meanwhile, your *friend*," the air quotes were obvious even though she hadn't made them, "appears to be a better investigator than the misogynistic Detective Morris. The florist connection is legit, and I think the threat on Richland Law is real. I want to do a sting operation. Can you smooth the way with the family?"

Max stared at her, waiting for the other shoe to drop, then decided that it wasn't going to. "Yes. I'll make it happen."

"Great. Go do it."

"You do realize that this will mean that I'll, you know, be working in your jurisdiction," he said.

"Nobody likes a smartass," she said with a flicker of a smile. "Go get to work."

# Dominique – Revelations

Dominique watched as Max talked to Jackson. Jackson had to know that Max was a Marshal. Why hadn't he told her? Did Max know about Jackson's prison record? Maybe that's why he'd said it wasn't that simple. Maybe he wasn't supposed to associate with ex-cons. She had really wanted the two of them to get along.

More cops came in and chatted with the paramedics. It was so strange to see her office and cubicle turned into an absolute disaster of a crime scene. She supposed it wasn't actually as terrible as it looked. Mostly, it was crowded and full of equipment. And everyone kept tromping by her cubicle to get to the emergency door and the actual crime scene outside. She could tell that the continued use of the door annoyed Sandra. Dominique tried not to enjoy that. She knew somewhere down under the layers of worrying about Max and *schadenfreude* over Sandra that she ought to be freaked out about the guys with guns. Or at least grossed out about the blood and the way that one guy's arm had *not* been bent at a natural angle.

But somehow, more pressing than all of that, was the fact Detective Morris was *still* droning on and she had no idea what he'd been saying for the last five minutes. She focused on three words and decided she didn't need to bother. She disliked his stupid bristly moustache and his entire face needed to be reorganized by someone who knew what they were doing—possibly Jackson Pollock or maybe Mike Tyson.

Dominique scrutinized Max and Jackson again. Max didn't seem antagonistic toward Jackson. Jackson had the same skeptical look he got when he didn't want to admit that it was the nonsense Aiden was spouting was hilarious. Max looked... slightly befuddled.

She wasn't sure what that meant. However, overall, they seemed like they were getting along. There were no crossed arms and Max wasn't even attempting to loom over Jackson. Not that Jackson was loomable. Jackson had his hands in his pockets and Max was scratching his head. But Jackson had always been incredibly cautious about involving law enforcement in Deveraux business. Why would he send Max to come get her? What the hell was her cousin thinking? As she watched, an older woman came in and barked at Max, making a preemptory gesture for him to follow her. Jackson immediately peeled off and headed in Dominique's direction.

"Are we clear?" demanded Detective Morris. "Are you even listening to me?" He sounded even more irate than when he had started.

"That would be a waste of my time," Dominique said. Behind the detective, she saw Jackson smother a laugh.

"You little—" Whatever the detective was about to say was interrupted by Jackson's arrival.

"Detective," said Jackson, "I believe the U.S. Marshal Director just arrived. Is our case being transferred out of your jurisdiction?"

"Like hell it is!" Detective Morris seemed to chew his whisker-like moustache in fury.

"She went out into the hallway," said Jackson helpfully and Detective Morris darted off like Jackson had thrown a ball. "Channeling your inner Evan today?" asked Jackson, looking at Dominique with a smile.

"That man is an idiot and my face hurts. I don't know why I should have to be nice to people who are stupider than I am." She frowned. "I wonder if that is how Evan feels all the time?"

"Evan is not smarter than everyone," said Jackson, sitting down next to her.

"No, he isn't, but I wonder if that's how he feels? Like he's surrounded by people who keep chatting on about things he doesn't give a shit about?"

Jackson hesitated. "Possibly. How are you—"

She cut him off. "Did you get a chance to talk to him?"

"I tried," he said, allowing himself to be diverted. "I got called away to a thing with Eleanor and then when I got home, Theo said he'd gone to work."

"He was supposed to stay home! His ribs have to be killing him! What the fuck is wrong with him?"

"It is my impression that Evan is used to being in pain."

She stared at Jackson. "That is an incredibly disturbing thing to say."

Jackson shrugged. "How are you—" he began again.

"OK, well, we'll table that discussion for later. I want to—"

"No," said Jackson, cutting her off in turn. "We're talking about you now. How are you?"

"I'm fine," said Dominique with the usual smile.

Jackson gave her a look.

"Some guy punched me," said Dominique, and saying it out loud made her want to cry. Jackson put an arm around her shoulders and gave her a squeeze. "Max broke that guy's arm though. And the other one's nose. I was kind of out of it for the arm breaking, so I didn't see it happen, but I'm pretty sure that arms aren't supposed to bend that way. Then I tore my skirt when he threw me through the door. Which, I realize is not the most important thing, but I really liked this skirt."

"Rough afternoon," said Jackson and Dominique sniffed back tears.

"Meanwhile, what the fuck is wrong with you?" she demanded, rallying and attempting to channel her emotions into something non-weepy.

"I have an unhealthy obsession with scones," said Jackson.

"What?" she looked up at her cousin with a half-laugh.

"You asked what was wrong with me. I'm telling you. Before I moved here, I didn't even know what a scone was and now I could eat them by the pound."

"No, you jackass, why didn't you tell me Max was a U.S. Marshal?"

"I assumed you knew. You said you chatted with his dad. You went to dinner with him. I mean, what the hell did you two talk about?"

"A lot of stuff that wasn't work," she said. "Grant said he didn't like Max's job and since Max carried a gun, I figured he was more like you. I didn't think he was law enforcement!"

"Why would I let you date anyone like me?" he asked. "That's a terrible idea."

"What's wrong with you?"

"Criminal record, lack of college education, and the previously mentioned scone problem."

"I would be beating you over the head with my purse right now except there are police around. And also, just to be perfectly clear, I date whoever the fuck I want to. You don't *let* me date anyone."

"Sorry. To rephrase, I would strongly state my objections if you tried to date someone with my background."

"You are not your background. But speaking of that, does Max know? Because we also didn't spend a lot of time discussing you over dinner."

"I have no idea," he said, with a frown. "The cops know, but it did sound like he hasn't exactly been invited to the party, so maybe he doesn't? Why?"

Dominque found herself blushing. "Well, because he's been somewhat resistant… I mean, not a lot, but…"

Jackson was watching her in confusion and then his expression cleared, and he laughed. "You are so spoiled. You don't have to work for it at all, do you?"

"I'm twenty-four, I have a relatively large bank account and a damn great pair of legs. Of course I don't have to work for it," said Dominique sourly.

"Well, it's not me that's cock-blocking you. It's his work. When he ran those photos, he got two hits off an INTERPOL list."

"That's not good," said Dominque, suddenly feeling that she was lucky to only have a sore jaw.

"Yeah, but it also flagged him as operating out of his assigned area."

"What does that mean?"

"He's between assignments. He says it's down to here or Virginia."

"Oh." Dominique tried to process that. The only thing she could grasp was that she disliked the idea of Virginia enormously. "Here would be better."

"Yes, everyone except the division director agrees with you. She thought we had asked him to use company resources to investigate for us."

"But we didn't!" protested Dominique and Jackson shrugged.

"That's how it looked, and she told him to stay away from the case. You're lucky I got him to turn up at all tonight. He's worried she'll block his assignment here."

"Oh crap. Can I explain it to her?" asked Dominique, chewing a fingernail.

"Yes, because that's what a guy wants his girl to do—explain things to his boss."

Dominique made a face. Jackson was very right about that. "Well, but... What do I do now?"

"No clue, but here he comes. Maybe he'll have some ideas."

Max walked across the floor and Dominique tried not to sigh. He really was dreamy. Those green eyes were to die for and that stupid little cowlick got her every time. "He's got serious face on," murmured Dominique. "I can't tell if it's good news or bad."

"That's cop face," said Jackson. "I think they train them at the Academy to do that. It's like an-hour-a-week class on how to look like you have a stick up your ass."

Dominique chuckled and then tried to stop as Max drew closer. He looked at them suspiciously.

"What?"

"Nothing," said Dominique and Jackson at the same time.

"I doubt that. Meanwhile, how is Eleanor going to feel about canceling her fundraiser?"

"Depends," said Jackson. "Why?"

"The director thinks Dominique's theory about Richland Law has merit, and she wants to set up a sting operation."

"Yes!" exclaimed Dominique, pumping a fist in the air. "I win. Detective Morris can suck it."

"Uh-huh, but maybe you could not say that where all of his colleagues can hear," suggested Jackson.

"I'm embracing my inner Evan, remember?" she said.

"Please don't," said Jackson. "One Evan is more than enough."

"I'm going to ignore this part of the conversation," said Max, "because I think whatever I say will go badly. But when we get back to talking about the mercenaries attacking your family, could you offer an opinion on Eleanor's cooperation?"

"Yes," said Dominique. "She's been looking for a way to beef up the pro-law enforcement portion of her brand. This would give her the opportunity to be seen as cooperative and friendly."

"I agree with Dominique," Jackson said. "I'm not sure about

the logistics of canceling an entire party the day before, or how you want to run a sting, but I think we can guarantee cooperation."

"Good," said Max, flashing a smile. "Because I already promised that we could do it."

"I feel like I'm being used for my connections and influence," said Dominique.

"She has a point," said Jackson. "What are you going to be doing for us in exchange? Can you kick Morris off the case?"

"Happening as we speak."

"What about additional security? I mean, for instance, Dominique's going to be home alone tonight, and I don't think that's safe."

"And I will personally take care of that," said Max, with enough fervency that Dominique wanted to giggle.

"Are you sure?" asked Jackson, and Dominique glared at him. He grinned unrepentantly. "We wouldn't want you to get in trouble with work."

"It's been taken care of," said Max, confidently.

"Oh good," she said. "In that case, bring wine."

"Not unless you text me what to buy," said Max. "I don't want to risk you embracing your inner Evan and chucking it out the window."

Dominique laughed, and then winced and gingerly felt her jaw.

"Ames," someone bellowed from the hall.

"See you in a few hours," said Max with a sigh, before turning and jogging away.

"OK, wingman. If you're so bright, tell me what am I supposed to do about the fact that I have no food, my apartment's a wreck, and there's not enough time to go lingerie shopping."

"Men like lingerie, but we do not *need* lingerie. Throw everything in a closet and order take-out," said Jackson.

# Maxwell – The Queens

Max watched Eleanor Deveraux spar with Gail Cabello. If the director had expected some sort of acknowledgment of sisterhood from Eleanor, she had been mistaken. Eleanor had no soft spot for sisterly solidarity. They negotiated the terms of the forthcoming operation with vicious certainty and the softest of tones.

Max watched them and tried to figure out the goal. Was it simply dick measuring, or whatever the girl equivalent was? He spent a few moments trying to decide if there was a female equivalent before deciding it was the wrong metaphor to begin with. It shouldn't have been this antagonistic. The U.S. Marshal Service was a presidential appointment and they worked for the judiciary. There was only so much even a sitting senator could do to affect them. Just as there wasn't much that a U.S. Marshal could do to impact a sitting senator. But the two women traded subtle insults and jabs while at the same time offering to help the other. Perhaps this was politics, but if it was, Max wanted no part of it.

They were in Eleanor's office at Deveraux House. Eleanor, in a simple blue pantsuit, sat on a floral print couch, her back ramrod straight, her ankles crossed, and her hands sitting gently in her lap. She had all the poise and manners of a princess or a Southern belle. In contrast, Jackson loitered behind her, leaning against a bookcase, his pose insultingly casual, and his jacket gaping just enough to show the gun tucked under his arm.

After Dominique and Jackson had left, and Max finally had two minutes to himself, he'd finally done what he should have done the day he met Dominique. He googled the Deveraux family and caught up on the news that he'd clearly been missing: Jackson Zane, now Deveraux, the genetically proven illegitimate son of Randall Deveraux, had been born in Chicago to a hotel maid who subsequently died of a drug overdose. When Eleanor's private detective had found Jackson, he'd been partway through a five-year stretch for armed robbery. With help from Eleanor's lawyers, the conviction had been overturned, and Eleanor, probably against all advice from every Deveraux lawyer, possibly including Aiden, had brought him back to Deveraux House and made the legal moves necessary to give Jackson the inheritance he should have had from Randall. Jackson had then taken charge of Eleanor's security, and appeared to now be one of Eleanor's most trusted advisers.

A fact that was clearly being ignored by Max's fellow Marshals. To them, Jackson was, and probably always would be, the thug who'd skated out of his conviction using his grandmother's money. Jackson, with his insolent expression, careless pose and martini glass full of clear liquid and an olive, played right into their beliefs.

But it all felt like play acting to Max. In all their encounters, Jackson hadn't ever been insulting or careless. In fact, Max would have bet money that there was nothing in Jackson's glass but water. Which made Max wonder: if Jackson was not the criminal low-life he was posing as, then how polite and perfect was Eleanor? Did all the Deveraux wear masks? Dominique certainly did—she buried her playfulness, competence and determination beneath an ice queen façade that she had clearly learned from Eleanor. But if that was her mask, then what was Aiden's? What was Evan's?

"Then we're agreed?" asked the director.

"Yes, my people will reach out to the guests and coordinate the cancellation. I will be at Richland Law to act as bait, and Jackson will approve all security measures regarding my safety."

Max could see that it bothered the other law enforcement in the room—the fact that they *had* to work with an ex-con who, in their minds, was not even *really* a Deveraux. Max wondered what Jackson thought of the Deveraux family. He seemed genuinely affectionate toward Aiden and Dominique, but Max couldn't help but wonder what Eleanor had done to keep him tied to the family. Max wondered if Dominique knew, or if she simply accepted it the same way she accepted that Jackson had low-jacked her phone. Perhaps when one was a Deveraux, that was just how it was.

"We will be in contact with Mr. Deveraux," said the director, scrutinizing Jackson with an unfavorable glare.

"I assume you'll use Marshal Ames to interface with us," said Eleanor, looking Max over with an equal amount of distaste.

"Technically Marshal Ames is on vacation," said the director.

"How fortunate, then, that he has been moved by his sense of duty to assist. Thank you for giving up your vacation time for us," said Eleanor, focusing on Max with a smile that was sincere and heartfelt.

Max recognized the trap for what it was. If he acknowledged the compliment or thanks then he was de facto agreeing that he would be available for her, thus end-running the director.

"I'm always happy to help friends," said Max, "but all of my assignments are handled by the director." He saw Jackson hide a smile behind his glass.

"How commendable," said Eleanor, turning back to the director, "that you have your people so well trained."

"If they can't follow directions, what good are they?" asked the director.

"I like mine to improvise," replied Eleanor.

"Creativity without constraint is wasted energy and effort," replied Gail.

It was like watching two fortune cookies battle.

"An interesting point," said Eleanor. "I'm so glad that you

could come by today. While I value our local police, I'm happy that these violent criminals will be met with a Federal level response. And I look forward to partnering with you."

Gail nodded and then stood up. "And I, with you." She held out her hand as Eleanor stood and they shook. Accord had been reached, terms negotiated, the Queens were satisfied. Max, however, still felt lost. He snuck a quick glance at Jackson, who gave the briefest smile and shrug.

# Jackson – Visiting Hours

Jackson dialed Pete for the third time while he waited for the crew to get in position. He didn't think there was anything Pete could add to the situation, but Jackson knew that the older man would be pissed if he got left out of the loop. Jackson shifted in the backseat of the van and watched as Garcia, Miller and Kerschel disappeared into the backyard of the white New Jersey McMansion. After three years in New York, he still wasn't sure why people didn't like New Jersey. Surely, it couldn't be the architecture. But with six different architectural styles jammed into one house, he had to admit that this seemed like a stupid house. He pondered the prejudice against New Jersey and waited for Pete's phone to go to voicemail. Cormin waited by the door of the van, ready to be his back-up.

"Kind of busy here, kid," said Pete, finally picking up. "But I got names."

"So did I. Nika's Marshal came through. At least two of them are on INTERPOL's Most Wanted list—check your email."

"Shit," said Pete. "Sending you a text."

Jackson switched to speaker so he could see the text. "I only have one of those," said Jackson. "This is good."

"The three names I got link to a matchmaker who works out of Jersey. I'm on the next flight back. He was going to be my first stop when I got back."

"Deepak Anand, right?"

"Yeah…"

"Good. I made a few house calls this morning to people we don't know and haven't even heard of."

Pete groaned. "Those are not good people."

"Then it's a good thing I never spoke to them," said Jackson. "But the people I didn't speak to all pointed me at Deepak Anand."

"Jackson, what are you doing?" asked Pete, sounding suspicious.

"Well, as with the rest of my day, I'm going to visit someone and listen to what they have to say."

"Jackson..." said Pete. "I think you should wait."

"I would love to," said Jackson. "It's been a long-ass fucking day and I would love to go home, make Theo bring me a Budweiser—because that's always funny—and call it a night. But the bastards attacked Dominique. If Max hadn't been there, God knows what would have happened. And that shit is not happening again."

"Don't do anything stupid, Jackson," said Pete.

"I'm not being stupid. I'll offer him money first."

"And if he doesn't take it?" asked Pete.

"I don't think I care to answer that question on an open phone line," said Jackson.

"Jackson, can't you wait for me?"

"No," said Jackson. "I can't. These guys are moving too fast, and I'm not waiting for them to attack another family member. Deepak is going to tell me who the client is, and he's going to tell me where I can find them."

"Jackson..."

"What?"

"Make sure it's a lot of cash," said Pete. "And fucking watch your back. I'll be there in a couple of hours."

"I've got the crew with me," said Jackson. "I'm not entirely stupid."

"Just partially?" asked Pete, sarcastically.

"You got it," agreed Jackson.

Jackson climbed out of the van, swinging his coat closed over the sling for his MP-5 and went into the house. The door was charmingly unlocked, so he didn't bother to knock. Jackson punched the first person that came at him and hauled him by the hair into the living room. By the time he'd reached the living room where Deepak was watching a Bollywood movie, Garcia and the others had closed in around the back and came in through the French doors that looked out over the pool. Deepak, in a wife-beater, sweats and a pair of Adidas slides, looked scared shitless. The three girls who were camped out doing coke off his coffee table also did not look particularly happy.

"Girls, why don't you take five," said Jackson, sitting down on the couch opposite from Deepak.

"No problem," said one of the girls, snagging a pile of cash as she high-tailed it toward the door.

"I'm just going to leave this with you," said another, handing Jackson a business card before following her friend.

"Uh…" said the third, before inhaling a quick line. "OK, bye."

The front door slammed three times in quick succession.

"Hi, Deepak," said Jackson.

"What the hell, man?" Deepak stared at his unconscious friend on the floor.

Jackson tossed two mug shots on top of the coke. "These guys: who hired them and where are they now?"

"I don't know what you're talking about, man."

Jackson looked up at Garcia, who stepped forward and punched Deepak. Deepak's head wobbled like a bobble-head and he had to grab the couch to stay upright. Garcia was about average height but had the barrel-chested shape of someone built for lifting things. Although, mostly Jackson used him for hitting things. People. Whatever.

"Have we established that I'm extremely serious?" asked Jackson.

"Yeah, man, serious, I got it, but I do not know these people."

"Deepak, I have a gun and a briefcase full of cash. Which would you prefer?"

"The cash?" Deepak was wiping ineffectually at the trickle of blood coming from his nose. Mostly he smeared it around his face.

"Then answer my fucking questions," said Jackson. "Who hired them and where are they now?"

"I don't know who hired them," said Deepak. "It doesn't work like that. I get paid in bitcoin. It's all anonymous."

"Someone hired you at some point," said Jackson. "Someone sent you an email."

"I don't know who," said Deepak. "And I don't want to know. That is not how my business works."

"Is that your computer?" asked Jackson, pointing at the laptop on a side chair.

"Well, yeah, but it's all dark web shit. I don't know who sends the emails."

Jackson looked at Kerschel. She grabbed the laptop and took it to the couch. "Log in," she told Deepak, opening it and handing it to him. Kerschel wore her dark hair short in a way that said she did not prefer men, but Jackson thought that some men found this aggressive and intimidating. As if simply noting that a woman was never going to be into them made them feel uncomfortable.

"This is illegal," said Deepak, leaning away from Kerschel. Deepak definitely looked intimidated by the hair. But then Deepak paid to have himself surrounded by girls who pretended to like him.

Jackson snapped his fingers at Deepak and Deepak tore his eyes off of Kerschel. "Do I look like I care?" asked Jackson. "Log in or I break something attached to you."

Reluctantly, Deepak typed in his password. "Show me the email," said Kerschel. Deepak grumpily navigated through the laptop. Moments later Kerschel took the computer back.

"All right," said Jackson. "Let's focus on question two. Where are they now?"

"How would I know? I set up dates between two people. They may or may not form a relationship. It's up to them, not me."

"But they are in your rolodex and you can contact them, so contact them now."

"I can't call people out of the blue! They'll be suspicious. Do you know the kind of people I'm dealing with?"

"Yes. The kind that get pissed off and visit your house," said Jackson, gesturing to the team scattered about the living room.

Deepak looked around the room and took in the guns and numbers. "Right," said Deepak. "So you want me to contact them?"

"Yes," said Jackson.

"I just have a text number. I don't know where it goes."

"That's fine," said Jackson. "Text them. Tell them you have more work."

"Fine," said Deepak, reaching too quickly for his phone on the coffee table. Garcia punched him again. "What the hell was that for?" demanded Deepak, swiping at his nose again.

"That's not your work phone," said Jackson.

Deepak looked pissed but didn't say anything.

"I'm good on this end," said Kerschel, shutting the laptop. "I'll have to dig in back at base." Jackson nodded.

"Work phone, Deepak," said Jackson. "Get it now."

Deepak stood up and went across the room, Kerschel following. Deepak opened a locked cupboard and Kerschel immediately removed the phone from his grasp. She plugged in a slew of dongles and handed it back to Deepak.

"If anyone finds out about this, I'm out of business. You're compromising everything." Deepak had moved onto whining.

"Fortunately, no one has to know," said Jackson. "We're not law enforcement, and I don't give two shits about you or your business. Give us what we want, and we will disappear again."

"I can find out who you are," said Deepak.

"Deepak," said Jackson, "you aren't even my target and I'm willing to shoot you in the fucking face. Do you really want to move up to being a threat to me?"

Deepak seemed to shrink down on himself.

"Send the message," said Kerschel, shoving the phone at him.

Deepak hesitated a long moment and finally took the phone and tapped in a message. Kerschel took the phone back and checked her equipment.

"Done," she said, unplugging everything.

"Great," said Jackson standing up.

"What am I supposed to do if they text back?" demanded Deepak.

Jackson handed over the hooker's business card. "I'm just going to leave this with you," he said.

"Funny," said Deepak sourly. "No seriously, what am I supposed to do?" He was following them as they walked toward the front door. "I can't tell someone they have work if there's no work."

"You worry too much, Deepak," said Jackson. "They're not going to be around long enough to call."

"These are serious dudes," said Deepak.

"And you think I'm not?"

"Yeah, OK, fine. You said there was money?"

Jackson made eye contact with Miller, who shrugged. Jackson shrugged too and then nodded. Miller dropped the briefcase and Deepak snatched it up, looking at the contents.

"I'm hope you get killed!" he yelled as Jackson swung the door shut.

"Good work everyone," said Jackson as they made their way back to the vehicles. "Kerschel, where are we on a location?"

"I'll have it as soon as it pings a cell phone tower."

"Great," said Jackson. "Let's head back into the city. Miller, where are we at on the hotel canvas?"

The group rotated to put Miller in front of Jackson. He was a big black guy with dreadlocks and swagger that Jackson envied. He was also quickly becoming one of Jackson's favorite operatives. "Hotel canvas is moving, but there's a lot of places close to the florist and they could have transportation we're unaware of, so we might still come up dry even if we hit them all. I'm also talking to a real estate agent named Argusen," said Miller.

They arrived at the vans and began the reloading process.

"Pete figured," continued Miller, opening the door, "that they might have gone for a short-term rental."

Kerschel, her head buried in her phone, walked into the van ahead of both Jackson and Miller. Miller gave her a what-the-hell look which she totally missed. Jackson met Miller's eye and they both laughed. Kerschel, already opening her laptop and typing at a furious speed, missed that too.

"Tech support," said Miller with a shrug. "Anyway, we've put out a pretty wide net. Hopefully, we'll catch something."

"Good," said Jackson.

They settled into their respective seats and quiet conversation.

"Got a text from Pete with an arrival time," said Garcia from the driver seat. "Also wants an update."

"Keep it vague," said Jackson. "Text messages can be subpoenaed."

"Right," said Garcia.

"I've got a ping," said Kerschel, looking up.

"I feel like Pete would ask us to consider informing law enforcement at this point," said Miller.

"Yeah, he would," said Jackson as he considered the angles. Max was going to be pissed if he found out that Jackson hadn't been sharing information. And while Jackson didn't want to mess up a potential relationship for Dominique, he had to consider family safety first. "One step at a time," he said at last. "Let's get eyes on the ping location first and then we can assess. If it looks like the authorities can handle it, then great. If it looks like there's an imminent threat, then we'll have to take action." There was a chorus of nods around the van. That seemed to sit well with the group.

Jackson's phone rang, vibrating in his pocket. Jackson saw Eleanor's face and picked up. "Hey," he said, trying to avoid her name or title. Nothing sounded less tough than *hi Grandma*.

"Dominique has done something strange," said Eleanor, without preamble.

"OK," said Jackson.

"She has contacted the family physician and requested a list of recommended mental health professionals."

"OK," said Jackson.

"You don't find that strange?" demanded Eleanor.

"No," said Jackson.

"You know what she's doing, then?"

"Yes," said Jackson.

Eleanor was silent for a long moment. "Is it something I should be concerned about?"

"Not at the moment," said Jackson.

"Hm," she said. "Very well. Moving on. Are you satisfied with the security arrangements from the Marshals?"

"More or less, but I'm attempting to ensure that we don't need them."

"I'm sure you will excel as always," she said.

"Thanks," said Jackson, who found his grandmother's compliments ambiguous. Did he always excel or was it simply her expectation that all Deveraux would excel?

An hour later, the team was taking in the view of a rundown hotel just south of the Brooklyn Bridge. Miller took a walk through and came jogging back.

"I've got a bad feeling," he said, ducking quickly into the van. "The hotel clerk thinks the guy with the broken arm and the broken nose are up in the room, but everyone else went out."

Jackson tapped his fingers on his phone and took out a piece of nicotine gum out of his pocket.

"You need to start transitioning to regular gum," said Miller.

"I need to quit already," said Jackson.

"Having something else to chew helps," said Miller. "Going cold turkey just makes you punch people." There was a pause. "Not that I would know. Obviously, I have no problems with anger management."

Jackson laughed. "Yeah. Obviously. Here's the thing, if it were me and two of my guys got busted up at the accounting firm, I'd be worried that someone was on to my plan with the lawyer and the fundraiser and I wouldn't wait."

"Not to mention that if two of my guys are out of commission, maybe my plan at the fundraiser no longer works," said Miller and Jackson nodded. "I'd be tempted to move up my timeline. The question is, who would they target?"

Jackson was about to answer when his phone chirped with an incoming text.

"Aiden," said Jackson, reading the message. "They're targeting Aiden."

# *Dominique – Almost There*

Dominique checked her hair in the mirror above the hall console table before opening the door. She watched Max take in the full-coverage apron and her long sleeves and not show the least bit of disappointment. He was either expecting nothing to happen tonight or he was being a total gentleman. She repressed the urge to laugh, because either way he was in for a surprise.

"Hi," he said, holding out the requested bottle of wine.

"Hi," she replied. She took the wine and his hand, backing down the hall so he wouldn't see the rest of her outfit. Her heels clicked against the parquet flooring. She'd selected them particularly for their strappy, spiky, slutty vibe. "I'm glad you're here. Tonight we are having the super-awesome, super special dish known as *pizza that I bought at the store.*"

He laughed.

"It's in the oven." They had made it to the kitchen. Max took off his jacket and dropped it onto the back of one of the kitchen chairs as he looked around. He eyed the vintage crown molding and high-ceilings before looking out from the kitchen into the living room with the French doors out to the roof deck. It had cost her a mint to tear down the wall between the kitchen the living room and it was worth every penny.

"Nice place," he said, swinging his gaze back to her.

"Thanks," she said and decided that now was as good a time as any to display the rest of her ensemble. She turned around and bent over, pretending to check the pizza.

"Jesus fucking Christ!"

"What?" she asked, hands on her knees, looking over her

shoulder at him. She tried blinking innocently but couldn't stop a giggle from escaping.

"You think this is funny?" he demanded, stepping out of his sneakers, kicking them across the kitchen and into the living room.

"It's a little funny," she said.

In response, he yanked his t-shirt off over his head. She straightened up and bit her lip. His body was just as good as she remembered from college.

"That apron is coming off," he said.

"I was assuming everything was coming off," she replied. He leaned in to kiss her, pushing her toward the oven and she yelped, bouncing back into him.

He took a step back, hands loosely on her waist, his face expressing surprise, confusion, and concern.

"Hot oven," she said, "on my ass."

"And here's you only wearing lace panties," he said. "We should really go into the bedroom and make sure you're OK." He bent at the knees and suddenly she was slung over his shoulder.

"Max!" She tried to sound outraged but couldn't stop laughing.

"I'm a trained first responder," he said. "Trust me, this is the right thing to do."

"Left down the hall then," she said, laughing harder. "First door on the left."

He made it into the bedroom and she felt him reach up and untie the apron a split second before he dropped her onto the bed, leaving him holding the apron in his hand, and revealing that her long-sleeve shirt was, in fact, a very short crop-top. "I love your sense of appropriate dinner attire," he said, flinging down the apron.

"I think you're missing the details of it from over there," she said. "Maybe you should come a little closer." She crooked her finger at him, and he grinned.

"In that case," he said, "incoming."

He jumped onto the bed and onto her. He caught himself on his elbows and while she felt the impact of his jump, she realized he was protecting her from his full weight. On impulse, she jabbed her hand upward into his elbow, shooting his arm out straight as she wrapped her legs around his waist and rolled him onto his back.

He made a tiny *woof* noise as he went and she ended up straddling him, sitting perched on his stomach, her hands on his chest. He blinked up at her in surprise, a ridiculous grin on his face.

"Where did you learn how to do that?" he demanded.

"Aiden found me a six-week course on MMA skills for self-defense," said Dominique proudly, then hesitated. She had forgotten that he had had been a nationally ranked college wrestler. "Did I do it right?"

His hand had been steadily sliding along her ribs and he used one finger to caress the full crescent of her breast as it peeked from beneath the edge of her shirt. She shivered at his light touch and his fingers progressed under the edge of the shirt.

"You did it perfectly," he said. His other hand drifted over her hip and then slid down her thigh, but that was hard to concentrate on because the hand under her shirt was drawing lazy circles and loops. "There's just one problem," he said.

"What's that?" she murmured, letting herself lean into his hand.

"I may know a little bit more about wrestling than you." He shoved her knee backward and wrapped an arm around her body, pulling her back down onto the bed with a twist. She went down with a little shriek of surprise as he ended up on top of her.

He flipped up her shirt and let his mouth pick up where his hands had left off. She breathed out a sigh of happiness and ran her hands down his back, pressing harder as she went lower. He gave a groan and picked up his head to kiss her mouth. Everywhere their bodies met prickled with electric energy. His skin was hot on her hers, and she could feel the rivets in his jeans as they pressed into her belly.

His hand pushed at the edge of her panties. And she stopped kissing him. "You first," she said. "You're the one that's still wearing pants."

"Fair point," he said but promptly went back to kissing her. "Totally doing that." More kisses, but eventually he pushed away from her, his lips losing contact last.

Dominique laughed as he stepped off the bed, clearly trying to exit his pants as fast as possible. She stopped laughing when his pants and underwear dropped past his ass. She flipped around on the bed and, leaning off the edge, sank her teeth into one of his cheeks.

"Whoa!" He jumped, unbalancing her and sending her toppling off the bed. She tumbled onto the carpet laughing. "Sorry!" he yelped, reaching for her, which only made her laugh harder. "Sorry! You surprised me!"

"I could tell," she said. He tugged at her hands, trying to help her up, but her heels were tangled in the bed covers. She finally made it to her knees, and reached down, clearly intending to help her up off the floor.

"Hey!" she said, looking up the long length of him to his green eyes. He stopped, standing there, staring down at her questioningly. "Are you watching this?" Might as well check something off his fantasy list.

"Watching what?" he asked.

She leaned in and licked his cock—top to bottom. He groaned and reached for the footboard of the bed for support when she continued, with tiny kisses and nibbles, to tease his cock into a full erection. She took it into her mouth, and he let out a gasp and buried one hand in her hair. She continued on, but she wasn't sure how far to take things. There was a breaking point to this kind of thing where she might end up not getting what she wanted.

"Nika, Nika!" he gasped. "You need to get on the bed, *right* now!"

Apparently, she had reached that point. She kissed her way up his chest and along his jawline. He pulled her shirt up and over her head and leaned in to kiss her. She tilted her head and then they both stopped as they heard a pounding on the door to the apartment.

"Seriously?" demanded Dominique, looking toward the front of the apartment. There was more pounding. "Seriously?" she asked turning back to Max. "Why doesn't the universe want me to get laid?" She was almost yelling in frustration.

"I don't fucking know!" he yelled back.

She let out a growl of pure frustration and stomped her foot. Then she reached into the laundry hamper and pulled out a long tunic shirt dress thing and yanked it on.

She was almost to the door when there was more knocking.

"Dominique!!" yelled someone from the other side of the door. "Dominique! Let me in!"

"I will fucking kill him!"

She stomped down the hall and yanked open the door. "What?" she demanded of Aiden. "What?"

He pushed past her into the apartment and hurried to shut the door and lock it. "We've got a serious problem. A serious problem! I think they followed me here!" He turned around breathing heavily and seemed to take in her outfit. "You're not going out in that, are you?"

"No, you asshole, I am not!"

Max came out of the bedroom, redressed in his jeans, and picked up his shirt off the kitchen floor.

"Right," said Aiden, his eyes going wide and turning back to Dominique. "Sorry," he whispered to Dominique. "Sorry," he called to Max.

"Someone followed you?" asked Max, leaning on the kitchen island with what Dominique considered a Zen-like patience.

"I think—"

There was more knocking on the door. "Nika! Nika, it's Evan." Evan was quieter than Aiden, but he sounded just as intense. She gestured to Aiden to open the door. Evan came in, clutching his side and looking pale.

"Christ," said Aiden, looking over their older cousin. "Are you OK? You look like death warmed over."

"Those guys are in your lobby," Evan said to Dominique. "I don't think they saw me, but I had to take the stairs."

"Those guys?" asked Max.

"The ones who fucking broke my ribs," snapped Evan.

"Yes!" agreed Aiden, nodding and pointing at Evan in agreement. "I think they were following me."

"So you brought them to Dominique?" demanded Evan.

"No! There was only two of them. I was worried that the other ones were coming for Dominique. I don't know!" Aiden looked frantically from Dominique to Max.

"Well, there's four of them now," said Evan.

"I'll call it in," said Max, reaching for his jacket. "Although, at this point, I feel like I'm waiting for Jackson to show up."

"I did text him," said Aiden.

Dominique looked in annoyance at her inconvenient relatives. "You call it in," she said turning to Max. "I'm going to put on pants."

"Might want to get a bra too," said Evan.

"Sorry," said Aiden again.

# Maxwell – Show Down

Max stared at Aiden and Evan, who were now in the living room. Evan lay on the couch. Aiden paced and tweaked Dominique's knick-knacks on the mantle with every pass-by.

The official response from the director was to sit tight and wait. Which was fine. He didn't know what the mercenaries in the lobby really had in mind, but his impression was that they were not stupid individuals. He didn't think that they would actually attempt an assault on the apartment. On the other hand, he didn't want to be surprised if they did.

"You two have phones?" he asked.

"Yeah," said Aiden, as if Max was being an idiot.

"They can do video chat?"

Aiden glanced at Evan. "Yeah," he said again. "Why?"

"Because I want to borrow them."

With a sigh, Evan reached in his pocket and pulled out his phone. "Here," he said, holding it up.

"Well, I mean," said Aiden, "what are you going to do with it?"

"What? Do you have porn on there?" demanded Evan.

"No! I just haven't run a back-up in a while. I make notes on here for cases!"

"Just give it to him," ordered Evan.

"It can stay in the apartment," said Max. "It's fine. I'll need you to video chat Evan's phone in a minute though."

He went back to the bedroom and knocked softly on the door.

"Almost done," said Dominique, irritation coloring her voice.

He poked his head around the edge of the door. "I need duct

tape." She had changed into a disappointingly prosaic set of jeans and a t-shirt. She was also in the process of whisking her hair back into a ponytail.

"I think I'm out. I know I've got electrical tape though. Will that work?"

"Yeah, electrical tape should do."

"In the cupboard over the washing machine. Are you taping Aiden to his chair or something?"

"No," he said grinning. "Just trying to get an eye on any killer florists."

"Sounds exciting. I'll be out to help in a minute," she volunteered. "I have to find shoes."

He nodded but didn't respond further. He found the laundry room, the electrical tape, a heavy duty flashlight, and a step-ladder and went out to the hallway. Aiden followed as if incapable of standing still.

"So what are we doing?"

"You're going to call Evan's phone, turn on the video chat. I'm going to tape it to the ceiling. That way if anyone comes up the elevator or the stairs, we'll be able to see them."

"Like a security feed! Cool!" They had just finished taping the phone up when Dominique came out to the hall. "Security camera," said Aiden holding out his phone that now showed the hallway.

"Smart," said Dominique, smiling up at Max on the step-ladder and he couldn't stop himself from smiling back. He was having a hard time switching to emergency mode. He wanted to… well, do a lot of things. But he would have settled for being able to kiss her, or at least put his arms around her.

"I do try to use my brain periodically," he said. "Now everyone back inside."

He shooed the Deveraux siblings back into the apartment and shut the door. Evan was still on the couch, now with his eyes closed.

"They won't come up here, will they?" asked Dominique, looking at him with a worried expression.

"I wouldn't count on it," said Evan from the couch. "I check the family accounts weekly. Jackson is throwing money at the problem like lemmings at a cliff. If he's worried..." Evan trailed off and Max watched as Dominique and Aiden made twin expressions of unhappy agreement.

"I don't understand what they want," complained Aiden, taking his phone to the couch, his eyes glued to the screen.

"To scare Grandma," said Evan. "We're the most convenient way to make that happen."

"Shows what they know," said Aiden. "Grandma doesn't get scared."

"Yes, she does," said Evan. "It's just that later, after she gets done being scared, she gets even."

"Well," hedged Aiden, "but after what happened at Nika's work... Why would they push their luck and try it a second time?"

"What happened at Nika's work?" asked Evan.

"They came to her work," said Aiden.

"What do you mean: *they came to her work*?" asked Evan, opening his eyes. "She's not even working under the Deveraux name. How'd they know where to find her?"

"I may have called the florist shop from work," said Dominique, sounding embarrassed. Aiden and Evan both stared at her. "I thought it was safe because Ace does their taxes! I thought it would seem legit. I didn't think they would attack me!"

"They attacked you? Nobody said anything about attacking!" Aiden looked shocked.

Dominique glanced nervously at Max. He wasn't sure what

he was supposed to add to the conversation. "I thought Jackson texted everyone," she said with a careless wave of her hand. She was doing the ice-queen thing again—pretending that everything was fine. Max didn't like it.

"I was in a meeting. I didn't read it," said Evan.

"Well, I read it," said Aiden, "but it just said you'd had another run in with them. You're OK, right?"

Dominique hesitated, glancing at Max again. "I mean, yeah, I'm fine. Just a bit..."

"A bit what?" demanded Aiden. "Max, what happened?"

"She got punched in the face," said Max. "And they pointed a gun at her."

"What?" Aiden looked horrified.

"Where the hell was Jackson?" demanded Evan, rising up on one elbow.

"With Grandma," said Dominique, "like he's supposed to be. He sent Max."

"Oh, well done, Maxwell," said Evan, collapsing back down onto the couch. His sarcasm was withering, and Max gritted his teeth, biting back an angry retort. Max went back to the kitchen to where he'd left his phone and checked for an update from the director. They were supposed to be sending squad cars and support right away. But *right away* could mean a half-hour while she dicked around with the cops.

"Hey, he broke one guy's nose," snapped Dominique. "And I'm also pretty sure the other guy's arm. So lay off. I'm fine. Just a little bit sore in the jaw. There's barely even a bruise. See? Everything's fine."

She tilted her head to display the area in question and, seeing barely a shadow under make-up, Evan and Aiden both relaxed, but Max frowned. He'd been in his fair share of fucked up situations.

The bruises were almost always the least of the problems. She really wasn't going to tell them that it had been scary as shit? He was starting to think Ice Queen was the wrong name for Dominique—Iron Maiden was more the description that was springing to mind.

"Well, OK, I'm glad you're fine," said Aiden. "But the question remains, why were they following me?"

"They probably wanted to collect the whole set of us," said Evan, going back to closing his eyes.

"Like driving a car at me wasn't enough?"

"They want to stop Grandma from going to work, right? That's what they told you, isn't it?" Dominique asked, looking at Evan.

"Yes," Evan agreed. "But if they're on the INTERPOL list then they're not some sort of crackpot lone wolf. I figure they have to have been hired by Absolex. Who else has the budget to hire mercenaries or motivation to get Grandma to stay home?"

Max watched the Deveraux family work from a front row seat. In college, he'd been aware of Aiden and Dominique as one unit and had thought of Eleanor and Evan as separate units. But watching the three of them, it occurred to him that no matter how much Dominique disparaged Evan, or how annoyed she was at Eleanor, she still went to family dinners on Sunday. And the same could be said of the others. They all showed up.

"That's what I thought too," agreed Aiden. "It's why I came over. I wanted to talk to Nika about whether or not we should be pushing the cops to investigate ties to Grandma's hearings and Absolex."

"Not to culturally appropriate," said Dominique, "but fuck the police. Detective Morris couldn't solve the mystery of why his zipper is down. I agree, Absolex is the most likely suspect, but how do we tie them to these mercenaries?"

"You let me do my job," said Max.

All three of them turned to stare. He could tell that they had forgotten that he was there. Evan looked like he was thinking it over. Dominique looked pleased. Aiden, of all of them, looked the least impressed.

"It's all very well for you to say that," said Aiden. "But the truth is that whoever hired these guys probably didn't pay them out of the corporate account. It's going to be difficult to prove."

"I just need one of them to flip," said Max. "Witness testimony goes a long way."

"We'll see," said Aiden. "Not to be a Debbie Downer, but Absolex has a long track record of corporate malfeasance. Pinning something on them is not going to be easy."

"You want me to not try?" suggested Max sarcastically. "Dominique and I could go down the back stairs and out to dinner—leave you two here to sort this mess out."

"Well, OK," said Dominique, "but it better be burgers or something not fancy because I'm not changing again." Max blinked, attempting to assess her tone. She gave him a flirty wink and he tried not to laugh.

"That is not what I meant," snapped Aiden, who was not as amused by his sister's blatant defection. "I'm just saying: nailing Big Pharma is harder than it looks."

"Yes, it is," agreed Max. "But these guys have enough on their resumes that they could get tried for terrorism. That's a pretty big stick to use as a lever. If I can get them in custody—they'll flip. That will at least tie them to whoever hired them, then the lawyers can start digging."

Aiden opened his mouth and then looked down at his phone. "You might get your wish," he said. "Three of them just got out of the elevator."

"Everyone in the back room," said Max, and he began flipping out lights.

"We could help—" began Dominique, but he nudged her toward Aiden.

"Go in the back bedroom, please," he said.

She went—reluctantly, but she went, taking the others with her. Aiden hovered for a moment in the hall, seeming on the point of saying something, but then shrugged and flicked out the hall light for Max.

Max went to wait by the door, flashlight in one hand, gun in the other. He heard the soft shush of footsteps across the carpet in the hall and then the barely distinguishable click of lock-picks being inserted into the lock.

Max felt his adrenaline start to kick in, but he waited, counting the seconds and trying to breath softly. In some ways he was used to it. The accelerated heart rate, the clammy hands, the same need to pretend to be calm. It was just like stepping onto the mat in college. He was only going to get one shot at this. He'd better get it right.

The door creaked open and Max watched a short-barreled Sig Sauer pistol come through the door, followed by the jay walking enthusiast. Max kicked the door shut on the man, slamming the edge of it into the guy's arm. The gun dropped from his hand with a sharp report, sending a bullet somewhere into the darkness. The man shoved back on the door and dove at Max, tackling him into the hall console table.

Max flicked on the flashlight, momentarily blinding his assailant and then punched him in the face. The man reeled back. "Get the girl and boy!" he barked over his shoulder, and then charged at Max. The second man dodged the pair of them and ran into the apartment.

Grabbing the man by the shirt, Max pulled, pivoted, and threw him into the console table, which broke with a shower of splinters. Then Max ran after the second man. He could not let anyone get to Dominique.

# *Dominique – Batter Up*

Dominique stopped by her bedroom first and picked up the child-sized aluminum bat that she kept under the bed. Evan eyed the bat skeptically, but she shoved him into the spare bedroom and gestured for Aiden, who snapped off the hall light and joined them. The three of them stood staring at each other and Dominique was reminded of the time when she was seven and Grandma's security officer had shoved them all into the safe room and told them to stay put. It had turned out to be nothing. Or at least Grandma had said it was nothing. Although, in retrospect, they had been driven to school and picked up by security guards for the next month. There had been a lot more threats and angry people when Uncle Owen and Uncle Randall had been alive. She glanced at Evan. He looked both tired and bored.

"I never liked this part," said Aiden. "It feels ridiculous to stand and wait for someone else to do something."

"Isn't that our entire lives?" asked Evan, going into the bathroom. He shut the door and turned on the fan.

"Either he's peeing or he's doing drugs," said Aiden.

"Possibly both," agreed Dominique.

"Either way, now is the time for that? He can't wait five minutes?"

"You're asking me?"

There was a gunshot and then a crash from the other room. Dominique gulped and fought the urge to go sprinting back out to the living room. She took a tighter grip on the bat and went to wait next to the door.

"I'm sure he's fine," said Aiden.

There was a second crash, and this one sounded more like splintering wood.

"That sounded like your console table," said Aiden, standing on the opposite side of the door.

"It was only about a hundred years old," said Dominique. "Barely an antique. I'm sure I can replace it."

There was another shattering crash and then a thump, this time closer to them.

"Probably the Venetian glass lamp and side table," said Evan coming out of the bathroom.

"Wasn't even part of a set," said Dominique, trying to sound as calm as Eleanor would in the situation.

The door was yanked open and a man advanced through, gun first. Aiden reached out and pulled whoever it was into the room. Dominique knew, although she couldn't have said how, that it wasn't Max, and she swung down on the arm that held the gun. The gun dropped, skittering away across the carpet. And Dominique swung again, this time low and hard at the man's knees. There was a pong of the bat hitting hard bone and the man yelled as he tripped, slamming into Aiden. Aiden seemed to pivot and spin in a surprisingly graceful movement and they both landed on the bed.

For a moment, Dominique thought her brother would punch the man. Instead, Aiden kicked their attacker off the bed, setting him up perfectly for Dominique. Dominique swung again, this time for the torso, connecting with a hard thump. Then she raised the bat, swung for his head, and got another satisfying crack. The man crumpled to the floor and Dominique stood breathing heavily and staring at him. Evan scooped up the gun from the floor.

The door was yanked open again, and Dominique spun, raising the bat, breathing hard. Max stood in the doorway, seemingly fine.

"OK," said Max, looking at the three of them. "Stay here. Be right back."

Then he turned and sprinted away. The three of them stood in silence for a moment.

"Jeez, Nika, repressed rage or anything?" asked Aiden, sounding annoyingly like Evan as he stepped off the bed and adjusted his shirt. He looked in the mirror and pushed his hair back into place.

"He came into my house with a gun," said Dominique, angrily. "What am I supposed to do? Stand around and scream? Fuck him!"

"I'm fine with it," said Evan. "Seemed appropriate." Dominique stared at him in shock. Had he and Aiden done some sort of accidental body switch? Even in a heightened state of emergency, Dominique felt a burst of strange emotions at having Evan's approval. He never liked anything she did. She was never up to Deveraux standards. Except for bashing intruders with bats apparently. Jackson said he'd talked to him. Maybe something had sunk in?

"Do you know how to use that thing?" asked Aiden, staring skeptically at Evan, still holding the gun loosely at his side.

"Jackson showed me," said Evan.

Aiden glanced at Dominique, who shrugged, then back at the guy on the floor. "Well, what the fuck do we do with him now?" asked Aiden.

"Tie him up," said Evan.

Dominique frowned. "My knot tying ability is limited to shoelaces. Also, I don't have any rope."

"Belts or scarves," said Evan. "I can do it."

"Great. I'll get those. Be right back," she said.

"Maybe you should wait," said Aiden. "You heard Max."

"And are we supposed to just keep bludgeoning this guy if he wakes up?" asked Evan. "It'll be safer for everyone if we tie him up. Come on, Nika. Aiden can do the bludgeoning while we get belts."

Dominique eyed Evan doubtfully. He still had one hand wrapped around his ribs and he looked pale. Also, he was taking her side now? Body swapping was starting to sound more plausible.

"There are people out there with guns," said Aiden. "I don't think we should go wandering around in the dark. Max might shoot us if nothing else. Also, I'm a pacifist. I'm not bludgeoning anyone."

There was a crash from the living area and all three of them jumped. Then they heard the front door slam open and the sound of running feet.

"Great Aunt Claudia's vase?" offered Aiden.

"I hated that thing anyway," said Dominique. "Evan, come stand by the door and shoot anyone that shoots at us. I'll go get stuff to tie this guy up." She took a firmer grip on the bat with one hand, cracked the door open with the other and peered out. The apartment was quiet. The only light came in from the windows and from the open front door. She made it out to the hallway and saw another unconscious person. Apparently, Max had been busy. She went back into the guest room.

"I think they left," she said. "Also, it appears there's another one in the hall. Aiden you'll have to drag him in here for Evan."

"Why do I have to touch them?"

"Stop being a weenie," said Dominique. "Evan has broken ribs. He can't move them."

"So? We can just leave that one in the hall!"

"No! That's so… untidy."

Evan began to laugh, then stopped. "Ow," he said leaning against the wall.

"Maybe I should take the gun," said Aiden, grimacing, but not reaching out to help Evan. They all knew that wouldn't go well.

"Do you know how to use it?" demanded Dominique.

Aiden shook his head.

"Then go get the guy in the hall and keep Evan upright." Dominique went back out to the hall. She jumped over the unconscious man and tip-toed to her bedroom. The apartment seemed silent, but she could hear the sound of a ruckus coming from the building hallway. She debated whether or not to go help Max but decided to deal with the immediate threat. She made a quick pass through her closet and ran back to the guest room.

"OK," she said, dropping her load of belts and scarves on the bed. "You guys tie them up. I'm going to go see if Max needs help."

"No," said Aiden. "He said to stay here."

"Whatever," said Dominique and ran back out into the apartment before her brother could stop her. The closer she got to the door, the more her heart began to jack-hammer. She wondered how Max did this kind of thing routinely. She wondered, if they continued to attempt dating beyond tonight, how she was going to deal with the fact that this was Max's job. The apartment door was ajar, and from the hallway, she could hear the sound of voices. They were chit-chatty type voices. They didn't even sound mad.

Dominique waited, then she peered cautiously around the door frame.

Max and Jackson were each pulling an unconscious person down the hall by the feet.

"See?" said Dominique, stepping out into the hallway. "You understand that you can't go around leaving bodies in the hallway. What's wrong with Aiden?" She knew she was focusing on trivial matters, but if she focused on the things like the fact that there was a blood smear on the wall of her building, she might lose it.

Both men paused—apparently, her brothers' opinion on body removal was a forceable change in subject. "I don't know," said Jackson. "Personally, I have always found it very disorganized and... untidy."

Max looked displeased. "It's comments like that that make law enforcement personnel uncomfortable."

"Why? I just said exactly the same thing," said Dominique, and Jackson grinned. "Doesn't anyone else think..." She trailed off seeing Max's face. He looked displeased.

"And how often do *you* have bodies lying about the place?" demanded Max.

"Well, this is, admittedly, the first time," said Dominique. "But, in general, I'm opposed to it. In fact, I find that I'm entirely opposed to everything that has happened since Aiden arrived." She lifted her chin up and assumed a very arrogant stance. She knew the effect was hampered by the fact that her voice had gone up an octave and a lump had formed in her throat, but she didn't know what to do about it. Jackson reached over and shoved Max at her.

Max took a few steps forward and hugged her. Dominique allowed herself a tiny moment to enjoy the embrace, but then caught Jackson's eye. He was looking too amused.

"I am fine," she said, stepping back. "I'm just very displeased about my furniture."

"Where are the guys?" asked Jackson, allowing her to pretend she was fine. But Max kept his arm around her shoulders, and she leaned into him gratefully.

"Aiden is kibitzing about being a pacifist."

"Ha!" Jackson barked out a laugh.

"And Evan is tying up the ones inside with my belts."

"Of course he is," said Jackson.

"What's that supposed to mean?" asked Dominique.

"Nothing," said Jackson.

"He's actually being helpful," she said, frowning at him. "And barely sarcastic."

"That's great," said Jackson. Dominique eyed him. There had been a tone. She just wasn't sure what the tone meant.

"Nika, get back in…!" Aiden leaned out the door, Evan just behind him, and saw Jackson and Max. "Oh. Hey. Problem solved."

"Nika says you're a pacifist," said Jackson.

"What would I know about hitting people?" asked Aiden.

"Mm," said Jackson. "I bet you could figure it out if you thought about it real hard."

Dominique glanced at Aiden. There had definitely been a tone that time.

"Nope," said Aiden blithely. "I leave all the dirty work to Nika. She hit that guy in the bedroom like it was Major League try-outs."

"Clearly, Grandma's investment in that tennis pro paid off," said Evan, stepping out into the hall. "You had a lot of follow through on your swing. Who wants a gun?"

"I'll take it," said Max, holding out the hand that was around Dominique.

"Great," said Evan, handing the gun to Max. "I'm going to lie on the couch and wonder why I left the house."

"Well, honestly, you really ought to be in bed," said Dominique. "I'll bring you some aspirin in a minute." If Evan was going to be nice to her, she could make a minor reciprocating effort.

"Whatever," said Evan, going into the apartment. Dominque looked at Jackson who shrugged.

"Is this all of them?" asked Aiden, looking at the two men on the floor.

"We're missing the two Nika and I saw earlier," said Max. "But I think this is the rest of them."

"They're in a hotel in Brooklyn," said Jackson.

"And you know that how?" demanded Max.

"Shh, Max," said Dominique. "We don't ask Jackson those kinds of questions."

"Well, I damn well do," said Max, looking annoyed.

"We have private investigators whose job it is to find the things we want found," said Jackson.

"And were you going to be sharing this information with the Marshals?" Max was being very stern.

"I would have, except Aiden texted me. This seemed more important."

"Definitely more important to me," agreed Aiden.

"Mm," said Max, looking annoyed but convinced. "Well, we better get a team out there ASAP."

"I've got some guys sitting on it," said Jackson. "They'll let me know if the others go anywhere."

"All right, why don't we—"

"Nobody move!" yelled a stern voice from the stairwell, cutting off Max's next statement.

"Hands up where they can see them," said Aiden, calmly. "And Jacks, try not to be yourself."

"I keep trying that," said Jackson, "but it doesn't seem to take."

A stream of police officers poured out of the stairwell and soon Dominique and the others were surrounded. Max was yelling back at them. Or maybe it wasn't yelling, maybe it was just the overly loud talking they all seemed to do. Soon, Dominique found herself and Aiden shoved back into the apartment, while Max and Jackson dealt with the police.

"We'll have to do statements in a little bit," said Aiden, slouching in one of Dominique's leather chairs by the fireplace. "Honestly, it'll probably be hours before we can go home."

"Oh joy," murmured Evan. He had returned to the couch. "Just how I wanted to spend my evening."

Dominique eyed them doubtfully. It was like some sort of flashback to her childhood summers. Sullen Evan, sulky Aiden, and no one was doing what they wanted to be doing.

"Why does it smell like smoke?" asked Evan.

"I'm not—" Dominique was cut off by the fire alarm and she jumped, letting out a shriek.

"The pizza!" she yelled, running into the kitchen. She yanked open the oven and got a face full of black smoke. Yanking on oven mitts, she pulled the pizza out of the oven and dumped it into the sink.

Max came into the kitchen, reached up and pulled the fire alarm off the wall. The horrible screeching stopped, and Dominique looked up at Max, not knowing whether to laugh or cry.

"Pizza's done," she said.

"I'm sorry, baby," he said, and hugged her.

"Seriously?" demanded Aiden. "Do we have to watch this? This is worse than that time Grandma went on a date."

"When can they go home?" asked Dominique, her face buried in Max's chest. She wanted nothing more than to stay right there, but he was already pulling away.

"I'm working on it," said Max, half-laughing. And then, with obvious intent, he leaned in and kissed her, and Aiden groaned.

"That's your fault," said Evan as Max went back toward the hall. "He wouldn't have done that if you hadn't said anything."

"Evan, why are you even here?" demanded Aiden.

"I'll be back in a minute or two," said Max to Dominique. "Good luck," he whispered as he slid out the front door.

"Aiden, stop being a pain," said Dominique, turning on the fan over the stove before going into the living room and dropping into the chair opposite Aiden.

"No, seriously," said Aiden frowning, "why are you here, Evan?"

From his prone position on the couch, Evan flapped a hand as if to wave away the question. "It doesn't matter."

"Actually, why *are* you here?" repeated Dominique, frowning. "Have you even been to my apartment before?"

"Yes, when you bought it," he said. She thought for a moment that he looked hurt. "You had me look it over before you made an offer."

"That's right. I appreciated your help. Thanks. And you're here tonight because?"

Evan was silent for a moment, poking gently at his ribs with one hand. "I was in the neighborhood for dinner. I keep meaning to talk to you about one of the accounts. I want to move it." Dominique thought that was a lie but didn't have a reason to call him out on it.

"Whatever you want to do," said Dominique with a shrug.

"Yeah, great, thanks," said Evan sarcastically.

"What's that supposed to mean?" snapped Aiden.

"Nothing."

"It didn't sound like nothing!" Aiden barked back, and Dominique looked at her brother in surprise. He didn't usually bother to fight with Evan. The stress of the evening was probably taking a toll on all of them.

"You really want to know? Fine. Then what I meant was that I just love how all of your financial decisions are always up to me. The entire fucking empire is built on what I do, but do any of you take a fucking interest? No, you do not. It's always all up to me."

"Oh, boo fucking hoo," said Aiden. "You want a gold medal for doing the Deveraux dirty work? Fine, sure, but get in line. I practice corporate law—corporate! But every time I turn around,

I'm getting pressed to do something I know nothing about. Here Aiden, read this contract. Here Aiden, get your cousin out of jail. Here Aiden, rewrite this bill that goes before fucking congress next month. No pressure!"

Evan stared at Aiden. "So what you're saying is that we're both pissed at Dominique for being smart enough to go into a field that Grandma can't sponge off of."

Aiden stared at Evan for a long moment and then flopped back into his chair, running a hand through his hair. "Yeah, that's what I'm saying."

They turned to look at her and she realized that she had missed the opportunity to gloat over the fact that she didn't have to do work for their grandmother. Nothing she said now was going to cover for the fact that she hadn't said anything—they wouldn't believe her. So instead she sat up straight and crossed her ankles. She brushed a piece of imaginary lint off her leg.

"What does she make you do?" asked Evan tiredly.

Dominique shrugged. "Does it matter?"

"Yes," he said.

Dominique shrugged again, but gave in. "I meet with Grandma's Campaign Manager once or twice a month to go over her marketing materials and make sure her brand is being expressed correctly. I also write or edit most of her public comments and script her press conferences. I estimate that it takes an additional six to eight hours a week, and now that we're approaching the election, it's going to double or triple that."

"You never said you did that," said Aiden, sounding shocked.

"Why don't you tell her to fuck off?" asked Evan, his voice strained.

She smiled the Deveraux smile. "I'm happy to help."

"Yeah," said Evan, staring at the ceiling. "I'm happy to help. I just wish I had a choice."

"That is the one luxury that none of us get," said Dominique. "But thank you for looking after all of our money."

"I don't really mind," said Evan with a sigh. "I'm just tired. Really tired."

"I wrote part of a law," said Aiden, fiddling with his hair. "And I did get Jackson out of jail. I mean, that's cool. I…" He looked from Dominique to Evan. "I always thought this was temporary. I thought when we were adults, we wouldn't have to be Deveraux."

"Joke's on you, then," said Evan. "I always knew I was going to be one."

Dominique licked her lips, then decided to take a chance. "But you don't have to be one like your father," she said gently. Evan was silent for a long moment.

"I'm not sure I know how *not* to be," he said.

"Well, for starters, you could stop doing drugs," said Aiden.

"Fuck you," said Evan.

With impatient fingers, Aiden dug his wallet out of his back pocket. He flipped through it until he found a well-worn business card. He got up and placed it on Evan's chest with a hard flick.

"They worked for me," he said, his voice flat and devoid of emotion. "I didn't even have to miss work."

Dominique held her breath. She and Aiden went to great lengths not to expose weakness to Evan. She knew he was taking a risk to do this, and she wasn't sure what Evan would do with the information.

Evan stared up at Aiden, and Dominique watched his hand curl gently around the card. "Thanks," he said.

"Whatever," said Aiden, then he dropped back down again

with a hard slap against the leather arm of the chair that seemed to express his emotions more than his words or face.

The door opened and Jackson stepped into the room, pausing like an animal who had caught a threatening scent on the wind. "How are we doing?" he asked, scrutinizing each of them.

"Evan is lecturing us about reading his financial reports," said Dominique, giving Evan a chance to tuck the card away.

"I read all of mine," said Jackson.

"You do not," said Evan.

"Yeah, I do. I mean, it takes me like a week and a dictionary to figure out what you're saying, but I read them."

"I could explain them," said Evan, sounding shocked.

"Can you?" asked Dominique. "Because maybe it's not a problem for Aiden, but it looks like a pile of gobbledygook to me. Also, I hate the font you're using."

"The intern did it."

"Multi-million dollar company and you can't hire a graphic designer?"

"No? I don't know. That's something people care about?"

"Your reports are visual representation of your brand. If your clients can't read them, then what message are you sending?"

"That's a good point," said Evan frowning. "I'll talk to Bob. I've had trouble reading the text too. Although, I might have to promote the intern. He's one of the VP's nephews or some shit."

"Just hire a graphic designer and shift the job duties," said Aiden. "It's totally legit as long as you rewrite the job description."

"Graphic designers cost about an intern in your field anyway," said Dominique.

"So..." said Jackson, "does this mean I get it explained to me or not?"

"Bring the most recent one to dinner next Sunday," said Evan, his voice gravelly, and his eyes drifting closed again. "We'll go over it."

"Don't put yourself out," said Jackson sarcastically. Dominique glared at him and he gave her a little head shake that said he was managing Evan. Dominique frowned—what was the percentage in annoying Evan while he was clearly exhausted and also making, what for him, was a supreme effort to be nice?

"I don't work for you," snapped Evan, "so don't worry, I won't."

Jackson gave her a little head nod of encouragement. She glanced at Aiden who shrugged his confusion also.

"Thanks, Evan," said Dominique sincerely. "I'd appreciate the help."

Evan opened his eyes and looked from her to Jackson, clearly uncertain which tone to respond to.

"Yeah OK," he muttered.

"Glad that's settled," said Dominique. "But I still want pizza. So I think I'm going to order delivery. Is everyone else in?"

"I'm not sure you're allowed to order a pizza to a crime scene," said Aiden.

"Neither am I," said Jackson, "but I am dying to see her try."

"I left my phone in the bedroom," said Dominique.

"Mine is still taped to the ceiling," complained Evan.

"I'm done letting people use my phone for the day," declared Aiden. It was one of his usual nonsensical proclamations, but for the first time, Dominique realized that his tone was exactly like Evan's when Evan declared something devastatingly arrogant and cutting.

"Fine," she said, standing, "but you're paying for the pizza."

"No, I'm not," he said. "Because the police will never let the delivery guy on the floor."

"We will find out," she said primly and went into her bedroom. Jackson followed her a few minutes later.

"What was that?" she demanded in a whisper. "He was being nice."

"He needs something to push against otherwise he doesn't feel like himself. I figured I'd be the designated asshole and you could be the nice one."

"Jackson! Did we just good-cop-bad-cop Evan?"

"Yeah, more or less. Why did he come over?"

"Some bullshit about wanting to talk about one of the accounts. I don't think that was true, but he... He really tried tonight. He acted like how he is at Christmas. You know, kind of bitchy, but still playing along. And Aiden gave him a card for that treatment place you sent him to."

"Did he take it?"

"Yes!"

Jackson grinned. "Good. We'll get him out of this yet." Jackson's phone pinged. "We need to talk about this more and we'll need to loop Aiden in, but right now..."

"You've got to disappear mysteriously?" she asked, picking up her phone.

"Just for a minute or two," he said with a grin.

"If you go out onto the veranda, you can hop onto the neighbor's deck, go in through their patio, and then go out their front door. It opens around the corner of the hall. If you're quick you can make it down the back stairs without being seen." She tried to layout her in-case-of-emergency escape route like it was no big deal so he would think she was cool.

"I think your neighbors might notice," he said.

"Nah, they're in Cancun. You can grab the spare key off the bulletin board in the kitchen and lock up on your way out."

"And how often do you use them as your back door?" asked Jackson, laughing.

"Hardly ever," said Dominique, although the answer was, in fact, never. "But you once told me that it was always important to have a secondary exit, and I always try to take your advice. Because contrary to popular belief, I do, in fact, listen."

Jackson laughed again. "All right, back in ten."

Dominique app-ordered from her phone as they went back out to the living room. Jackson stepped out through the French doors and was across the roof deck within seconds without so much as a backward look.

"Did Jackson just jump over your balcony?" asked Aiden, coming out of her kitchen carrying the bottle of wine that Max had bought.

"I don't know what you're talking about," said Dominique, finalizing toppings and hitting the check-out button. "I'm sure he stepped into the restroom for a few minutes.

"I'm absolutely certain I saw him go into the bathroom," said Evan, without opening his eyes.

"I don't appreciate the double-team on gas-lighting me," said Aiden, but without any animosity. "Meanwhile, Evan, will you drink this if I open it."

Evan opened one eye and squinted at the wine label from his place on the couch. "Yes," he said.

Dominique sighed. "That was my date wine."

"Well, I'm sorry, but I don't see why we should have to suffer wineless through a police interrogation just because you have shitty dates," said Aiden.

"I'm with Aiden," said Evan.

"It was a perfectly lovely date," said Dominique. "At least until the pair of you showed up!"

"I don't know, Nika," said Aiden popping the cork. "This Max guy, isn't he going to come into conflict with Jackson?"

"Jackson likes him," she said. "I thought you did too."

Aiden gestured awkwardly with the wine opener. "You hated him in college. Can't go around liking people your sister hates."

"Well, I no longer hate him, so you may feel free to like him."

"Oh good," said Aiden. "I always thought he was a nice guy. Couldn't figure out what the hell he'd been thinking when he said that to you."

"He was drunk, and he says he was not thinking, and he has apologized."

"Good for him," said Aiden. "Couldn't ever get the hang of apologizing myself. I always sound like an idiot. I mean, most of the times that I do things, I do them on purpose. Being sorry about it later just makes me sound like an indecisive twat." Aiden watched Evan as he poured out glasses of wine.

Dominique snorted. "Just because you did it on purpose doesn't mean you're married to that decision for the rest of your life. I've done lots of things on purpose that I later realized were a terrible idea."

"When have you ever done anything you regret?" muttered Evan.

"I stole McKenzie Hubbard's iPad," said Dominique. "And once I pantsed Liam Dover in the lunchroom."

"Ooh, that was you?" asked Aiden, sucking air through his teeth. "That wasn't cool. He was really embarrassed. Why'd you do that?"

"Well, I was kind of a bully for a while in high school. I got tired of everyone saying I was *just like Genevieve*."

"I don't think that meant you had to go the other direction," said Aiden drily.

"Well, I figured that out after a bit and I have tried to apologize and make amends, but Liam still won't talk to me."

"Some things are just broken," said Evan.

"But some things *can* be fixed," said Dominique firmly.

# *Maxwell — Afterwards*

Max said goodbye to the last of the Marshals and went to find Dominique. She was in the kitchen staring at the pile of pizza boxes, a depressed look on her face. He didn't blame her. The apartment was a wreck. The living room was covered in crime scene markers, fingerprint dust, and broken furniture.

"Thanks for ordering pizza for everyone," he said, putting his arms around her. "I think you may have secured the popular vote for me getting assigned here."

She leaned into him. "It's fine. Grandma wants the police union endorsement, and every little bit helps."

"I can't have you buying half a squad's worth of pizza though. What do I owe you?"

"Don't worry about it."

"I am worrying about it. Pretty sure the Marshals ate more than their share."

"No, I mean, don't worry about it because I made Aiden pay for it."

"Oh, well, all right then. Never mind."

She chuckled tiredly and snuggled against his chest.

"Dominique?" He tried to figure out the right way to ask what he wanted to ask.

"Mmm?" she replied without moving.

"Are you OK?" he blurted out.

She made a questioning noise and looked up at him, her blue eyes worried.

"This has been a fantastically shitty day for me, and I'm at least trained and somewhat used to this bullshit. How are you holding up?"

She blushed. "I'm fine."

"Nika, baby, don't bullshit me."

"I feel silly when people ask me how I am," she said. "I never know what to say. Yes, I'm upset. I'm sure I'll be more upset later. But right this minute, I'm more traumatized by the mess and the fact that I'm going to have to explain to Grandma how Great Aunt Claudia's vase got broken. I mean, having it get broken is practically the only good thing about the situation, but I'm sure she'll get all pinch-faced at me like I put it out just for mercenaries to break. Which is ridiculous. Although, had I known they were coming I certainly would have. But on the whole, I'm still standing. The apartment is... structurally still sound. Except for that one bullet hole. Max, I have a bullet hole in my wall!"

He hugged her tighter, and she put her head back on his chest. He liked the way she fit just under his chin.

"Sorry," he said. "But on the upside, everyone I know in this state thinks you're a badass. That guy is going to be in the hospital for a while."

"I hit him really hard," she said, sounding smug. "But... really, your entire day was shitty?" She sounded wistful and he felt himself grin.

"Well, I cannot pretend there weren't some definite high-points," he said. "If it weren't for the mercenaries, I think you could safely say that we *almost* had a great date."

"I really wanted it to be a great date," she complained.

"And up until your brothers, cousins, and whatevers showed up, it was a fucking great date."

She looked up at him and frowned. "Well, at least we're a matched set," she said, reaching up to gently touch the bruise and scuff that were forming by his right eye. "Is dating you always this difficult?"

"Me? No, this was all you. Those were your monkeys and your circus."

"I don't want it to be my circus!" she wailed, hugging him tighter and shaking him a little.

"I'm assuming that your circus will leave town eventually," he said with a laugh.

"God, I hope so. I don't think I can have any more armed gunmen popping around for dinner. The stupid police took my bat for one thing."

"It was evidence."

"It was my security system."

"Yes, Jackson was complaining that you wouldn't let him install anything."

"The walls are plaster. He was going to be drilling and pulling wires. And that meant having more contractors around and I finally got the remodel for the kitchen done. I couldn't take the idea of having more saggy pants electricians wandering around. That much ass crack is not OK."

"I don't think you have your priorities in order," said Max.

"You didn't have to look at them. Max?"

"Yes?"

She picked up her head again and looked at him nervously. "You're right, they really are my monkeys," she said. "The circus may leave, but Evan and Aiden and Jackson, they're always going to be around. Are you going to be OK with that? Because I would really like this to be more than a... great date."

"I like them," said Max. "Evan, maybe, not so much."

"I actually have hope for him," said Dominique. "I'm not sure what happened, but tonight he was… human. And if he could stop doing drugs, maybe, well, I don't know, maybe he could be OK."

"Maybe," said Max with a shrug. "Of course, I would like them a whole lot more if they would stop coming over in the middle of a date. But basically, yeah, I'm fine with them."

"And the stupid fundraisers and galas and benefits? I go to a lot of those. And I have to go be a, well, a Deveraux a lot."

"I like Dominique Deveraux. I like Dominique Casella. I like naked Nika on the bedroom floor."

"You like that one the best, don't you?" she asked, grinning.

"Yes," he agreed. "I really do."

"We could try that one again," she suggested.

"OK," he said and bent over and picked her up, slinging her over his shoulder.

"Max!" she protested. "That isn't what I meant!"

"No?" he asked, heading for the bedroom. "Should I put you down?"

There was silence. "Well," she said, "I mean, on the bed."

He did put her down on the bed. Gently, this time. Then he stepped back and untied her shoes, tossing them over his shoulder one at a time. It made her laugh, which was kind of the point. Then he undid the button and zipper on her jeans and pulled them off of her. She hadn't changed her entire outfit—she was still wearing the red lace panties from earlier. He pulled off his own shirt and kicked off his shoes, before climbing on to the bed.

"Max," she murmured, "please tell me you locked the door."

"Door is locked, with a fucking chair under the handle just to be sure," he confirmed, kissing along her stomach as he worked her shirt up.

"And if the phones ring…"

He silenced the rest of that sentence with a kiss. "We are not answering," he said pulling back.

"OK," she said with a happy sigh. She sat up a little to wriggle out of her shirt and he unsnapped her bra as she did. He went back to kissing her, pleased to find so much skin now in contact with his. He kissed along her neck as she reached down to un-do his jeans, when she stopped. "Max?" she said. "I realize this is a bit late to be bringing up, but you did bring condoms, right?"

"Condoms? What? Oh, no!"

She froze, eyes wide.

He reached in his back pocket and pulled one out. "Yeah, I got you," he said, tossing it on the bed next to her.

"You are such a jerk," she said, smacking at him. Max laughed and dropped his weight onto her, flattening her out beneath him. "Jerk," she repeated around a kiss, but her hands were still working the zipper on his fly. He cleared a little room to let her work. She slid her hand inside his pants, and he groaned as she made contact with flesh. She pulled her hand away, which was not at all what either of them wanted, but then she pushed at his pants. She was entirely ineffectual, but it was clear what she wanted. He pulled back, and she followed him, going up on her knees on the bed, kissing him as he removed his pants.

Her hands pulled him back to her as soon as he was naked, sliding down his back taking a firm grip on his ass. He paused and looked around.

"What?" she asked, breathing heavily.

"I'm naked. You're in your underwear. Last time, this is when shit went wrong. I'm just giving it a moment. If someone wanted to jump out at us, now would be the time. Because after this, I'm not stopping, I don't care who comes through the door."

She laughed and then stood up on the bed. Slowly, she began

to peel the red lace off her body. He leaned in and gripped the edge with his teeth, yanking the lace gently over her hip bone. He heard the way she inhaled, and he kept his mouth there even as he pulled the underwear off.

Max looked up at her. She was biting her lip, and with one finger he pushed her backward. She toppled onto the bed with a giggle.

He kissed along her thigh. He wanted to hear the little inhale of breath again and he wasn't disappointed. He trailed his fingers along her other thigh. Dominique moaned as his hands explored her body and his tongue tasted her sweetness.

"Oh God, Max," Dominque moaned, running her fingers through his hair. "Max... God, Max, I want you inside me."

He was more than willing to comply, but some things took time to do properly. He kissed his way up her body, keeping one hand between her thighs. She was wet and writhing under him by the time he reached her breasts. She moaned again, one hand flailing out. She grabbed the condom, ripping it open while he ran his tongue over her nipple. She was breathing hard by the time she got the condom out.

"Put it on," she ordered, shoving it at him.

"My hands are busy," he said, sitting up. "You put it on."

"Oh God," she moaned, arching up as he stroked harder. She looked like she was torn between wanting to object to his order and not slowing the process down. She took a deep breath and reached for his cock, then stopped, arching back again. With his free hand, he helped her slip the condom on. Her fingers left him breathing heavily. Too hard to be slow anymore, he grabbed her by the hips and pulled her down the bed to him. He eased inside her and she moaned, her hips opening up to him.

"God, you feel good," he groaned.

He pushed into her, again and again, kissing her as their bodies met. He dragged his teeth across the lips that drove him wild, and she wrapped legs around him, her heels digging in, locking him to her—as if he would ever want to separate. Their bodies moved in rhythm, and he felt the building pressure, the urge to speed up. She alternated between biting her lip and holding her breath and he grinned, recognizing the signs.

"Faster, Max, faster."

He did as she urged, slipping one hand underneath her to offer a little more resistance. Her eyes flew open and she gasped, her hands flexing involuntarily.

"God, fucking, yes! Yes, Max, yes!"

Her fingernails dug into him as he drove into her and he found himself hovering on the brink of losing control. She came, arching under him and he let himself go, coming with a blinding force.

When he was finally able to form a coherent thought, he realized that she had her arms and legs wrapped around him. He made as if to move, but she let out a very disagreeing noise. He levered up a little and rotated them to the side, so that he at least wasn't squishing her. He was still breathing heavily, but then, so was she.

He pushed a lock of hair out of her face so he could kiss her, and she relaxed her hold on him a little.

"God, I'm an idiot," he said, looking down at her.

She made a questioning noise, a wrinkle forming between her eyes.

"We could have been doing this in college if I had just been less of an idiot."

She laughed and let go of him, rolling away to lay like a starfish in the middle of the bed.

"We'll have to start on a debt repayment plan," she said. "Six years is a lot to make up for."

"I always pay my debts," he said, kissing her again, before disposing of the condom in the trash on the far side of the bed.

"Then there's interest," she said, nibbling at his shoulder as he stretched over her. "I have a lot of interest."

He chuckled and flopped down beside her. She shifted to snuggle up against him and he found his eyes drifting closed.

"I'm getting up," she said.

"Why?" he asked.

"So that I can brush my teeth, because otherwise morning sex is going to be not good."

He pondered that. "I don't have a toothbrush."

"I have a travel one you can use."

"Great," he said, not moving. He watched her ass as she went into the bathroom. "I wonder if I should text my dad?"

She peered around the door. "Uh, why?"

"I still have his car," he said. "He'll probably miss it eventually. On the other hand, maybe I shouldn't, because if I tell him, then he'll know where it is and where I am. And maybe that's too much information to share with a parent."

Dominique burst out laughing and ran back into the bedroom to grab for his phone.

"What are you doing?"

"I'm texting your dad that you have the car."

"No, I just said that maybe wasn't a good idea."

He reached for the phone, but she held it away. "Max, in case you didn't notice, basically everyone in my entire family knows what I'm doing tonight. I don't see why you should get to escape sharing that embarrassment."

He groaned as she hit send with a giggle.

"Oh, who cares," he said, dropping back on the bed. "I'm too tired to worry about this shit. It'll probably just make him happy. He thinks we're a good fit."

"Yeah, we were," said Dominique, with a leering grin as she went back into the bathroom.

"I'm going to be so tired tomorrow," he said around a yawn.

"I already called in a sick day," said Dominique from the bathroom. "I'm not waking up for anything but sex tomorrow morning."

In the bedroom, he grinned at the ceiling. This really was turning out to be the best vacation ever.

## *Dominique — After that*

Dominique lay on the green velveteen couch in the study at Deveraux House, the dish of M & M's from the coffee table balanced on her stomach and waited for her grandmother to finish whatever she was doing. In the meantime, Dominique plucked out the peanut M & M's from the dish, tossed them into the air and caught them in her mouth.

"You going to eat that whole bowl of M & M's?" asked Jackson, picking up her feet and sitting down underneath them.

"Just the peanut ones," said Dominique, and Jackson laughed, his blue eyes twinkling.

"What exactly did you two say to Evan last night after I left?" said Jackson, kicking his feet up onto the coffee table in direct violation of Eleanor's commandments.

Dominique hesitated. "What do you mean?" she asked.

Jackson stole a few of the non-peanut M & M's. "Well, he came by this morning with the most recent financial report and went over it with me."

"Oh, shoot. I thought he said he'd do it on Sunday. I actually did want him to go over it with me too."

"He said he'd do yours on Sunday because we're diversified differently or something."

"Oh, good," said Dominique.

"Anyway, he looked like shit, and he refused to talk about anything but the damn financial report, but he was hardly even sarcastic. I thought we left things in a pretty good place last night, but I mean... actually responding to requests? No sarcasm? Even when I pushed him on looking for a therapist."

"Oh my God, you actually suggested therapy?" Dominique was shocked. "I'm not sure I would have had the courage to say anything. What did he say?"

"He sort of shrugged, but he didn't actually say no. It was weird. If Evan's not swearing at me in Ukrainian, how will I know he still cares?"

Dominique chuckled. "Is that what that means?"

"That is what I have chosen to believe," said Jackson.

"We don't make it easy on you, do we?" asked Dominique. "I don't know why you stick with us. You could be on a beach in Greece or something."

"On a beach with who?" asked Jackson. "Beaches or a shitty apartment on the west side of Chicago—it's exactly the same if I'm by myself."

"You know what I envy about you?" asked Dominique.

"My hair," said Jackson. "I know. It's hard to be related to hair this perfect."

Dominique laughed so hard she missed her next M & M. She retrieved the candy out of the couch cushion and popped it in her mouth. "No. I envy your ability to be emotionally honest with others. Max keeps expecting me to be honest about my feelings."

"Oh God, the horror," said Jackson, sarcastically.

"It is a bit," said Dominique seriously. "I hadn't realized how often I deflect the question *how are you*. And Max actually wants an honest answer. And he keeps being... supportive when I do answer."

"Isn't that good?" asked Jackson, looking like he was trying not to outright laugh in her face.

"Yes! It's great. It's weird. And I feel like you have a much clearer understanding of your own emotions than I do sometimes. Or at least you're more comfortable with expressing them."

He nodded. "My mom was fucked up about a lot of stuff, but one of the things that she was really clear on was that being honest about feelings was the only way to be happy. You can't expect anyone to meet your needs if you don't say what those needs are and in return you can't be someone's partner without listening to theirs."

"Yeah," said Dominique, "I'm not sure Deveraux are allowed to have emotional clarity."

"Yeah, well, maybe they should," said Jackson, stealing more M & M's.

"It would be kind of nice for a change," said Dominique.

"Speaking of feelings," said Jackson, around a mouthful of chocolate, "how are you doing?"

"Agh!" Dominique sprawled out in disgust, trying to melt into the couch. "I'm fiiiiine!"

"You got attacked in your home," said Jackson, chuckling. "You're not freaking?"

Dominique frowned. "Yeah. A bit. It really helped to have Max spend the night last night. I think it will be better once I get everything cleaned up at home."

"You can always come stay here," offered Jackson, but Dominique shook her head.

"That would make it difficult for Max to come over and protect me again tonight," she said, knowing that she was grinning like an idiot.

Jackson laughed. "Whatever floats your boat," he said. "Meanwhile, I've talked to Aiden. I'm going to stop by his office on Friday and grab lunch so we can compare notes on Evan. You want in?"

"Yeah, definitely. We need to work out a game plan. If Evan can be not … well, himself, that would be nice for everyone."

"You're not convinced?"

"He's nice at Christmas and then he's not. I just think I would like to be cautious for a while."

"Definitely a wait-and-see situation," agreed Jackson. "So, you and Max, huh? What happens if he gets assigned to Virginia?"

"They called this morning. He's officially going to be here. So, problem solved, as Aiden says. I think we're a green light for, you know, actual 'shipping.'"

"Great!" said Jackson, patting her foot affectionately. "But, um, word of warning, I'm not sure Eleanor is going to be super pleased with you pairing up with him on a more serious basis."

"Why on earth not?" demanded Dominique in surprise.

"Not entirely sure," he said. "It's just the vibe I'm getting. I don't think she likes that he's law enforcement."

"But if you don't have a problem with it, why would she?"

"No clue," Jackson said with a shrug. "I like him. He's funny."

Dominique laughed and tossed another peanut M & M into her mouth. "He really is."

"And of course, if you keep dating him, I can skip assigning you a security detail, which saves on my budget."

"Oh, ha ha. You know I was never going to let you give me a bodyguard anyway."

"I'm not saying it wasn't going to be a challenge. I'm just saying I would do it if you kept playing detective."

"Well, fortunately, I don't have to," said Dominique. "Didn't last night take care of the problem? Max didn't have any updates by the time he went into the office, but he seemed confident."

"Well, we'll find out in a few minutes. Eleanor's getting briefed right now on the phone."

"So best case scenario is that those guys flipped, named names, and she can publicly have what's-his-face Granger, the CEO of Absolex arrested on the floor of the Senate when the hearings re-convene on Monday."

"Yeah, that would be the dream," agreed Jackson.

"What's worst case?"

"They all say nothing, the cops turn up nothing and Absolex takes another run at us."

Dominique frowned. She didn't like the sound of that.

"Jackson, Dominique! Feet off the furniture!"

Jackson reluctantly dropped his onto the floor. "Mine are on Jackson," protested Dominique.

"Don't prevaricate," said Eleanor sternly.

Dominique gave an exaggerated sigh and swiveled to barely upright, slouching on the couch.

"I fail to understand how none of you were raised together and yet you all display the same disregard for proper treatment of antiques."

"Maybe there's a yet to be identified gene for indifference to furniture," suggested Dominique and Jackson chuckled.

"I suspect that there must be," agreed Eleanor, settling herself on the edge of a wing-backed chair and straightening her skirt. Dominique rolled her eyes.

"Grandma, don't keep us in suspense. What did they say about the guys, mercenaries, whatever?"

"Well, apparently the one you repeatedly struck with a bat is still in the hospital."

Jackson held up his hand and Dominique hit the high-five with a resounding smack.

"And thanks to Jackson's efforts, they also have the remaining two members of the group in custody."

"But what are they saying?" demanded Dominique. "Are

they going to rat out their employers or what? I want Absolex on a platter."

Eleanor's smile was a tight, thin line. "The investigation is on-going. However, it would appear that a few of the gentlemen in custody have provided information that will lead back to their employers."

"That doesn't sound like you get to have them arrested," said Dominique. "That sounds like it's boring detective work and we hope they haven't shredded everything and maybe six months or a year from now they'll arrest some VP and he'll get a severance package before going to white collar prison. Meanwhile, Granger or whatever asshole it was at Absolex thinks he can get away with coming after us."

"Language, Dominique. We do not describe our opponents as *assholes*."

Dominique raised an eyebrow. "They're not opponents. They are literally the people who were trying to kill us."

"Apparently, the goal was to kidnap Aiden and blackmail me into canceling the hearings. Then they thought they would take both of you when he went to your apartment."

"Stupid plan," said Dominique.

"As it turned out, yes," agreed Eleanor.

"But that kind of thing can't go without a response," said Dominique. "It's unacceptable. And I appreciate that the law has to work through things or whatever, but I'm not sure they're going to be fast enough."

"An interesting sentiment for someone who seems to be intent on pursuing a relationship with a U.S. Marshal," said Eleanor.

"Well, Max is wonderful and, of course, I fully support law enforcement," said Dominique. "But as I keep saying, I really can't have people going around trying to squash Deverauxes. It's a very bad precedent to set. I say we chop up his favorite horse and put it in his bed."

Jackson began to laugh.

"His favorite horse?" repeated Eleanor, looking horrified.

"I don't mean that," said Dominique. "Animal cruelty is really not OK. But there must be *something*. I dislike that this is going to go unanswered."

Eleanor smiled at her affectionately. "Don't worry, dear. It won't. But, you must remember, patience is a virtue."

# *Maxwell – Fatherhood*

Max was laying on the couch with his laptop on his stomach when he heard his father come into the condo.

"Hey, Dad!" he yelled. "Do you have a printer hooked up to the wi-fi?"

"Do I have… Where the hell have you been?" demanded Grant, yelling from the foyer.

"I texted!" Max yelled back.

He heard his father's keys being tossed down forcefully into the bowl by the door.

"Yes, that you're at work. You're with Dominique. You have my car. Which is it?"

"Ended up being all of the above," said Max as Grant stomped into the living room. "But it worked out. I'm going to be assigned here. But I need to fill out some paperwork for HR. So do you have a printer?"

Max looked up and found his father looking at him in horror. Grant grabbed him by the chin and twisted his head around into the light. "What the fuck did you do?"

"I didn't do anything," said Max in irritation, pushing his father's hand away and sitting up. "There were some mercenaries that wanted to kidnap Dominique and Aiden. It's fine."

"Fine?" repeated Grant. "Fine? I… I can't. I just can't. I hate this, Max. I hate it."

"Hate what? Dad, take it down a notch."

"No, I will not. I hate your job. I hate that you put yourself in danger. I hate it. I couldn't take it when you were in wrestling. I can't take it now. Every time one of those big kids came after you,

I wanted to run down and yank you off the mat. Only I can't yank you off the damn mat if you keep doing it for a living. Why can't you just be a fucking accountant or something?"

Max blinked up at his father and found that he had no response.

"We sent you to a really good college! You liked law! Why couldn't you go be a nice, boring, *safe* lawyer?"

Max put his laptop down and sat up. "OK, a couple of things there. Dad, you do realize that by high school I was the big kid on the mat? I lost like three matches in my entire high school career. I was the one other parents worried about."

"That's not the point!" yelled Grant.

"OK, well, my point is that I was a good wrestler and I'm a good marshal. I'm not in constant danger. So stop freaking out."

"Not in…" Grant gestured angrily at Max's face.

"OK, yeah, I see your point. But there's a bit of extenuating circumstances there. And it's not likely to happen again. At least, I don't think so. I'm assuming that Dominique isn't being threatened by mercenaries working for pharmaceutical corporations every week. Although, I guess I'll find out."

"What?"

Max realized he'd wandered off his point. "I'm fine. I'm going to continue to be fine. And the reason I'm not a lawyer is because I'm not ready to go back to law school yet. I want to really get an understanding of how the law functions on this side of the table first."

"I hate your job," said Grant.

Max stood up, leaned down and hugged Grant. "Sorry, Dad. But I really am fine, and I like my job."

Grant sighed and patted him on the back. "You're really going to date Dominique?"

"Yes," said Max.

"I like her. Why is a pharmaceutical company trying to kidnap her?"

"They want Eleanor to stop the Senate hearings into Absolex."

Grant stepped back and squinted up at him. "What's wrong with people?"

"I don't know.

"Are you really thinking about law school?"

"Not for at least another five years, so don't get your hopes up. But I am going to need your real estate friends to help find me an apartment. Also, can I list your place for mail delivery while I'm looking?"

"You can't get a PO box?" demanded Grant throwing up his hands. "I think I'm still getting mail from when you were in college. Like I need your junk mail *and* mine."

"Sorry, Dad," said Max again, but this time, he smiled.

## *Dominique – Here Now*

Dominique climbed out of the cab, collected all her bags and, staggering a little under their weight, headed toward the front door of her building.

"Let me help you with that, ma'am," said Max in an artificially deep voice and appearing out of nowhere to open the door for her.

Dominique found herself beaming at him. "Hi!" She went up on tip-toe to kiss him.

"Hi," he said back, dropping into his normal voice and kissing her back.

"Ahem."

Dominique looked around and saw her neighbor carrying a bag of groceries and giving them the eye. "Sorry, Mrs. Salazar!" she said, trying to make it into the lobby and clear the doorway.

"You were obviously busy," she said smirking at Max as he continued to hold the door. Dominique tried not to blush as Mrs. Salazar cheerfully waggled her eyebrows at Dominique in passing.

"Are you coming in?" asked Dominique as Max seemed to be holding the door for too long.

"Nope. My uber eats is almost here."

"What?"

"I ordered food from the train after you said you had been meeting with Eleanor's campaign people."

An uber car pulled up and he let the lobby door swing closed while he went out to the curb and collected their dinner.

"So let me get this straight," said Dominique as he came back in, "we're not going to have the usual fruitless conversation about what to eat while we're both starving? Is that even allowed?"

"It is when I plan ahead," said Max with a grin. "I just figured you had a job interview, a Jackson-Aiden lunch, and the campaign people today and you should probably not be forced to make decisions and plans tonight."

Dominique had to physically restrain herself from blurting out that she loved him and his beautiful, thoughtful brain. They were two whole weeks into dating. The *L* word was the kind of thing that sent people running. And seriously, she shouldn't be saying that. It was only two weeks! Even if she kind of, seriously, thought that she meant it. She hit the button for the elevator and leaned against his arm, enjoying the half snuggle and the support.

"But you had your first day of work today!" she said. "You shouldn't have to make decisions either."

"Ah, but I'd already met almost everyone thanks to you and your family, so basically it was me learning where the bathroom was and finding my desk. Plus, I ordered before I got hungry, so I still had brain cells to spare. How'd the job interview go, by the way?"

"Good. I really wish I wasn't moving on this fast, but the whole mercenaries attacking at work thing kind of blew my cover. I think these guys will offer me the job. Although, honestly it might be because they're tech company nerds and I may have melted their brains a little. I would feel bad about trading on my looks except that I am one hundred percent confident I can rock the job. They've got a solid brand, a great product, and the worst marketing ever."

"Sounds like it was a good day then?" he asked as the elevator doors slid open. They had the car to themselves and Dominique hesitated as they got in. Even with the movement, he still spotted her pause. "What? Not good?"

"I was supposed to have lunch with Jackson and Aiden to

discuss Evan. Apparently Evan is going to a therapist. Which is great. Although, I'd feel better if he'd picked someone off the list I'd already pulled. But that's not the point. The point is that he's getting help."

"That's great," said Max. "Even if he didn't use your approved vendor list."

Dominique chuckled at Max's teasing tone. "It's not like I even showed it to him. I just thought he'd pick someone with a bigger practice. I mean what if this person is a total blabbermouth or something?"

"And you don't think you might be being a tad paranoid?"

"Oh, probably," admitted Dominique. "Jackson will check her out and if he says she's fine, then she's fine. Anyway, we were supposed to talk about strategies for supporting him that wouldn't annoy us or him too much, but then Aiden no-showed. I don't understand how he manages to space out on these things! If this was the first time he'd done it I'd get over it, but I swear he disappears periodically. Where the hell does he go? But as a result, I ate lunch super late and got back late. And then Grandma's campaign manager was being an asshat and not wanting to use the scripting I sent over. Mine tests better with the younger demographic, but I think he doesn't like that I backseat drive stuff. And I get it, I really do, but that's the gig. I'm sorry that Grandma prefers to use the unpaid labor of her grandchildren. I'm sorry that nepotism is real. But it is what it is. I have a hard enough time convincing people I know what I'm doing at work. I don't need it from that douchebag too."

"So rat him out to Eleanor," said Max. The elevator slowed as they approached Dominique's floor and he reached out and grabbed her laptop bag and her gym bag off her arm. She let them go with a sigh of relief, then fished in her pocket for her keys.

"He's doing a good job otherwise," she said, with a shrug.

"He's probably just stressed with the election coming up. I'll wait it out."

She stared at the keys in her hand as they exited the elevator and realized that if things continued going well with Max, she was going to have to get him a key. She'd never given a guy a key to her place before. That was a monumentally weird thought.

"What did you get us for dinner?" she asked unlocking the door.

"I got Cashew Chicken and pot stickers from the Chinese place you like, Red Curry from the Thai place I like and cheesecake from the diner we both shouldn't be allowed to visit on an empty stomach."

Dominique giggled. "Modern eating at its finest." She dropped her purse on the new console table and Max delicately put her other bags down next to it before proceeding into the kitchen. Dominique let him get a few steps ahead of her so he would see her surprise.

She heard him laugh and followed him into the kitchen.

The giant balloon bobbed happily in her kitchen with the teddy bear anchoring it to the counter.

We're Beary Excited for You!

"I was going to have it delivered to Grant's," she said, taking the food bag from his hands. "But then I realized you were meeting me here, and plus, the bear has some lingerie in the little bag."

"That must be some teeny tiny lingerie," he said, picking up the bear, and attempting to peer into the red sack the stuffie held. "Because that is a teeny tiny bag."

"Lace compresses into surprisingly small packages," agreed Dominique with a grin. "I'm really glad that you're officially here now."

"Yeah," he agreed, putting the bear down and sliding his arms around her. "I'm officially here now."

She put her arms around his neck and leaned in for a kiss. When she finally pulled back, he was looking down at her with a bemused expression of happiness.

"God, I love you," he said, then his face froze in an expression somewhere between panic and assessment. Dominique giggled in delight.

"You said it first," she crowed softly and kissed him again.

## EPILOGUE: THE DEVERAUX BOYS

## *Evan Deveraux – Last Week*

Evan sat on the couch and tried to control the nervous jiggling of his leg.

"You seem nervous," said the therapist. Dr. Nicholas seemed like a perfectly nice woman, round in shape, with curly hair, glasses and a soothing energy. He wasn't sure he cared about nice. What he cared about was whether or not this would work.

"I'm not nervous. I just don't want to be here."

"Why not?"

"I don't like… this feels like I'm not in control."

"But you set the appointment time. You can leave at any time, refuse to answer any question. You have as much control as you need."

Evan took a deep breath. She was right. That was right. He chose. He could walk out if he didn't like it. She couldn't tell anyone. Those were the rules.

"So, why did you choose to be here?"

"I think I have to be."

Dr. Nicholas tilted her head and caught his eye with a smile. "That explains why you don't feel in control. Nobody likes feeling like they have to do something. Did somebody tell you to come here?"

Evan felt his shoulders drop a fraction of an inch.

"No. It's me. I just think…"

"Think what?"

"I can't afford to not be here," he said.

"What does that mean? What happens if you don't come to therapy?"

Evan swallowed hard. This was it. This was the moment when someone was going to know how screwed up he was. "I think I'll probably try to kill myself again."

"Again," she repeated. "When did you try to kill yourself?" She didn't take any notes. She didn't look shocked or concerned. She just asked the question. Like this was normal. Like *he* was normal.

"Last week. I took most of a bottle of sleeping pills and all of a bottle of Scotch." He found himself just blurting out the truth, tricked by her calm expression.

"Then what happened?"

"I woke up and had to go to work," said Evan. That had been the worst part.

"You didn't get any medical help?"

"Not exactly," said Evan. "I mean, yes, but not for that."

"What do you mean?"

"I got... uh... mugged, I guess, on the way to work, and had to go to the hospital." He felt himself smiling.

"You liked the hospital?"

"No. I hate the fucking hospital. I find it humiliating. But they called my cousin to come and get me," he said.

She stared at him, waiting for the good part.

"And she did."

"That surprised you?"

"Yes," said Evan. "I really didn't think she would. I thought my cousins hated me."

"But if she came to get you, then maybe she doesn't?"

"She ought to," he said. "But she still showed up."

"And if she maybe doesn't hate you, then maybe you could not hate you?" suggested Dr. Nicholas.

He shrugged. It seemed far-fetched when it was said out loud.

"So, how does this work?" he asked. "Do I tell you about my mother or whatever? How do you fix me?"

"I don't fix you. It's *we*. We fix you. And we only talk about your mother if you want to talk about your mother," said Dr. Nicholas. "I think it might be better to focus on current issues. It's great to understand why a problem is a problem, and we'll probably cover whatever went wrong in the past as we go, but understanding doesn't necessarily fix anything. You need to take concrete actions now."

Evan relaxed back into his chair. That was a much better response than he'd been bracing himself for. He didn't want to spend hours dredging up the past. He wanted to move forward.

"But, if we want to have a solution, I do have to know what the actual problem is. So, you tell me, what do you think is wrong with you?"

"I'm an abusive asshole," he said.

"We can fix the abusive part," she said confidently. "The asshole part is probably up to you."

# Aiden Deveraux — Last Night

Aiden blocked, used a sticky hand technique, and grabbed his opponent by the neck. There was a tussle, a push and pull of strength, and Aiden lowered his center of gravity and pushed upward, sending his opponent onto his heels. Aiden shoved harder, running the man backward and slamming him into the fencing. He knew there would be a bounce effect as the chain-link flexed and his opponent would shoot back toward him. Aiden waited for it, then took the opportunity to drive his knee upward twice—once in the groin and once in the gut. He felt the hard clack as his kneecap rammed into the plastic shell of the other man's cup.

What was this guy's name again?

Aiden genuinely couldn't remember. He didn't actually care. He'd just picked up the fight because he was starting to lose it. He'd nearly blown it in Nika's apartment and punched the shit out of her attacker. Evan's derision had been almost too much to bear. But everyone knew that clueless Aiden was a sweetheart. Aiden Deveraux didn't get mad and he certainly didn't punch people. That was the trade-off for no one ever suspecting that, every few months, Aiden could be found in a *lucha libre* mask at a highly illegal underground fight.

But tonight's fight was stupid.

Using the family's private jet to fly to Mississippi was something that Jackson would probably notice. But maybe, as long as he got it back tonight, no one would blab and he could just say it was a work thing if questioned.

His nameless opponent shoved Aiden off and tried to punch. Aiden dodged and then struck back. The guy wasn't bad, but his stamina wasn't what it needed to be. He was sucking in air too hard. The knee to the gut probably hadn't helped.

The bell rang, ending the first round, and Aiden went back to his corner.

"Keep doing what you're doing," said his coach. Josh was an ex-MMA fighter who'd been banned for steroid use. Aiden's corner-man popped in and swabbed Aiden down, looking for cuts under the blood flecks and smears, and didn't find any. The blood was all from the split eye and lip on his opponent.

Aiden knew this fight was a mistake. It lacked planning or a proper cover-up. And truthfully, it didn't meet the goal he always claimed to be fighting for—to find her.

Cinderella.

The girl behind the mask in Mexico. The only girl who had ever made him feel like a true Prince Charming. But Cinderella had probably done exactly what he'd told her to do—run and never looked back.

Maybe he should stop doing this.

The bell rang and he stood up again.

Maybe he should keep going.

His opponent cracked him one across the jaw and Aiden felt annoyed. He couldn't afford any facial bruising. He punched back and then kicked.

Aidan knew that he ought to stop fighting. His last girlfriend had been horrified by the bruises and injuries that he claimed came from practice matches. She had begged him to stop. When he wouldn't, she broke up with him. That had hurt. So why hadn't he stopped?

The truth was that he was no longer fighting for Cinderella. He was fighting for himself. Because he liked it.

He hit the man across from him again and then waited for the left hook he knew was coming. Aiden side-stepped with a hook of his own, then he stepped back, going in for the uppercut. The man staggered and hit the floor, and there was a roar of disappointment from the crowd. The favorite was down and out.

Josh hustled him out of the ring. He had already collected the money for Aiden. It never paid to stick around. But just as they were getting in the car, Aiden thought he caught a flicker of movement in the audience. A slender waving hand on a dark-haired girl. He looked out the window as the car pulled away, but it was too late. Whoever it had been wasn't there. He was never going to find her.

# *Jackson Deveraux — Right Now*

"Mr. Zane," said Dr. Nicholas, standing up and holding out her hand as he entered the office. "It's nice to meet you."

Jackson surveyed the therapist, deciding he wouldn't insult her by shaking her hand since she was about to be pissed at him. "My name's not Zane. At least not anymore. It's Jackson Deveraux." Dr. Nicholas looked shocked, and her hand dropped to her side. "Sorry for the subterfuge of making an appointment, but we want to know what Evan talks to you about and I thought it would be better to talk in person."

"No." Her expression was angry. "This is unacceptable."

Jackson moved away from her, prowling around the office. "We will pay you a lot of money."

"Absolutely not."

"We could cover your rent for a year."

"This is a complete invasion of Evan's privacy. You need to leave."

Jackson checked out the sight lines from the window. Everything was oblique. No windows looked directly into the office.

"We're his family. It would hardly count."

"Of course it counts!" Dr. Nicholas was outraged. "You need to leave. I'm not discussing Evan with you or anyone else. Get out!" She emphasized her directive with a hand and arm pointing toward the door.

"That's good," said Jackson, sitting on the couch. "Is there anything you would like to ask us?"

"What?" Dr. Nicholas looked utterly befuddled.

"We're very excited he's getting help. Is there anything we can add?"

"Mr. Deveraux, I don't think you understand how client confidentiality works."

"I do actually," said Jackson. "I'm glad that you do as well. The family would like to support him. What is the best way to do that?"

"Stop going behind his back and talking to his therapist!"

Jackson grinned. "This will probably be the last time you see me. Please. What should we be doing?"

Dr. Nicholas stared at him, then sat down. "You know what. Fine. You're his HIPAA emergency contact. I'm required to contact you for safety planning anyway, but I'm going to bill you for this hour."

"Please do. Does Evan need safety planning?"

She tapped her pen on her notebook but didn't answer the question. "How abusive was he toward Dominique?"

Jackson winced. Dr. Nicholas apparently did not pull her punches. "Verbally and he hit her once."

"Just once?"

"That's what she says."

The pen tapped again.

"How forgiving of that is she? I'm not asking what you would like her to be. I'm asking how she actually feels."

"We all discussed it," said Jackson. "She is... tentatively interested in reconciling, assuming he continues to change. She considers his father's abuse toward him a mitigating factor."

"What about you?"

"What about me?"

"He says he argued with you."

Jackson laughed. "When?"

"Recently. He says you tried to talk to him after he was mugged, and he threw a glass at your head."

"It's fine," said Jackson.

"It worries him."

"It shouldn't," said Jackson. "I've forgotten about it."

The pen tapped again. "All right. He is interested in connecting with all of his cousins, but specifically with you."

"OK."

"His uncle apparently promised that you would be his brother."

"Really?" asked Jackson, surprised.

"When he was a kid. Apparently, Randall made some off-hand comment about bringing Evan home a brother and he has it in his head that you're it."

"Cool," said Jackson, feeling pleased. "I didn't know that."

Dr. Nicholas raised an eyebrow. "You think that's acceptable?"

"Yes?" She didn't seem to think that was a good answer. Jackson tried again. "No? Which part?"

"That your father, if he was referring to you, would not bother to recognize you for your entire childhood and then expect you to be someone's brother."

"Oh." He shrugged again. "As far as I can tell, Randall and Owen rarely checked in with what was acceptable human behavior. Evan can't control what random shit Randall decided to do."

"Yes, but Evan believed his uncle. He thought that you would be his brother."

"OK," said Jackson again.

"But he's not your brother."

Jackson shrugged. "I would have been if Randall had lived. So... Why not now?"

"OK, well, no, you would have been and are his cousin."

"I don't think Randall and Owen differentiated much between

what belonged to the other person. I think they had to rely on each other so much as kids that their boundaries on what was Randall's and what was Owen's were pretty blurry. So in Randall's head, that probably worked out."

"Thank you, Dr. Phil," said Dr. Nicholas sarcastically.

"I'm just saying if you look at it from their perspective, it makes sense. Ish."

"No, not really. But aside from the extreme boundary issues between Evan's uncle and father, there's the fact that you don't know these people. Or at least you didn't until, what? Three years ago. You're fine with just instantly being Evan's brother?"

"I always wanted a brother," said Jackson. "Everyone else I knew had one. Why shouldn't I have one? Aiden has Dominique. Why should Evan and I be left out? Although, really, I don't see why I should stop at Evan. I've decided to take all of them."

"Siblings aren't something you go out acquire," said Dr. Nicholas practically.

Jackson shrugged. "Well, apparently you can if you're a Deveraux. And now I'm a Deveraux."

"And how do you feel about that?"

"Really? Isn't that question a *little* cliché?" asked Jackson, delighted to be able to fight back with something. Dr. Nicholas was clearly very smart, which was great for dealing with Evan, but Jackson hadn't signed up for a headshrinker.

"There's a piece of paper on the wall that says I am legally required to ask that of everyone if they're sitting on the couch," said Dr. Nicholas.

"Doesn't mean you'll get an answer," he answered, with a smile.

The doctor lifted an eyebrow and then wrote a brief sentence in her notepad. Jackson shrugged, annoyed. "Well, I don't care what you think. He wants to connect? How do I do that?"

"He doesn't trust you," said Dr. Nicholas.

"Seems reasonable. We haven't known each other that long in the greater scheme of things and I am having him followed."

Dr. Nicholas glared at him.

"For security reasons."

"I don't have time to get into that, but if you could find a way to grow trust between you, that would be a start."

"OK."

More pen tapping. "He needs support and he needs people who believe that he can be different, because he is extremely unsure about that fact."

"Easy," said Jackson. "I absolutely believe that."

"You do?" Dr. Nicholas looked skeptical.

"Evan quit going to Fetish on his own and hasn't been back. To me, that says that he does not require violence in his life. The fact that he's seeing you tells me that he is looking for another option. We pushed him, but he's the one making changes. I think he can do this. Also, I think I should probably hug him more."

"What?"

"He hugs a lot when he's drunk. He probably needs more hugs."

"Is that what you do?"

"Hug people? Not generally, no."

"Give people what they need."

Jackson felt surprised. Most people couldn't spot it. "Yes. That's my job. And to keep everyone safe. So far, I'm only doing a middling job. It's taken me longer to figure out what everyone is up to than I thought it would. I think I should have ignored Eleanor and tried harder to get Evan help sooner. It's embarrassing that Dominique managed it over me."

"So you're here to please Eleanor?"

"Oh," said Jackson, recognizing her confusion. "No. I'm here to please myself."

"And collecting siblings and getting Evan healthy pleases you?"

"Yes. I always wanted a family and now I have one. It's what I wanted as a kid. This is my happily ever after. But it only works if they're all healthy, safe and happy."

"You don't think maybe that's a bit too much responsibility for one person? You can't make an entire family happy."

"Watch me," said Jackson.

FIND OUT WHAT HAPPENS NEXT IN...

# THE CINDERELLA SECRET

# ABOUT THE AUTHOR

Bethany Maines is the award-winning author of action adventure and fantasy tales that focus on women who know when to apply lipstick and when to apply a foot to someone's hind end. When she's not traveling to exotic lands, or kicking some serious butt with her black belt in karate, she can be found chasing after her daughter, or glued to the computer working on her next novel.

# OTHER WORKS BY BETHANY MAINES

**Carrie Mae Mysteries**

Bulletproof Mascara (#1)

Compact With The Devil (#2)

Supporting The Girls
*A Carrie Mae Mini-Mystery*

Power Of Attorney
*A Carrie Mae Mini-Mystery*

High-Caliber Concealer (#3)

Glossed Cause (#4)

Tales from the City of Destiny
*Short Story Collection*

Wild Waters
*A Paranormal Suspense Romance*

**Galactic Dreams**

When Stars Take Flight
*Volume 1*

The Seventh Swan
*Volume 2*

**San Juan Islands Murder Mysteries**

An Unseen Current

Against the Undertow

An Unfamiliar Sea

**Shark Santoyo Crime Series**

Shark's Instinct (#1)

Shark's Bite (#2)

Shark's Hunt (#3)

Find out more at:

**BethanyMaines.com**

Made in the USA
Columbia, SC
08 January 2020